Killing the Blood Cleaner

A Novel

by

Davis Hewitt

TELEMACHUS PRESS

This book is a work of fiction. Names, characters, places and incidents are either the product of the author's imagination or are used fictitiously. Any resemblance to actual persons, living or dead, or to actual events or locales is entirely coincidental.

The publisher does not have any control over and does not assume any responsibility for author or third-party websites or their content.

Cover Designed by Telemachus Press, LLC

Cover Art:
Copyright © iStockphotos 11661137, iStockphotos 2864372

Published by Telemachus Press, LLC
http://www.telemachuspress.com

Visit the author website:
http://www.davishewitt.com

ISBN: 978-1-939337-29-0 (ebook)
ISBN: 978-1-939927-49-1 (paperback)

Version 2013.11.12

Printed in the United State of America
10 9 8 7 6 5 4 3 2 1

ONE

IT DID NOT matter that Dr. Amy Bridge had turned from
Georgia Highway 189 into Georgia Maximum Security Prison
outside of Lester, Georgia, hundreds of times in her three-year
career as the prison doctor. Each time, the massive gray structure
with its soaring guard towers and miles of tall, chain link fences,
topped by shining razor wire startled her as it rose mightily out of
the flat Georgia pine forest like a heavily armed castle. She pulled
her powder blue truck under the guard tower and pressed the black
communications button on the ground level monitor.

"Beulah, it's just me," the doctor said with a wave to the black
female guard whose broad, smiling face appeared at the window of
the tower, high above the truck.

"I will let you in this time Dr. Bridge, but only if you promise
to stay out of trouble," Beulah replied in an electronic crackle on
the monitor. The heavy steel crossbar in front of the truck slowly
rose to allow entrance into the compound. Dr. Bridge turned her
vehicle to the left and into the employees' parking lot. Even though
it was seven in the morning, the hot June sun had already heated
the thick air, which she immediately felt as she stepped from the air
conditioning of her truck onto the pavement of the parking lot. She
breathed in the warm air deeply and looked up at the cloudless blue
sky. She was not expecting it to be her last day.

An inmate trusty in a bright orange uniform was busy sweeping the walk to the entrance, occasionally stopping to remove a piece of trash.

"Good morning, Dr. Bridge. I'm going to come see you today for my arthritis," the older, black inmate called to her.

"We will get you fixed up, Jimmy," she replied, with a smile, thinking to herself how she wished every inmate patient were as decent as Jimmy.

The entrance to the prison was guarded by a long concrete tunnel which led to the main Administration building. She had often thought it looked like an elongated igloo as it rammed toward the front of the older building. The entrance to the tunnel was the entry point past a second, sixteen-foot fence, again topped with razor wire. The black metal entry door to the tunnel was further garnished with two gray security cameras mounted at the top of the fence.

As she approached the door she waved again to the tower and Beulah Burns smiled, nodded and pressed a button. Dr. Bridge heard the loud metallic click which indicated that the electric lock in the door had been opened. She grasped the silver steel handle and pulled the heavy metal door open to enter the tunnel. The door closed behind her and locked with the same metallic click.

She made her way down the tunnel which was brightly lit by recessed lighting protected by bulletproof glass. She walked past four security cameras, each with a small brightly lit red light to show she was being monitored in her progress through the tunnel. She thought to herself that this was like being in some sort of futuristic subway station.

As she reached the end of the tunnel she stood in front of a huge gray door made of steel with a small window of thick, bulletproof glass. The guard on the other side of the door looked at her and nodded. Again, the metallic click was heard and she pushed on the door to enter the Administration building of the prison. It was the only original structure in the prison compound and had been built in 1938.

She entered the vast rotunda which was a marvel of WPA architecture and art from the thirties. She stood on a clean and polished mosaic floor. The thousands of ceramic bits created the State Seal of Georgia underneath her feet. The front wall held a huge Soviet style mural showing white inmates laboring in the fields watched over by clean-cut white officers wearing thin black ties with their blue uniforms.

The guard stationed in the rotunda was a middle-aged white officer with a touch of grey in his well-styled hair. He gave Dr. Bridge a long, approving glance, taking in her blonde hair, her fortyish athletic figure and her elegant, low black heels. "The Warden wants to see you, Dr. Bridge. I don't think it is anything urgent, though," he said with a slight sigh, looking her over, top to bottom, again.

"Thanks Ben. You doing okay?" she said, knowing, like everyone else in the building, that Ben Johnson's young wife had recently left him for a major at Fort Stewart.

"Yes, ma'am. It is always good to see you," he said, appreciating her comment and hoping that, perhaps, there was more to it.

She turned and walked to the Warden's office on the right side of the rotunda. The Warden's outer office was large with tall ceilings graced by intricate plaster moldings and an ancient red leather couch and armchairs for the benefit of visitors. On the wall above the couch was a massive, illuminated, oil portrait of one of the Confederate generals responsible for losing the battle of Atlanta. Behind an antique wooden desk was seated the Warden's secretary, Darla Cooper. She was a hefty, red headed, older woman, much more formidable than the guard outside.

"Warden Hammond will be with you in a minute. He is still dealing with Arnold O'Berne, the inmates' class action lawyer from

Atlanta. That always takes a while when they go over all of Judge
Valentino's Orders on the prison," she said, briskly pointing to the
closed door of the Warden's inner office. Behind her, on a credenza, a fax machine was grinding out its latest message. Mrs.
Cooper stared as an inmate trusty entered the office, who was then
directed by her pointing finger to a large trash bag full of shredded
documents. The inmate silently picked up the bag and left the
room. Mrs. Cooper walked over to the fax machine and inspected
the documents received.

"Another Court Transfer Order from Central Office in Atlanta.
It looks like Judge Valentino is going to give them all some kind of
hearing. The Court sends the Order to the Attorney General's office
in Atlanta. They look at it for a day or so and then they send it to
Corrections Central Office. Central Office lets it sit for a while and
then they fax it to us. By that time we are a few days from the
hearing," she said as she read the fax and dialed the phone.

"Jimmy, we got an Order from Judge Valentino sent from
Central Office. We got four inmates going to Court in Brunswick
on Friday, this week. You come up here and pick up the Order and
arrange for the transfer van," she commanded quickly into the
telephone. "You can also pick up these shanks for the disciplinary
hearings tomorrow. You will need them for evidence," she continued as she pulled a large, clear plastic bag from a desk drawer.
Inside the bag were four homemade knives, one metal, two made
from carved and sharpened wood, and one especially sturdy stiletto
knife made from plastic. Each knife was carefully tagged for use as
evidence.

"I would be careful about handling those," Dr. Bridge commented.

"Don't worry. I always have them cleaned with bleach. We
don't need the fingerprints. There are always plenty of witnesses,"
Mrs. Cooper replied.

The door of the Warden's inner office opened and Warden Greg Hammond, a six-foot, red faced, balding man with bushy black eyebrows entered the outer office. He was dressed in a dark green suit which was garishly accentuated by a neon green tie. The Warden was accompanied by a short, thin, fortyish man wearing a rumpled blue suit which clashed with his luminous red hair and eyebrows. The thin man stopped and peered at the plastic bag.

"Darla, the Warden tells me that you are down to only four stabbings this month. Is this the evidence?"

"Yes, and fortunately none of these were really serious. Just a few stitches in disputes over gambling debts and one M Building altercation," she replied.

"Four stabbings a month. That's probably even with your old High School in Atlanta, Arnold," the Warden commented.

"Maybe slightly better, actually," Arnold replied, still eyeing the plastic bag. "I guess one of these involves the sally port?"

Darla nodded and pointed to the metal knife. "Yes, this is the one where Officer Lucas thought he would speed things up by opening both sally port doors at the same time and running a herd of them through the metal detector. With that many going through at one time it didn't catch this little metal knife which then figured in our altercation," she responded with irritation.

"Arnold, I have fired that officer. Everybody knows that it is bad security practice and a violation of Judge Valentino's Orders to have both sally port doors open unless it is an emergency," the Warden responded.

"And the State Merit System will put him right back to work when he files his appeal. You may get a month's suspension to stick if the Attorney General's office gets fired up," the lawyer said as he picked up the metal knife and examined it closely.

"Arnold, unfortunately, you are probably exactly right. That would be the State Merit System protecting the rights of government employees. Darla, you make sure that Mr. O'Berne gets to see all his inmate clients. And you make sure that there is plenty of security. I don't want his wife suing us if one of them gets unhappy," the Warden commanded with a smile. "Arnold, here is Dr. Bridge," he continued.

"Yes, we correspond regularly. Every time one of my folks has a medical problem," the lawyer replied. "We have also gotten to know each other very well as we deal with Judge Valentino's Medical Monitor, Dr. Price, and his regular reports on your compliance and of course, noncompliance," he continued.

"I wanted her to drop by in case you had any problems with medical," the Warden stated.

"My problems with medical are that you need about two more doctors and four more nurses. But that is something that I have to take up with Judge Valentino. After I have talked to my clients I'm sure I will have some specific questions for the doctor," the lawyer replied.

Dr. Bridge squinted at the attorney and stated crisply, "We are just doing the best we can. I think the Medical Monitor's most recent report to the Judge showed a bit of improvement. Let me know if I can help with your individual clients," she replied, exhaling.

"How are the renovations to the Medical Unit coming?" the lawyer asked in a more conciliatory tone.

"We have modified the examining rooms to provide more privacy and better security. We have redone the pharmacy formulary to comply with the Judge's Order on medications. We have also hardened security on the controlled drugs in the supply room. Entrance now is by palm identification only and the Warden and I are the only ones with the combination to the controlled drugs safe inside," she replied.

"Palm identification? Now that we have the security up to the Juan Peron level, I assume we won't be having any more overdoses for drugs pilfered from medical like last year?" he asked.

"Hopefully not, and that system kept Mr. Peron's secrets for as long as he lived," she replied, smiling at the attorney's reference to the Argentine dictator's famous office safe and the subsequent removal of his hands from his corpse. She noted the Warden, frowning, obviously mystified by this obscure historical banter.

"All right folks. We all need to get back to working on the chain gang. Arnold, if you would like to tour the medical renovations at the end of the day that would be fine. Darla, I need to talk with you for a minute in my office," the Warden stated. It was clear that this comment amounted to a dismissal of all involved, and Dr. Bridge turned to leave toward the Medical Unit as two officers arrived to escort Mr. O'Berne throughout the prison.

TWO

AT DAWN THAT day, in M Building, Henry Kirk lay on his concrete bunk and thin institutional mattress going over his preparations. Looking furtively around the cell he confirmed that all the needed items were at his disposal. With a smile he reached under the mattress and retrieved a slightly crumpled photo of a nude blonde woman which had been torn from a magazine. The woman was bent over in a seductive pose and wore nothing except a white nurse's cap. He stared at the photo for some time and thought again how much the photo looked like Nurse Tacy in the clinic, and how finally, today, he would be enjoying that pert little body all to himself. Putting the photo away he heard the initial preparations for the delivery of breakfast with the clanging of gates and the sound of voices.

An inmate trusty, accompanied by a guard, made their way with the metal breakfast cart and its eleven insulated food trays into M Building.

M Building squatted in the southern corner of the huge courtyard of Georgia Maximum Security Prison. Between it and the Administration Building were four electronically locked sally port gates. M building was a one-story whitewashed cinder block building surrounded by its own ten foot, razor wire fence and "sanitized" perimeter which was made of white bleached stones. Any item thrown over the fence could be easily detected. Its seven windows were narrow glazed slits with thick opaque glass encased in heavy, gray, gunmetal frames.

There were three guards assigned to the building. One guard was always stationed in the bulletproof glass enclosed Control Room. The glass was heavy enough to give the officer inside from four to ten minutes of safety, depending on the size and weight of objects thrown against it, if the inmates took control. The Control Room operated the electric lock to the front gate and to the two heavy metal and glass sally port entrance doors to the building. From the Control Room there was a clear view of the outside fence gate through the sally port doors, along with the electric locks to the individual cells. Six video monitors in the Control Room also added to the security of M Building.

Two inmates swept the path leading up to the fence gate of M Building. The Control Room officer watched them carefully that day, occasionally glancing at the monitors. Another armed guard in a tower outside the prison, from time to time, would glance at the sweeping inmates, leaning on the rail of the tower and making sure they knew they were observed. All involved were aware of the problem of two days before. Somehow, a piece of sharpened white plastic had made its way into the building. Fortunately, the inmate was quickly overwhelmed by his two escorts and the injuries to one officer were minor. This shank was one of the four in Darla Cooper's desk to be used in evidence.

Beyond the Control Room was a row of twelve single cells. The doors to the cells were one piece of solid metal with only a slit for a food tray and a small barred window at face level. Inside each cell was a concrete slab where the inmate's mattress was placed, along with a stainless steel toilet and sink. The hall in front of the cells contained four televisions mounted near the ceiling. There was also a treadmill and a rowing machine in the hallway in front of the cells. At the end of the row was a metal door which led to an outside exercise courtyard which was about twenty feet square and enclosed by white cinderblock walls.

In M Building, inmates were only allowed out of their cells one at a time and only with two guards present. The inmates were allowed one hour of exercise per day, five days a week. On clear days they were allowed to use the walled courtyard. On rainy days they used the exercise equipment in the hall. The televisions ran twenty four hours a day, seven days a week. Usually, most of the inmates who were not the individual being allowed to exercise were to be found at the metal window of their cells watching the televisions with slow blinking eyes.

One of the cells had been converted into a "law library." Inside this cell was a metal table bolted to the wall and a lightweight plastic chair. Inmates were allowed to request legal materials from the main prison law library and to review these legal materials in this cell for four hours a week. Once a month they could request a trip to the main law library under heavy escort. While only a few inmates used the law library on a regular basis, Henry Kirk always made a point of using all his law library time and always requested a trip to the main law library.

This cell was also used by the Pill Call nurse to examine inmates for very minor ailments and to dispense medications. If the problem was anything beyond a cold or headache the inmate would be taken to the Medical Unit. At all times when the nurse was on the floor she was escorted by two officers and the door to this cell was left open.

M Building was the highest security area in the Georgia prison system, outside of Death Row. It took quite a bit of bad behavior for an inmate to end up in M Building. Once there, the stays were typically two years or more. Because of the intense staffing, the Department was very selective on the use of these high security resources. In general, an inmate had to demonstrate on several occasions that he was unpredictably violent and dangerous, especially to staff. Occasional fighting or even the killing of another inmate was not enough. There were lots of inmates who stood their ground against aggressors and time and time again were involved in fights and sometimes killings. There were other security environments for these inmates.

M Building was also not technically a "punishment" environment. Typically, the inmates in M Building had already been punished for their particular infractions by incarceration in a separate Lockdown Unit which consisted of single cells, limited exercise, no visitation and no television. The inmates called this area, "the Hole," and to an outside visitor it seemed quiet and peaceful with no televisions blaring and most of the inmates sleeping quietly in their cells. However, deprivation of interaction with others and loss of contact with the outside world via television was sufficient for most inmates to consider it punishment to be avoided.

The inmates in M building were allowed to watch television, have limited visitation, and were allowed such personal items as radios and books. The point was to create a controlled environment where these inmates could not attack each other or staff and where they could serve vast stretches of time without endangering others.

The rest of the prison had a variety of security environments. Most inmates who qualified for general population were housed in a dormitory with fifty other inmates, supervised by an officer in a Control Room. Another officer, from time to time, entered the dorm to make checks and to provide a security presence on a regular basis. In addition, there were other specialty areas such as the "Sissy dorm" for active and aggressive homosexual inmates and the "Sick" dorm for inmates with chronic diseases such as diabetes and high blood pressure. There was also a Protective Custody dorm for inmates who claimed their lives were in danger and for former police officers and the like.

For general population inmates there was some freedom of
movement within the prison. There were movies, church services,
sports teams, job assignments, library and law library visits and regular visitation with relatives. A Classification Committee of officers
classified each inmate as to his housing assignment within the
prison. The crime committed by the inmate was of less importance
to the Committee than his ability to get along with others. This
classification system often had peaceful murderers with lower security classifications than supposedly nonviolent offenders such as
burglars. The system had long ago determined that a murder done
out of passion or under the influence of vast amounts of alcohol or
drugs did not necessarily predict the capacity for violence of an
inmate once he was detoxed and behind bars. The emphasis of
classification focused on the inmate and how he acted. In general,
the classification system worked very well at keeping the peace in
the prison. Indeed, murderers tended to heavily populate the Law
Clerk positions in the law library as they most often fit the criteria
of inmates with long sentences who were unlikely to hurt others
and who had the education and mental capacity to understand the
workings of a law library.

That day, officer Jason Tibbs, in preparation for his contact
with the inmates, switched on his tiny digital recorder and placed it
in his pocket. His partner, officer Roger Sims, watched as the two
of them stood outside the Control Room in M building. "I know I
am paranoid, Roger, but since that plastic shank got in here the
other day I like to have my very own record of what is said. If we
have to fuck up somebody like Kirk he will no doubt say we tried
to grope him or something," officer Tibbs explained. Officer Sims
nodded his approval and they began their walk of the hall of M
building, looking into each cell where there was not a face watching
television. The Control Room officer busied himself making coffee
and watching the monitors.

Officer Tibbs noticed inmate Henry Kirk lying quietly on his mattress with his face to the wall. Once the officer had passed, Kirk sat up and picked up his transistor radio from the floor by his mattress. He pulled the battery out and attached a small wire from his pocket to the terminals of the battery. He jerked out the small plastic receptacle into which the battery terminals had been plugged and threw it on the floor. This allowed enough room in the battery compartment for the battery and its newly attached wires. He clicked the plastic cover over the battery and wires into place. Kirk then reached over and picked up his shoe. With his fingernail he pulled a sliver of a razor blade out of the rubber heel. He used the blade to make a small cut inside his lip. He pressed the cut with his fingers and allowed the blood to pour down his chin. He spread the blood with his fingers around his mouth and cheeks. He then rolled up his sleeve and made another cut which produced a slightly larger amount of blood. Using his fingers he grabbed the remains of his breakfast and mixed it with the blood on the front of his shirt.

It was about thirty minutes later when officer Tibbs was again at Kirk's window. "You OK Kirk?" he yelled without really expecting a response.

Kirk turned over exposing his red face and reddened scrambled eggs on his shirt. "I think I have been throwing up blood," Kirk said as he rolled back into the wall with a dramatic cough.

"How long has this been going on?" Tibbs asked.

"All night, but it has just gotten bad recently. I'm okay though," was Kirk's response.

"We will be getting you to medical. So get ready," officer Tibbs responded, looking at Kirk and his soiled shirt.

"I don't want to go. Last time the medicine made me sick," Kirk said.

"You're going to medical. And change your shirt," officer Tibbs ordered.

Once officer Tibbs had moved on, Kirk removed his dirty shirt. Kirk then reached for the vent and again using his fingernails inched a nine inch piece of white sharpened plastic from the space inside. He carefully taped the plastic knife to the center of his back. He then put on another shirt which had been lying crumpled on the floor. He put the transistor radio and a small earphone in his pocket. He again reached for his breakfast tray and spread a small amount of blood and his leftover scrambled eggs on the front of the shirt. Just enough of a mess to deter an officer from a thorough pat down search.

Officer Tibbs had moved on to the cell of inmate Brannon. Brannon was at the window of his cell yelling to the officer, "Tibbs, I got me the runs real bad. Can you take me to medical?" he asked.

"Are you going to fight us all if I let you out?" Tibbs asked.

"I can't fight anybody today, Tibbs. Yo Mamma could whip my ass," Brannon replied.

Tibbs could see the brown splashes all over the stainless steel toilet and could smell that there had been a problem. "My Mama could whip us both on our best day and I think you remember that from when you and your brother used to see her at the football games. But I'm going to take you medical even though you are trying to mess with my Mama," Tibbs replied with a smile.

Officer Tibbs walked to the Control Room door and signaled the officer. The lock clicked and Tibbs, followed by officer Sims, entered the Control Room. Inside the Control Room was a metal control panel which stretched out along the full length of the glass front. On the control panel were red and green lights for each lock in the building. All the locks were lit red showing that all locks were locked. Above the panel were the six video monitors which gave the Control Room officer a view of the cells, the cell block hallway, the front gate, perimeter views of the building, the exercise courtyard and the Control Room itself. These same videos could also be displayed in the Main Control Room of the prison if desired. In general, only the view of the M building Control Room was monitored in the Main Control Room of the prison.

At the back of the Control Room was a rack of nightsticks, hand held electric shock devices and a rubber bullet gun which had a three inch barrel like a blunderbuss. These were the only weapons allowed inside the prison. Each officer carried a nightstick, but the use of the electric shock devices had to be approved by a Captain or higher except in an emergency. The use of the rubber bullet gun had to be approved by the Warden or the Deputy Warden of Security. As security was tight in M building, the shock devices and rubber bullet gun were rarely used. From time to time, an inmate would attempt to attack one of the two officers when allowed out of his cell. The nightsticks were generally more than sufficient when wielded by two trained officers to regain positive control over most inmates.

On a table on one side of the Control Room was a large bound Logbook in which the officers recorded the daily activities of M building. Tibbs walked over to the Logbook and wrote quickly, "Hall clear and Kirk and Brannon complaining of being sick. Observed vomit on Kirk and evidence of runs on Brannon. Will request medical." He then picked up the telephone and dialed the extension for the Medical Unit.

"We got two from M building. Henry Kirk says he has been throwing up blood and it looks that way. Booger Brannon has the runs. They both look sick," he stated, detailing his observations. "Yes ma'am, we will bring them right up," he replied. Once he had hung up the telephone he went back to the Logbook and made a notation.

The Control Room officer pressed a button on the control panel to talk with the Main Control Room of the prison. "We need two officers to escort Kirk and Brannon to medical," he requested.

"We can send you one. Have Tibbs go with him. We are short officers today," a commanding voice boomed back over the speaker.

"Shit, they are short officers, everyday. Somebody's going to get hurt with guys like Kirk and Booger," the Control Room officer said to Tibbs, making sure the communications button was off.

"Well, at least they are both throwing up sick. Booger is not much of a problem for me. I was friends with his older brother, Jackson, when he was a kid. We played football together at Lester High. Jackson was Captain of the team the year my old girlfriend Cindy Jessup was Homecoming Queen. Their Momma's boyfriend shot Jackson and hit Booger on the head with a wrench which caused him to act funny. But it didn't take but a few years before Booger grew up a little and got him back. That's how Booger got here in the first place," Tibbs responded.

"I remember Cindy Jessup, she was a piece. Did Booger kill the Mama's boyfriend?" the officer asked.

"Killed him good. Gouged his eyes out with his bare hands and then snapped his neck. He won't be picking on anybody anymore," Tibbs replied. "Booger's in M building cause with that knock in the head you can't tell when he is going to lose his temper. Two inmates and an officer here found that out when they pestered him a little. As for Cindy she didn't see much future with me working for the prison," Tibbs continued.

"Doesn't she work in law enforcement herself, over for the Sheriff in Ossabaw?" the officer asked.

"Yeah, but somehow, I think she makes a lot more money than the average police," Tibbs replied.

The Control Room officer looked at one of the monitors and saw the requested escort officer at the front gate. He pressed the button to unlock the front gate and then separately, the sally ports to let him in the building. Tibbs opened the door to the Control Room and stepped out to meet him. Officer Sims remained in the Control Room.

"Shall we pick up our dance partners?" Tibbs said to the officer. The other officer nodded his agreement and handed Tibbs a pair of handcuffs and a heavy metal belly chain, keeping a set of each for himself. They walked down the cellblock hall and stopped at Booger Brannon's cell.

"Hands through the slot, Booger, so we can cuff you up," Tibbs instructed. In a few seconds a pair of huge brown hands appeared through the slit. Tibbs snapped on the stainless steel reinforced cuffs which then disappeared back into the cell. Tibbs signaled the Control Room officer and soon there was the familiar click of the electric lock on the inmate's cell door. Tibbs pulled back the heavy door while the second officer stood back several paces with his hand on his night stick. "Okay Booger, let's get on your belly chain so you will be presentable the nurses," he continued. The inmate stepped out of the cell and Tibbs circled his stomach with the belly chain and clicked it into place. "Sit down on the bench while we get Kirk," he ordered.

The officers moved on to Kirk's cell. "Okay Kirk, you know the program. Give us your hands so we can cuff up," Tibbs ordered. The officers waited a few seconds but there was no response. "Kirk did you not hear me? I said cuff up!" he continued.

"You fuckers, Leave me alone. I will be okay," was the response from inside the cell. The officers looked at each other and shook their heads. Tibbs signaled to the Control Room officer to unlock the door to Kirk's cell. Again, in a few seconds the click of the electric lock was heard and Tibbs pulled the cell door open. The second officer stood behind him with nightstick in hand.

"Kirk you're going to medical. I hope we won't have any extra injuries for them to look at other than the puking," Tibbs said in a voice of authority with his left hand touching his night stick. Kirk rolled over on his mattress and presented his hands in the air to Tibbs. Tibbs entered the cell and quickly snapped on the cuffs. "All right, get out here so we can do the belly chain," he continued. In a few seconds Kirk had rolled off of the mattress and stood outside the cell, with his handcuffed hands in front of him. Tibbs quickly snapped on the belly chain while the other officer watched carefully, night stick in hand.

The officers did a quick pat down search of each inmate. Tibbs pulled the transistor radio from Kirk's back pocket along with its attached ear piece. "You planning on rocking out up in medical?" Tibbs asked, looking at the device.

"That radio won't hurt anybody. If I got to sit in medical half the day maybe I can catch a ballgame," Kirk responded.

"All right. It can be a long day up there," Tibbs said returning the radio to Kirk's hip pocket. "Okay, now that everyone is cooperating we can go upstairs," Tibbs continued. The inmates walked toward the cellblock door followed by the two officers. Officer Tibbs again signaled the Control Room officer for the door to be unlocked. The group then passed through the sally port and the front gate of M building.

They went through three more gates with Tibbs each time requesting movement and unlocking by using his radio as they approached each gate. The final gate had an airport style metal detector which was manned by two officers. This gate led to the Administrative Building which housed the Warden's office, the Medical Unit and other offices. Tibbs walked the two inmates through the metal detector which buzzed loudly because of their handcuffs and belly chains. "Give them a pat down. We aren't going to take all this metal off," he said confidently. One of the officers began a pat down search of inmate Brannon beginning with his shoes, moving up the inside of his thighs, across his back and over the front of his chest and under his arms.

The officer began the same process with Kirk starting with his shoes. The officer hesitated when he got to Kirk's shirt and saw the small amount of crusted eggs and dried blood. He touched Kirk briefly under his arms and ordered him to turn around. He continued the search inside his thighs and touched his shoulders briefly. The officer noticed the bulge in Kirk's hip pocket and pulled out the transistor radio and examined it. Tibbs nodded at the officer and the radio was returned to Kirk's hip pocket. "Good to go," he stated to officer Tibbs.

"Let's go see the doctor," Tibbs responded and the four men moved on toward the infirmary. Kirk smiled as he moved his shoulders slightly and felt the plastic knife securely in place.

THREE

DR. BRIDGE WAS not expecting a busy day in the Medical Unit. Sick call had been light that week with less than thirty inmates a day being seen. On a busy week there could be as many as seventy five a day. As Dr. Bridge arrived, the two nurses were already busy with the morning routine. The first nurse, Hattie Bishop, an older black woman with many years of experience at the prison, was checking the supplies on the emergency Crash Cart. The second nurse, Tacy Crandall, was seated at a metal desk and reviewing sick call requests. Tacy was a twenty six year-old local who had once been Miss Lester and a runner-up as Queen of the Ohoopee Onion Festival. Her blonde hair tossed as she looked up and smiled at Dr. Bridge.

"Tibbs brought up Kirk and Brannon. He says they have been sick overnight," she said as she gestured to the two inmates who were in the Medical Unit Holding Cell, quietly seated on plastic chairs behind white metal bars and a white metal door with the standard electric lock. Their handcuffs had been removed for their examination, but they still wore the metal belly chains which could be used to quickly bring them under control if necessary. The Holding Cell was designed to hold up to ten inmates and it was brightly lit so the activity of those inside could easily be observed by those outside and by a security camera which was aimed at the bars of its gate. Nearby, and seated at another metal desk, drinking coffee and reading a newspaper, was officer Tibbs. Once the inmates had been deposited in the Holding Cell the accompanying transfer officer had left and returned to his other duties.

"Hattie, you finish up replenishing the Crash Cart and Tacy and I will start taking a look at Mr. Brannon," Dr. Bridge instructed. Nurse Hattie nodded and looked at her checklist for the Crash Cart. She noted that the small oxygen tank had expired and that a few other supplies were needed. Taking the oxygen tank, she walked over to the door of the Supply Room and placed her palm on the security plate near the door and in a few seconds the door to the Supply Room popped open. She used the oxygen tank as a doorstop to hold the door open and entered the room. In a few minutes she returned with a fresh oxygen tank and supplies for the Crash Cart. She returned to the cart and began replacement, noting each item on the checklist attached to the cart. In her concentration on her tasks she forgot about the oxygen tank holding the Supply Room door open.

Nurse Tacy pressed her code into the keypad of one of the four examination rooms. The door unlocked with the familiar metal click. Inside each examination room was a gray metal examination table which was covered with shiny, black padded vinyl. Each table had an additional paper covering which was changed after each examination. There was also a metal chair, a sink and two wastebaskets. One wastebasket was made of stainless steel and contained an orange plastic liner and warnings that it contained biological waste. Each examination room contained a security camera discreetly mounted near the ceiling above the door. Except for emergencies, it could only be activated by pressing a switch near the sink or by the Central Control Room on the direct order of the Warden or Deputy Warden for security. The door to the examination room was solid metal, painted white with the exception of a one foot square glass window.

Nurse Tacy looked around the room to make sure it had been properly cleaned by the inmate orderlies. She walked over to the examination table and made sure the paper was fresh and glanced over to check that the sink was clean and the wastebaskets were empty. "Tibbs, you can bring Brannon in here," she said as she readied her blood pressure cuff and electronic thermometer.

Officer Tibbs got up from the metal desk and walked over to the key pad of the holding cell.

"Brannon you are first, so I want you up here near the door. Kirk I want you in the back of the cell while I let Brannon out," he ordered. Brannon moved toward the front of the cell and Kirk slunk back to the rear.

"I don't want these bitches sticking me today," Kirk shouted.

Tibbs ignored Kirk as he tapped his code into the keypad of the holding cell. He opened the gate once he heard the metallic click of the lock and after carefully closing it he moved Brannon to the examination room. "Sit on the table and behave yourself. I will be right outside the door. And remember, these ladies are trying to help you," he cautioned Brannon. Nurse Tacy began her examination as Tibbs closed the door. He could see her using the blood pressure cuff as he looked through the glass window. Satisfied that Brannon was calm and cooperative, Tibbs returned to his seat at the metal desk, glanced at Kirk in the holding cell and continued reading his newspaper.

In a few minutes a green light flashed on the door outside the examination room, signaling that the nurse was ready for the doctor to examine the patient. Dr. Bridge appeared from her office holding inmate Brannon's thick medical file. Officer Tibbs watched admiringly as her heels clicked across the polished floor and she entered the examination room.

"Mr. Brannon, I see from your Sick Call Request that you have had bad diarrhea for several days. Is that right?" Dr. Bridge asked, looking at the medical records, "Tacy, are his vitals okay?" she continued.

Nurse Tacy responded first, "His vitals are all okay. I think he is a little dehydrated," she said.

"I have had the runs for two days and a headache," Brannon stated. "I have been a little better in the last few hours."

"Mr. Brannon have you still been eating roaches?" Dr. Bridge asked in a soft, kindly, tone as she looked at her notes from previous encounters. "You do remember us telling you that roaches could make you sick?" she continued.

"Miss Doctor, I try to do what you and Nurse Tacy say. But sometimes the voices they tell me to eat the roaches. They say if I don't eat them the roaches will eat me if I go to sleep," Brannon replied, blinking his eyes.

"Mr. Brannon, you know those roaches can't hurt you. Unless you eat them. Then they can make you sick. Are the voices telling you anything else?" Dr. Bridge asked.

"The voices say that bad men in this prison want to hurt you and Nurse Tacy. The voices fly around my head and talk to me. I try to bat them away and sometimes that works. But you need to be very careful. The voices have been flying around a lot today," he said ominously while he stared at the floor.

"I don't think we need any voices for us to know that," Nurse Tacy replied in a soft voice.

"Today be different, I think," Brannon said still looking at the floor and shaking his head.

"I'm going to get you some medicine from the Supply Room that will take care of your diarrhea. If that doesn't work, fill out another Sick Call Request and we will do a culture to see if you need an antibiotic. I'm also going to schedule you for mental health to get you some help on the voices," Dr. Bridge said as she made notes in the medical file.

"I will be glad to get that from the Supply Room," Nurse Tacy replied.

"That's okay. I want to try out my palm print on the new security door. I haven't tried it yet since they hardened the security on the Supply Room and I gave them my palm print," Dr. Bridge replied as she stepped outside the examination room.

An announcement began on every loudspeaker within the prison. It was especially loud in the Medical Unit which for some reason had two speakers. "It is now time for morning Count. All movement within the prison is to stop immediately until the Count clears. All designated officers will report their Count numbers to the Central Control Room immediately. You will be notified when the Count clears and movement is authorized," an authoritative voice ordered.

The Count of the inmate population was taken every day at the prison, three times a day. The purpose of the Count was to make sure that no inmates had escaped or were hiding within the prison. Given the number of inmates, their various assignments and movement within the prison, the Count made sure that all inmates were accounted for every eight hours. In times of turmoil counts were done more often or sometimes the entire prison was locked down and all inmate movement stopped.

Tibbs watched Dr. Bridge walk across the medical area toward the Supply Room. He then got up and walked to the examination room door. He knocked on the window and then using his code opened the door to the examination room. "Tacy, you and Mr. Brannon need to be out here while Count is going on," he said. The nurse and inmate left the examination room and stood beside Tibbs. Nurse Tacy left the examination room door slightly ajar as she expected the Count to be over quickly.

Tibbs had his back to the Holding Cell and was about to say something to Nurse Tacy when inmate Brannon shouted, "Hear the voices! He coming," as he pointed to the door of the Holding Cell. Tibbs turned and could see that inmate Kirk was at the gate of the Holding Cell with a white plastic knife in his left hand. In Kirk's right hand was the transistor radio that he was manipulating around the locking mechanism to the cell door. Across the room the click of the electric lock opening the Holding Cell could be heard. Kirk then stepped outside the Holding Cell waving his plastic knife.

Tibbs unsheathed his nightstick and reached for his radio. "Code 10–31, Medical Unit, inmate armed," Tibbs shouted into the radio as he faced Kirk. Tibbs then noticed the door to the Supply Room being held open by the oxygen tank. Tibbs looked around the room frantically for Dr. Bridge and Nurse Hattie. He shuddered as he heard movement in the back of the supply room. Nurse Tacy froze as she felt Kirk's eyes level with hers.

"I tricked the lock. We get to fight for pussy now, Tibbs," Kirk snarled, his eyes moving all around the medical area in a strategic fashion.

A noise distracted Tibbs from his faceoff with Kirk. He turned slightly and saw that Brannon had opened the examination room door and was pushing Nurse Tacy inside. "You stay there," Brannon said as he closed the door behind her and heard the familiar metallic locking sound. For a second, Tibbs felt relieved as he was sure that he and Brannon could overpower Kirk. "Get back in there," he shouted at Kirk.

At that moment there was the sound of something being dropped in the Supply Room. Kirk instantly moved several steps to the left and with one sweep of his huge hand, scraped the palm sensor to the Supply Room off the wall. Tibbs and Brannon lunged toward the Supply Room as Kirk kicked over the oxygen tank and closed the heavy metal door to the Supply Room behind him which immediately locked, just as it was designed. As the door closed, everyone in the Medical Unit could hear screams from within the Supply Room.

Tibbs grabbed the tangled wires to the security plate at the door, but with no effect. He then pulled with all his strength at the handle to the massive door which remained unmoved. Just then, three helmeted officers with shields and a rubber bullet gun entered the room. "He's got Dr. Bridge and Hattie in there. We need to crack the door," Tibbs screamed.

One of the officers looked at the remains of the palm plate on the floor, tugged at the door and then yelled at his radio, "We need some crowbars and sledgehammers." The other officer ordered Brannon to lie on the floor. The prison sirens wailed and there was an announcement on the all the loudspeakers in a loud, modulated voice which sounded prerecorded and mechanical, "Entire prison is on lockdown. Only emergency movement allowed." The message continued to repeat in a weird automatic way every minute. After the first message, the red lights to all the security cameras turned off.

Within seconds the Warden arrived with two additional officers armed with crowbars and pickaxes. It took exactly thirty-nine minutes after the door to the Supply Room closed and locked for the officers to reopen the door. Tibbs, the Warden and the four other officers stood with their shields and the rubber bullet gun ready as an officer finally pried the door loose with a crowbar.

As the door opened, they could see Kirk standing naked with his hands in the air. He was covered with blood and there were pills all over the floor. Behind him could be seen the nude, blood covered body of Dr. Bridge. The white plastic knife protruded at an angle from her bloody neck. The clothed body of Nurse Hattie lay at Kirk's feet, her head snapped back and nearly touching the top of her back.

"I swear I didn't do it. I want a lawyer. I have rights," Kirk said as he laughed, his eyes glazed. Tibbs lunged at him, but was held back by the Warden.

"Tibbs, we will take it from here. There is nothing you can do," the Warden said as he wiped his eye. Two officers stepped forward and placed Kirk in handcuffs and leg irons, and tightened his belly chain to the point that he grimaced in pain despite the medication he had consumed. Tibbs left the room and walked toward the Warden's office.

Nurse Tacy emerged from the examining room and began to cry. "That should have been me!" she sobbed.

On the floor, his hands cuffed behind him, Booger Brannon cried as his huge body shook convulsively, "the voices laughing," he said as he sobbed.

FOUR

IN ATLANTA, ONE week later, Dr. Jack Randolph opened his crusted eyes at a little after ten that morning. He could hear the delicate sound of Annabelle Royce throwing up in the bathroom next to his bedroom. His clothes and hers were strewn about the room along with two champagne bottles, one smashed to bits and a half empty bottle of rum lying on the floor on Annabelle's side of the bed. On the bedside table next to him was a squashed tube of personal lubricant jelly with a sizable puddle of glistening liquid spreading towards his alarm clock. Jack's dinner jacket and formal shirt were crumpled into a compact ball on the faded blue wing chair next to his bed. His suspenders were wrapped around the bed post on Annabelle's side and her peach colored thong panties hung loosely from the middle of the bed post on his side of the bed. He noticed that Annabelle's expensive platform heel shoes were lined up like bookends on either side of a crystal glass that Annabelle had loaded with rum atop the bedside table. The covers and sheets to the bed were in a heap at the front of the bed and only the uncovered mattress remained. It was marked with various stains of unknown origin, in a variety of colors, some of which were still wet.

Jack lay naked on the bed with his head supported by one down pillow and a decorative green pillow with a small rip in the left corner. He looked around the room wondering where he had left his shoes and cufflinks. Casting his gaze to the armchair he could see the golden shine of a cufflink still safely attached to his formal shirt. He felt relief as the cufflinks had been a gift from Annabelle and with the price of gold these days it would have been overly expensive to replace these golden balls.

Annabelle was still in full charge of the bathroom as could be heard from the noise of the shower, sink and toilet all of which seem to be operating at the same time. Jack was about to step out to the other bathroom when the telephone rang. He looked at it on his bedside table and thought about not answering. However, the call indicator showed that it was Annabelle's uncle, Dr. Randall Cannon, and he was not a man to be ignored.

"Jack, this is Randall. One of my partners has been checking you out with your prior employer, the Centers for Disease Control. He shouldn't be doing that, but he is friends over there with a guy named Dr. Anten. Dr. Anten says you are a drunken, Buckhead wild ass and that you seduced about half of their nursing staff. I need something to tell my partner before we can get you in the firm. He is mostly retired so I don't think he really gives a shit," Dr. Cannon crisply announced.

Jack gazed around the room and his eyes focused on Annabelle's panties wrapped around the bed post near his face. It was far too early for serious conversation and especially for job-related discussions. However, he exhaled, shook his head and proceeded.

"I resigned from the CDC voluntarily to be in private practice and there is no disciplinary record of any type. I'm still a consultant to Dr. Howard Clayton who is a Deputy Director of the CDC on the HIV Task Force. As to my personal life, I would admit that I'm a young man who is full of life and enjoys a good time. And while there have never been any questions asked about me at the CDC, at least on the record, there have been a lot of questions asked about Dr. Anten. I recall a few times time when the Controlled Substances Room was missing cocaine and he appeared on the video monitor a little more than would be expected. Caring doctors like Dr. Anten sometimes need a little snort when their patients don't respond well to treatment," Jack said.

"That's the stuff, son! You should have been a smartass blackmailing lawyer. I will shut him up with this and we will be on board with you next week. I know Howie Clayton would back you up in front of a firing squad. And by the way, you better not be showing your ass working for me or you will regret it. If anyone is fucking the nurses, that will be me. Do we understand each other?" Dr. Cannon said, knowing full well that Dr. Anten's description was not only accurate but probably a conservative description of his new associate.

"Yes sir, I will follow your medical leadership completely," Jack said, feeling relieved.

"You better. We are hiring your ass under a cloud from the CDC. No doubt you appeared on the Controlled Substance monitor also. Howie has somehow kept your record clean. I am old and tired of this medical shit. I expect to bill your work as mine while I am relaxing down at my house in Palm Beach. I need to make sure you are someone who is on the program and will not rat me out to those dammed insurance companies or Medicare. Also, I want a response on those tough cases I let you look at. Fixing them will also help placate my partner," Dr. Cannon continued brusquely.

"You can count on me. I will be running those patients past Howard to get a little outside help," Jack replied quickly without argument. "We will both make plenty of money while serving our fellow man," Jack continued, as he hung up the receiver to the laughter of Dr. Cannon. Jack thought to himself how lucky he was to have found this old rascal and his gold mine of a practice which was no doubt highly lootable.

Jack looked up and saw that Annabelle had reentered the bedroom. She looked surprisingly good, considering the savage sounds he had been hearing from the bathroom. She was naked except for a bath towel around her waist. Her light brown hair, still slightly wet cascaded down to touch her tanned shoulders. Her tanning salon tan continued to her athletic breasts which she scratched slightly while speaking to Jack.

"Who was that on the phone?" she asked.

"That was your Uncle Randall. We were talking about some information he needed to help me join his practice," Jack said.

"Oh good. I know he has been keen to have you work with him. He is been totally irritable since that female doctor he hired two years ago killed herself with sleeping pills last month. Now he has to actually work in Atlanta instead of spending most of his time in Palm Beach with his slut girlfriend," she said.

"I'm sure I'll be a great help to his practice," Jack replied with a smirk.

Annabelle moved around the room picking up her clothes and reordering the contents of her purse. She retrieved a blouse and a pair of white slacks from her overnight bag which was on the floor near the door to the bathroom. She playfully threw the towel at him and dressed herself with the slacks and the blouse. She fished into the bottom of the overnight bag and retrieved a pair of gold sandals. She stuffed her clothes from the previous night into the overnight bag and looked around the room for any remaining belongings. Her eyes stopped at the panties hanging on the bed post.

"I'm going to leave those with you until next time. Maybe they will remind you what a cute little bottom I have," she said proudly. "Perhaps then you will concentrate on me instead of always playing doctor. I thought you were going to operate on that awful redneck at the bar last night. The medics were already there and you were trying to jump in."

"He was choking. If his airway was blocked it would cut off the circulation to his brain and he would be a vegetable or dead in a few minutes. But if you punch a tiny hole in his windpipe it allows the air to get through and gives him a much better chance. The medics aren't very experienced with that but I have done it hundreds of times. But you were pulling on my arm and I stopped and let them do what they could do. So it doesn't matter anyway," Jack replied.

"Well, nobody knew you were a doctor. He probably would've sued you if it hadn't gone right," she said knowingly. She continued gathering her belongings and stopped at the entrance to the bedroom.

"I want to make sure you're on time for lunch at the Capital City Club, downtown, at one with your friend, Howard Clayton. You are the one that set this up, so the least you can do is be on time. You and Howie can talk medicine while I cruise the Club and find out what's been going on in Atlanta," she said in an instructional tone, clearly indicating she was doing Jack a great favor by taking her time for this lunch with his old friend. She turned and with a click of her gold sandals walked out of the bedroom and down the hallway to her car which was parked outside.

Jack, still naked, pushed back in his bed and lustfully enjoyed the view of her tight white slacks as she departed.

"You can count on me, Annabelle. And I do love it when you show me your bottom," he said.

FIVE

INSIDE THE LITTLE white house in Lester, Georgia the television was tuned to the latest reality show. On the coffee table was a gallon jug of chilled chardonnay, the local grocer's best value wine. Tacy and two of her friends, Myrtrice Beckham and Alice Wass, were seated on the brown sofa which also could be converted into a spare bed, sipping wine from paper cups. Myrtrice and Alice were both Tacy's age but looked considerably older. Each sported a small diamond ring on their left hand and each had a similarly chubby figure indicating that at some point in the recent past a decision had been made that child care would take precedence over dieting and fitness. In the black vinyl lounger by the side of the couch presided Tacy's mother, Clarice Crandall, dressed in a plaid flannel robe over blue cotton pajamas. She nursed a potent rum and tonic in a short green glass with both hands. On the small mantle was a slightly faded picture of Tacy's father, Sergeant Roy Crandall, in full uniform. The picture had been taken a few weeks before he had been killed in Vietnam. Only Mrs. Crandall was intently watching the show.

"Tacy, you were so lucky you weren't murdered by that creep," Myrtirce stated as she took a long sip on her wine. "He was obviously planning on getting you from what you told us," she continued, with a slight glance at the activity on the screen.

"Myrtrice is right. You could have been raped and murdered. Kirk is still over at the prison. He may yet try to get you. I don't care how much security they have, there have always been problems. I know these things, my Dad worked there twenty years. The inmates are always figuring something out," Alice added, also partaking of her wine and stopping to refill her cup from the jug.

"It does scare me. I think about Kirk all the time now. I have nightmares about Dr. Bridge and Hattie, the way they looked. It also scares me about the way that inmate, Booger Brannon, talked about the voices. It gives me chills," Tacy responded.

"Well, if there is any place on earth with evil spirits flying around it would be Georgia Maximum Security Prison. Just think about some of the people who have lived and died in that place," Myrtrice said.

"Tacy, why don't you just quit and get a job in Atlanta. There are lots of jobs for RNs up there. The hospitals are having to import nurses from the Philippines. And it would be a lot easier to meet some decent men," Alice added, briefly glancing at one of the couples on the television.

"She is right, Tacy. Alice and I have our husbands and children down here, but you don't have anything holding you back," Myrtrice added.

"I have thought about moving to Atlanta a lot since Dr. Bridge was killed. Or even moving to Savannah or Brunswick, which might be less of a culture shock. But I have just started my job and I do need to look after my mother, even if she doesn't think so," Tacy said as she motioned over to her mother who was now asleep and snoring with her face toward the ceiling. "Also, it is not so bad a job. I get to help people who definitely need help. And it is interesting and exciting sometimes."

"What is interesting about that monster, Kirk? Why would God put such a creature on the planet?" Myrtrice said, holding her cup in one hand and fingering the small gold cross which hung from her neck with the other.

A loud blast of music from the television woke Mrs. Crandall with a start. "God works in mysterious ways. Maybe those voices are a sign of a battle going on over something. Something important," she said mystically, evidently having heard more of the conversation than was apparent.

"Or maybe we are not giving Booger Brannon enough psychotropic medication," Tacy said with a nervous laugh. "And I do remember thinking that retarded drunk, Oscar Henderson, who used to hang around Lester was completely worthless, until the night my friend, Ellen Jameson and her twelve year old son were getting beaten nearly to death by her husband. Oscar was on the street and heard their screams. He kicked open the door to their house and got stabbed by the husband, but not before he broke his neck and put an end to him. The jury let Oscar go on Ellen's testimony,"

"Don't be placing any bets on Kirk doing any good deeds, even violent ones," Myrtrice commented wryly.

"You are probably right about Atlanta. I would love to meet someone I could care about. You all have your husbands and families. I want that too. That is probably not likely to happen in Lester, Georgia. I guess I was just too serious in getting my nursing degree and ran all the boys off," Tacy continued.

"You are right about that, honey!" Tacy's mother snorted, taking a long pull on her drink. "I can't count how many you have run off or ignored."

"Well, I am serious about it now. Maybe I should move to Atlanta or someplace. But if I do find somebody good, you can be sure I will give them both barrels," she said sticking out her impressive chest and tossing back her long blonde hair.

"Lord help him!" Myrtrice said with a lusty laugh. "Here's to both barrels," she said, hoisting her glass in a toast which was quickly joined by all the ladies, including Tacy.

SIX

THE CAPITAL CITY Club sits on the corner of Peachtree and Harris Streets in Atlanta. Since 1887 it has been a second home to corporate presidents, prominent lawyers, businessmen, physicians and the occasional entrepreneur. Many generations of members have watched decades of Christmas parades from its porch overlooking Peachtree Street, or partaken of an elegant lunch in the Mirador room upstairs to the accompaniment of a jazz quartet. The Club is generally unmarked except for a few well-shined brass plates with the Club name and insignia.

A discreet entrance on Harris Street allows ample valet parking even on the busiest days. Members are greeted by their names as they step from their cars along with a welcome to any guests. Once inside, there are again personal greetings as coats and reservations are checked. A large portrait of Robert E. Lee along with imposing portraits of several past Club presidents from the nineteenth century preside over the walnut paneled hallway. There are also bronze plaques to commemorate members lost in WWI and on the Titanic.

The ground floor of the Club provides several choices for eating and drinking. Near the entrance is the Three Cs room which is dedicated to the Atlanta Olympics of 1996, in which many members were early leaders. The room contains an assortment of Olympic memorabilia from the games including the Olympic torch. It is a somewhat casual place with a buffet loaded with covered silver cauldrons filled with the works of the Club's European chefs. It is a good place for a quick lunch or dinner with clients or old friends. In the winter a fireplace crackles with nearly the warmth of the head waitress, Zena Pounds. Zena is an expansive black woman who has been with the Club for thirty years and knows the names of all Club members and many of their children.

Past the Three C's room is the Main Bar and sitting room. The bar shines with brass and varnished mahogany and is presided over by its longtime bartender, Leah Crawford. Several members have known Leah since she was the bartender at the Officers Club in Seoul Korea, right after the Korean War. To the right, the sitting room is again decorated with the portraits of past Club presidents. There is also a portrait of a favorite Democratic president, Grover Cleveland, who was aggressive in wiping out the last traces of reconstruction in Georgia. Ample couches and armchairs allow for comfortable waiting or a leisurely drink.

At the end of the hall is the Peachtree Room. Diners here have a choice of being seated inside or in appropriate weather, meals are served on the expansive porch overlooking Peachtree and Harris Streets. It is a more formal room requiring coats and ties for gentlemen and serves a sophisticated variety of foods ranging from continental classics to Southern favorites. It is presided over by Carlos Amaya and his brother Julius. It is a favorite lunch spot for downtown lawyers who can often be seen at their regular tables.

Today, Dr. Jack Randolph was running late. Clifford Moss, another long time, Club employee who presided at the front desk, greeted Jack and noticed his minor irritation.

"Hello, Dr. Randolph. Dr. Clayton and Miss Annabelle are waiting for you out on the porch," he said with a bright smile.

"Thanks Clifford. I hate being late. Annabelle gets mad," he replied.

"I know that's right," he said with a knowing smile, thinking back to the many tantrums of Annabelle Royce he'd witnessed since Miss Royce was a small child.

Jack walked briskly to the Peachtree Room, still anticipating Annabelle's displeasure. "Dr. Randolph, your friends are here," the distinguished Carlos announced with a hand gesturing toward the porch. Jack followed him to a large table overlooking Peachtree Street. The full glasses and bottle of wine chilling in a silver wine cooler gave him a hope that they had been enjoying themselves and Annabelle would overlook his tardiness.

"Howie and Annabelle, have you missed me?" he asked. Dr. Clayton rose to greet him. Annabelle stayed seated with a faint smile and a glass of wine in her left hand. "We were forced to start without you, Jack," she said with a little pout as Jack was seated at the table. "Jack, if we are going to be married I'm going to have to train you better," she continued in her smooth Southern voice, waving the wineglass slightly.

"Jack is past training, Annabelle," Dr. Clayton responded as Carlos smoothly took further drink and lunch orders.

"Howard, have you cured AIDS today over at the CDC? I hope you washed your hands before you left. We don't need an outbreak of river blindness or Ebola here at the Club," Jack said, hoping to move the conversation past his being late.

"We are working on AIDS but it's a difficult rascal. Thank God it hasn't mutated to spread like Ebola or we all probably wouldn't be sitting here," Dr. Clayton replied.

"Jack and I are going to Sea Island this weekend," Annabelle injected, always bored with medical conversations.

"I will be there, too. The CDC has an HIV Viral Load Subcommittee meeting there together with the CDC Homeland Security Committee and we are expecting doctors and researchers from around the world sharing information. Jack, you're welcome to attend. You might learn something useful for that Buckhead practice you are joining since you left us," Dr. Clayton continued.

"Jack will be too busy with me to go to some meeting about nasty germs," Annabelle volunteered.

"I do have a couple of cases from the practice I would like to talk to you about. They are a little complicated and I would need about an hour of your time," Jack said.

"Why don't you come out to the CDC tomorrow morning? I'll look at your files and see if we don't have something helpful. I will also show you the research I'm presenting to the committee," Dr. Clayton replied.

"Thanks, Howard. These patients have got me puzzled. The new blocking drugs should be working, but aren't. I will be there around nine, if that is OK," Jack responded, as Annabelle stood and blew an enthusiastic kiss to one of her former sorority sisters across the room. She excused herself and walked over to give the girl a hug and began an animated conversation.

"Jack, are you really ready for Annabelle to whip you into husband material?" Dr. Clayton said with a kind smile of concern for his friend.

"Oh, that's just Annabelle. She's always like that. We both have known her forever," Jack replied.

"That's what worries me. She is just the same as when we were all at Westminster and she was the Peach Prom Queen. Of course, she wouldn't actually talk to me then. But she has always liked you, since you were on the football team and especially since you got out of medical school," Dr. Clayton said, as they watched Annabelle across the room. She was now all smiles with an attractive young man who was wearing a crisp and perfectly fitting seersucker suit. "I see she is now finished with Deb Timmons, Queen of the Omegas, and focusing her laser charm on her brother, Bill Timmons," he continued.

"At least BT could maybe afford her, if he got the full cooperation of his trust officer," Jack replied. A full twenty minutes passed before Annabelle returned to the table, just as lunch was being served. Carlos was assisted by two waiters in serving the group with quiet perfection.

"Queen crab from Charleston, my favorite. They are not often on the menu," Jack commented, looking at the artistically presented dish before him.

"Usually you can only get this on the Coast. I love it too," Dr. Clayton agreed.

"How can you men eat that messy crab?" Annabelle asked, questioning Jack's judgment in all things. "I mean crab meat is good, but it is so much work!" she continued.

"This has never been a favorite of the ladies here. It was always a favorite of my Dad's. He once told me that the fishermen from Charleston were having a slow fishing day and they decided to lower their crab baskets about a mile down into the Atlantic just to see what was down there. They were shocked when they came back full with these big crabs, almost as big as the King crabs in Alaska," Jack replied. Carlos and an assistant attended at a discreet distance, being careful that the crystal glasses always brimmed with wine.

Annabelle enjoyed her steak and after another few glasses of wine relaxed in her chair with a contented smile. "Howie, I know all about what Jack does as a doctor. It's like what my Uncle does over at his internal medicine practice. But what is it that you really do over at the CDC? I see it on television a lot. They are always talking about bird flu or some plague someplace," she said with a slight slur in her voice.

"I am the Deputy Director of Research for the HIV Task Force. We do research on potential cures for AIDS and ways to fight the virus. I review the work of researchers at the CDC and around the world. I also do my own research. My research often deals with blood samples from human volunteers," Dr. Clayton replied, somewhat surprised that Annabelle had any interest in his work.

"Can you make any money doing that?" she replied, her slur increasing.

"When you work for the government they make you take a vow of poverty," Jack injected. "That is why I left the CDC. The work was really interesting but you can make so much more in private practice. I also liked actually treating patients."

"Jack, honey, anytime you take a vow of poverty, you might as well go ahead and take a vow of chastity," Annabelle said, a little too loudly. Carlos and his assistant, who were well within earshot, discreetly looked out across Peachtree as Jack shook his head and signaled for the check.

"Howie, I will see you tomorrow," Jack said as he rose to assist Annabelle from her chair. Dr. Clayton also stood and thanked Jack for the lunch.

Annabelle stayed seated. "You boys run along. Howard, it was good to see you. I am going to stay a bit and catch up with my friend Deb and her brother, BT."

Jack and Dr. Clayton looked quizzically at each other for a second and then headed for the parking lot.

SEVEN

THE NEXT DAY Jack allowed plenty of time to make sure he arrived at the Centers for Disease Control by nine in the morning. The CDC was located next to Emory University which was at least a half hour ride from his apartment in Buckhead. As he turned onto Clifton Road he could see the compound of new buildings which made up the CDC. He noticed several security cameras on the buildings and uniformed guards in the parking lot and patrolling the buildings. It was rumored the CDC had been a target of the 9/11 bombers, but the plane designated for it was grounded in the Atlanta airport once trouble was reported on the other planes. Since then, security had been greatly increased, as was appropriate for buildings which contained samples of every variety of dangerous bacteria or virus on the planet. Many of these had never been seen in North America, but had inflicted immense damage in parts of Africa. Ebola was one of these plagues which had wiped out whole villages and a good portion of the medical personnel in hospitals where the victims were sent. The building contained every variety of the HIV virus along with a multitude of other threats such as avian flu virus and antibiotic resistant tuberculosis bacteria.

These samples were tested, evaluated and categorized by the researchers inside as to their virulence, changeability, method of transmission and numerous other factors. The watch was always on for a virus which was deadly but difficult to transmit, mutating or combining with another virus to produce a new creature which was deadly and easily spread among humans. Once such a problem was identified, a team from the CDC was dispatched anywhere in the world to help the local health authorities contain the problem. Mostly this involved the destruction of livestock and the isolation of human victims. So far, these methods had been enough to keep such plagues out of major population centers throughout the world. Still, every day, many researchers in the building watched the data and samples as they arrived daily and prayed silently that this would not be the day where unlikely combinations lined up to produce the Apocalypse.

Jack walked through the glass doors at the entrance of the Main building. There were three guards who looked at him carefully. Even though it had only been a few weeks since he had left his job at the CDC, he felt like a stranger.

"Good morning sir. Do you have an appointment?" the most senior of the guards asked him.

"I am Dr. Jack Randolph and I have a meeting with Dr. Howard Clayton," he replied. "I used to work here myself," he added. The guard was silent as he looked at the computer screen listing today's appointments.

"I see your appointment, Dr. Randolph. Now if you would just show us your driver's license and then step through the metal detector you will be on your way," the guard said. Jack complied, and once he was on the other side of the metal detector the guard handed him a clip-on identification card which read "VISITOR" in large red letters. "Officer James will accompany you to the third floor to Dr. Clayton's office."

Jack nodded and the second officer escorted him to the elevator and then to a waiting area on the third floor. It was only a few seconds before Dr. Clayton arrived to greet his guest.

"Jack, it is good to see you. Sorry we have tightened things up even for an old alumni like yourself," Dr. Clayton said as the guard departed.

"It doesn't bother me. I'm glad they are guarding you and all the germs in this building so well. The CDC has come a long way from the days, years ago, when those two maintenance workers came down with Rocky Mountain spotted fever over the weekend and died while they figured out there was a problem," Jack said.

They walked back to Dr. Clayton's office which was a bright glassy room which overlooked the woods of the Emory University campus. There were stacks of papers on his desk, on the floor, and on his polished wood conference table.

"I see the mortality and morbidity reports just keep rolling in," Jack said as he looked at some of the stacks of papers.

"Yes, and the surveillance reports, blood samples and the HIV testing algorithm reports and on and on keep coming. Every day, I wonder whether something great or awful will be arriving," Dr. Clayton replied.

"Let's hope it's something great. So what is new going on?" Jack asked.

"Well, there are a lot of new studies that have been done, now that we have been doing HIV testing for several years. We are seeing groups of folks that had the virus for a long time and are still doing well and are not sick. You remember, I think you did some work on these HIV Controllers. Of course, by testing their blood we came up with these new drugs that block the replication of the virus and slow down the onset of full-blown AIDS. Anything that decreases the viral load of HIV virus in the blood is a good thing," Dr. Clayton said.

"I recall working with you on some of those HIV Controllers, but that was a while back before they moved me to antibiotic resistant TB. What testing groups are you looking at now for these HIV resistant folks?" Jack asked.

"The HIV tests are required of the military and for the prison systems on a general basis. We also get some tests and monitoring from hospitals. The problem with the military is if they have the virus they won't let them in the service and we lose track of them. The prisons have much more controlled populations but with all the privacy laws, and the prisoners not wanting to cooperate, we get a lot of interesting statistics but not a lot of human volunteers that we can monitor throughout their infection," Dr. Clayton replied.

"Let's not forget the somewhat sordid history of experimenting on prisoners to add further difficulty. So you don't have anyone yet to look at who had the virus and resisted the virus back to the point that there is no virus in his system?" Jack asked.

"You mean like someone who gets an infection on their finger and fights it off and is completely bug free?" Dr. Clayton responded.

"Yeah, not just somebody who is still infected, but is doing okay. I know you have a lot of those. A lot of times something happens and they get sick later on and they can still spread it," Jack said.

"No, not yet. But somewhere there must be somebody like that. That is the person we are all looking for, the Elite HIV Controller. They are the Blood Cleaner. Everyone researching HIV is looking for the Blood Cleaner," Dr. Clayton said looking wistfully at the pile of papers on his desk.

"Just like when Dr. Jenner figured out that the milk maids never got smallpox because they had already been infected with a mild disease like cow pox," Jack replied.

"Exactly, and that is the breakthrough we are looking for. We send researchers all over the world when some doctor gives us a report that he has a patient who tested positive for HIV and is now clean. So far, they just turn out to be a false positive for the first test, or when you give them a full blood workup they still have the virus someplace, even though they are doing well. If we could find a person who had cured himself of the virus completely it would be a medical breakthrough equal to the discovery of penicillin. Actually better. Not only would we be able to make a vaccine to prevent the HIV virus from making people sick, we could also cure the people who already have full blown AIDS," Dr. Clayton replied.

"Well, maybe someday. Sounds like a prison is your best bet. You can be sure they started out with it, because of the initial testing," Jack said as he reached into his briefcase and produced two files. "Howie, take a look at these. At first the HIV replication blockers worked and they had a reduced viral load. But now they're getting sick," he continued.

"Have they been compliant with their drug routines?" Dr. Clayton asked as he opened the first file.

"They all swear they are taking the medicine, but you never know. Patients do lie. At least these are pretty responsible people. They are not out there infecting anyone," Jack said.

"That's good. I hate to think of all the noncompliants out there spreading the virus and letting it mutate to defeat these blocking drugs. Like the damned street patients with antibiotic resistant TB. They come in sick to the emergency room or some jail. They get third generation antibiotics that cost in the thousands for free. They feel better, so they stop taking the drugs. Then they get sick again with the superbugs that survived these exotic antibiotics," Dr. Clayton said as he continued to study the file. "For this guy, I would recommend that you greatly increase the dosage. He has already taken a course of antiretrovirals and they helped him at first. We have seen some good results with much higher dosages. I think that should give him a shot. If that doesn't work we can try something experimental," Dr. Clayton continued as he turned his attention to the second file.

Dr. Clayton looked at the file and searched his computer records. He also looked at several reports scattered around his office.

"This patient is really headed downhill. You have already increased his dosages. Given his blood work it is unlikely he would respond to a higher dose. There is not much left for him. I do have an experimental clinical trial I can get him into. It is a crude type of chemotherapy. Sort of like how they treated syphilis with arsenic before antibiotics. It may kill him, but it helps some people. You need to be clear with him about the risk," Dr. Clayton continued.

"Since that would be his last chance, I think he will do it. He is a tough little guy. Can I have him call you?" Jack asked.

"Of course, just don't get his hopes up too high," Dr. Clayton replied

Their medical work finished, Jack stood up and looked at the greenery of the Emory campus. "Are you going to have any time for fun when we get down to Sea Island?" Jack asked.

"These conferences are strategically designed to take place at locations like Sea Island so we can have a little vacation at the taxpayer's expense. I plan on getting to the beach and over to St. Simons in the evenings," Dr. Clayton said with a slight smile, thinking of the pleasures of the Coast.

"You know Annabelle will be ready to party, and I will have trouble getting loose for any meetings," Jack said.

"Let me give you a copy of the research summaries and my presentation. You can read them on the beach or in bed with Annabelle," Dr. Clayton said, handing Jack a large stack of documents and a binder containing the presentation. "Maybe your curious mind will see something important that we all have missed."

EIGHT

JUDGE AUGUSTUS VALENTINO had set the monthly meeting of the Homeland Security Coastal Region Advisory Committee for ten that morning in his Courtroom at the Courthouse in Brunswick, Georgia. Judge Valentino was the titular Chair of that committee which was the product of some complex political maneuvering when it became apparent that the infamous Sheriff of Ossabaw County, Roger Odum, was to be appointed as Director of Homeland Security Law Enforcement for the Georgia Coastal Region. In addition to his title as Director, the Sheriff had received high level security clearances which allowed him access to all sorts of Federal criminal investigation databases along with access to classified military information including real time information from military satellites. This high level intelligence access also included the construction of a sophisticated compound on the tidal Arkola River which bristled with satellite dishes and antennae towers and was completely under the control of the Sheriff. This boon was the result of the Sheriff's long time friendship with the local Congressman, Jarvis Ray, whose vast seniority and powerful Committee memberships made him a force in Washington. Congressman Ray was also assisted at the State level by his choice for successor to his seat, his son-in-law and Georgia legislator, Roy

"Soapy" Tilman. Together they had totally overwhelmed all local opposition to the appointment of a Sheriff that the Georgia Attorney General had once called "a fountain of corruption," in an unsuccessful local prosecution of one of his Deputies. The Homeland Security Coastal Region Advisory Committee was a small fish thrown to the objectors as a gesture of minor oversight of the Sheriff in his new role. The Advisory Committee at least allowed some input from other law enforcement agencies such as the Georgia Bureau of Investigation, the Georgia Attorney General's office, the Judiciary and the Georgia Department of Corrections who were less than delighted at the Sheriff's appointment. Judge Valentino's leadership gave the group more authority than the Committee's limited advisory powers would have indicated. Judge Valentino was a legendary figure in the Coastal area. During the Korean War he had been the sole survivor of a Chinese assault on a small, sad hill which killed fifteen other soldiers. He was captured and spent two years as a POW. After graduating from Georgia Law School, he arrived in Brunswick and set up a solo practice. In a few years and with some big cases won, he ran against a sitting Judge, Ezra Benton, who was getting along in years and was famous for his erratic comments and rulings. Judge Benton had gone unchallenged for years as the local attorneys feared him, with good reason. The entire local bar was relieved and delighted when Valentino won the election and established order in what had been a chaotic and unpredictable Court.

In attendance would be Fitz Davis, Special Assistant Attorney General who handled the Georgia Maximum Security Prison class action case for the State and other high profile State cases in the Coastal area for the Georgia Attorney General; Albert Pindar, the Regional Director for the Georgia Bureau of Investigation; Jack Templar, the Regional Director of the Georgia State Patrol; Dewey Lawson, the District Attorney; Commander Stanford Dalton who was in charge of the local Coast Guard Station and of course, the Director himself, Sheriff Roger Odum.

Fitz Davis hurriedly left his house on St. Simons Island at 8:45. He understood that the Judge would want to talk to him privately before the meeting began. Fortunately the traffic on the causeway to the mainland was light that day and he was in the Judge's office at 9:15.

"Good to see you, Fitz. The Judge is expecting you. Go right on in," was the cheerful greeting from Judge Valentino's Clerk, Albert Rogers. Davis lightly knocked on the mahogany door to the Judge's inner office as he opened the door, closing it behind him.

Judge Valentino looked up from the papers on his desk and stood to greet Davis, holding out his hand. "Fitz, I appreciate your being here early. It gives us a chance to talk and make sure the Sheriff doesn't get too far afield," the Judge said as Davis shook his hand and settled himself in one of the brightly upholstered armchairs in front of the Judge's desk. "We can also have a little chat about the class action at Georgia Maximum Security Prison."

"It may take more than this advisory committee to keep Sheriff Odum from unloading all the cocaine in South America right into the Coastal Region," Davis responded with a slight laugh.

"Well, look on the bright side. At least we are safe from terrorists," the Judge replied. "So what do you hear is going on? Anything new that the Sheriff is up to?"

"I understand that the DEA will be boarding the Columbian freighter, the Cabeza Rioja, off Miami which has a big load of cocaine. It is headed for Savannah. So at least the Sheriff won't get his hands on that."

"Are you having any more luck with that informant, Cindy Jessup, who works for him?" the Judge asked.

"Cindy knows she is in deep and is in trouble. She keeps giving me little bits and pieces, but nothing we could use to really bring him down. She is playing lots of games right off TV and expects to get full immunity and maybe keep a million or two in drug money. I worry about her if the Sheriff figures her out. It did shake her up when I told her about the Sheriff's handmaiden, Major Knowles, getting two hundred pounds of nice bloody beef trimmings from the slaughterhouse in Jasper for the Ossabaw jail the day before her brother got attacked by the sharks when he was fishing in his waders at his usual spot. Of course, I am sure that the Sheriff's records show that all two hundred pounds of meat was used to make sausages and other delights for the inmates at the jail. And they probably did use some of it for that. I did find it a little unusual that Major Knowles went out to the slaughterhouse himself," Davis said.

"Yeah, I imagine if you dribbled a little bit of that meat from the channel to that inlet where he liked to fish and then dumped about a hundred pounds right where you knew he would be you could expect to have several very excited sharks around in a hurry," the Judge replied. "I also remember the Coroner's inquest. Not much evidence of anything. You can't make a murder case on a few bits of beef in what was left of his clothes."

"Indeed. It was either an accident or very well done. But since he was just beginning to talk with me about his work at the Bank of Lanier I tend to think it was not an accident. Especially right after he stupidly sent me an email directly from his computer at the bank," Davis replied. "I have heard from my sources at the Banking Commissioner's office that the Bank of Lanier does seem to process a lot more millions in cash than you might expect from a little country bank," he continued.

"Do you think that's because Judy's Waffles N' Grits and the Ossabaw Crab House are just packing them in?" the Judge responded with a smirk.

"Probably. Everyone likes waffles. So that is where we are. One potential informant dead and another one acting kind of strange. Oh, and of course the Cabeza Rioja seems out of his range," Davis reported.

The Judge glanced at this watch. "The rest of the group will be here soon. I want to know what the Department of Corrections is doing about medical coverage at Georgia Maximum Security Prison since Dr. Bridge was murdered. Are they having any luck finding a new doctor?"

"Would you like a job where the previous occupant was murdered? I have explained to the Warden and the Commissioner of Corrections that they need to deal with this vacancy in a hurry. They have hired a search firm specializing in doctors and they are covering medical out of the Correctional Medical Institution in Augusta. They are also making a lot of extra trips to the local hospital," Davis responded.

"Fitz, you know that won't do for long. Am I going to have to order one of those doctors in Augusta to be transferred to Lester? Or if I move a bunch of those sick high max guys from Lester to Augusta it will mean a whole lot more security in Augusta. You know Arnold has been calling about this situation for the inmates. I think I will set it down for a Status Conference with both of you and the Warden to move it along," the Judge said.

"That's a good idea. I know how persuasive you can be," Davis said, thinking back to many changes of attitude produced by the Judge looking down the barrel of his reading glasses at the end of his nose and carefully explaining the options to some reluctant miscreant. "Also, maybe the Attorney General's office can get busy and convict some of those hotshot Atlanta doctors with Medicare fraud. You remember what a good doc we had for years, a while back, when the illustrious Dr. Bernard Austin, Board Certified in internal medicine and University of Virginia graduate, got himself in trouble for drugs," Davis continued.

"I remember Dr. Austin well. Somehow the Department of Corrections worked a little magic over at the State Medical Board and Dr. Austin received a limited license to practice medicine at Georgia Maximum Security Prison. They made him a trusty and let him live in a State house on the compound. They even gave him a car as I recall. I believe you used him as an expert witness in my Court several times with good effect," the Judge commented with a smile.

"I did indeed. He was a good doctor and an even better witness. Amazingly, no one ever asked if he had ever been convicted, he was so authoritative with his white coat, his deep voice and his silver beard," Davis responded with a laugh.

There was a knock at the door as Albert, the clerk, entered. "Judge I got all the players now assembled in the Courtroom except you and Fitz."

"Let's not keep this illustrious Committee waiting," the Judge replied with a slight wave to Davis as they headed for the Courtroom. "Albert, once we get in there, you and the Bailiff make sure nobody else enters. These Homeland Security meetings are one of the few things around here that are supposed to be confidential."

NINE

THE CLOISTER HOTEL at Sea Island, Georgia is a venerable resort which has catered to the well-to-do since its opening in 1928. The hotel was built by the Coffin family, along with the development of the "cottages" of Sea Island. The property descended to the Jones family who owned it for several generations until its sale in bankruptcy in 2010. The hotel and the beach club have been a prime destination for generations of Atlanta families. It was the sort of place where parents could rent a cottage and safely turn their children loose with their beach club number and bicycles, subject only to stern warnings to stay on the island and that they were only allowed to charge in the snack bar.

For years, bingo on Tuesdays and Thursdays has been seriously played by children, parents and grandparents alike. The cash bingo prizes were always generous and it was not uncommon for a child to turn over a well-worn bingo card to find the comment of a parent written long ago. "This card stinks!" or "I won $50," were common themes.

The grounds of the hotel were filled with ancient live oaks laden with Spanish moss. Many an Atlanta child had been disappointed when their shopping bag of the gray moss from the island

failed to prosper over the winter when transported to the trees of
Atlanta.

Parents and children enjoyed the freedom staying at Sea Island
brought. Connected to St. Simons Island by a bridge and then a
long causeway to the mainland, Sea Island was a world of its own.
Children were safe to roam on their bicycles, swim and play with
their friends, discretely supervised by a staff of attractive teenagers
hired by the Cloister for this purpose. Adults could have an elegant
dinner and drinks by themselves, safe in the knowledge that the
hotel would keep the children amused and happy, away from their
boring parents. Later in the evenings couples could drive over to
St. Simons which had a variety of somewhat more lively establish-
ments where drinking and dancing could continue into the night.

Many generations of Atlantans had moved down the path toward adulthood by boldly presenting fake IDs at the drive-in liquor
store window of the Geechee Club which was one of the few black
nightclubs on St. Simons. These questionable identifications were
always graciously accepted, especially when accompanied by a large
order and a five dollar gratuity.

Another St Simons favorite was the Altamaha Fish Ranch,
owned and presided over by owner and cook, Gerald Hopkins. It
was located in a cinderblock building on the south end of the island
decorated with strings of white electric light bulbs and served the
best seafood and steaks in South Georgia. Gerald was an Atlanta
lawyer who had left the practice of law and escaped to the quiet of
St. Simons. The decor was eclectic with ancient mounted local fish
on the walls near many of the better tables. It also featured a crackling fireplace in the winter and leather sofas and chairs, along with
a repeating tape of South Carolina beach music for added effect.
On a good Friday or Saturday night the parking lot was crammed
with scores of expensive automotive hardware from Sea Island
with a total value of about three times the construction cost of the
restaurant itself.

In recent years Sea Island decided to reinvent itself, much to the dismay of its longtime visitors and leading inevitably to its eventual bankruptcy. A gate was constructed at the entrance of the bridge to Sea Island and the Cloister declared itself to be a private club, open only to hotel guests and club members. "City" charge accounts (meaning Atlanta) which had been in effect for years were abolished, which meant that the more thrifty of Atlanta's gentry holding these accounts could no longer book an inexpensive room on St. Simons and then wander over to Sea Island for dinner and drinks.

The gate and the heightened security also eliminated the time-honored practice of teenage residents and young visitors to St. Simons sneaking into the beach club and its evening dances in hopes of meeting an attractive Sea Island visitor.

These changes and Sea Island's attempts at grander real estate development had pushed the resort into vast debt and forced the layoff of a good many employees. There was one sad day when hundreds of employees were let go. However, even with these problems, Sea Island and the Cloister remained a haven of tranquil Southern charm in a chaotic world and continued to be so under the new owners.

Jack was not concerned about the gate or any of the changes as he drove across the bridge to Sea Island after being properly identified as an authorized hotel guest by the pleasant guard. He'd been there scores of times beginning as a child and each trip blended in with the ones before and produced an immediate sense of comfort and relaxation the minute he was on the island. The salty marsh air thickly rolled over the windshield of his white Mercedes convertible. He could hear the familiar crunch of sea-shells that had made their way to the blacktop as he slowly turned into the entrance of the hotel past the old oaks and their heavy Spanish moss. As he pulled into the entrance he thought about the red MG automobile he remembered from his childhood which was always parked at the entrance to the hotel. As a child, he had been told that it belonged to Mr. Jones, the Cloister's owner, but it had disappeared years ago.

Jack handed his keys to the valet and waited as a bellhop took his bags from the car. "Welcome back, Dr. Randolph," the bellhop chirped, obviously alerted to his arrival by the guard at the gate.

"It is always good to be at Sea Island," he responded as he walked up the stairs and into the lobby. Once again, like the perfume of an old lover, the crisp distinctive smell of the Cloister lobby greeted him. Instantly he felt a pleasing sensation as his unconscious recollected a long assortment of happy memories.

"Good afternoon Dr. Randolph. Are you ready to check in?" the attractive thirtyish woman at the mahogany and brass reception desk asked. "We have you over at the River House. Is that okay?" she continued as she handed him the usual forms to be signed.

"I remember the old River House. My Dad used to let me catch crabs off the dock next to it. We always used a rope with chicken necks tied to the end. I would slowly pull it through the water and the crabs would jump on and he would scoop them up with a net. I suppose you don't allow chicken necks over there now," he replied.

"Would you like me to order you some chicken necks?" the woman replied with a smile. She was quite used to this sort of banter from the old Atlanta regulars.

Jack laughed. "Not right now. Maybe later. My friends from the CDC tell me they are full of germs. We didn't know that when I was young."

In a few minutes he was well ensconced in his room in the River House. He mixed up a bourbon and water from the minibar and opened the French doors to the balcony which overlooked the Blackbanks River. Leaning on the rail he could see the river and marsh which separated Sea Island from St. Simons. It was low tide and scores of sandpipers were busily poking into the slick and muddy banks of the river in search of their dinner. Jack waved to an elderly black fisherman on the opposite bank. The man waved back and proudly pulled a string of fish from the river, showing off his catch. Jack raised his glass in salute to his neighbor's fishing prowess. Another fisherman in a motorboat cruised slowly past, being careful to keep in the center of the river to avoid any sandbars that had popped up during low tide.

Jack thought of the many times he had fished on that river, thinking back to one particularly good catch of ten large sea trout off an oyster bed right around the river's next bend. He had been twenty and was still a student at Vanderbilt and he well remembered the trout and his willowy companion that day in her red bikini.

He walked back into the room and picked up the telephone. In a few seconds the hotel operator had connected him to Dr. Clayton.

"Howie, let's head over to St. Simons for some dinner. We need to scout up a wild woman for you. I'm worried that you might be headed for erectile dysfunction from lack of use," he said.

"What about Annabelle? I'm surprised she doesn't have something big planned for you tonight," Dr. Clayton replied.

"Annabelle and I are done. Seems like BT has won her heart and her vagina. She went out with him the night we had lunch. You remember her talking to him that day at Capital City. Apparently that evening was a major erotic bonding for the two of them. He invited her to a big house party at his place at Lake Rabun this weekend. Her touching goodbye call lasted all of a minute. So I am now history. But I had already paid for our room down here so I just came on down," Jack said.

"Good man. As bizarre and mean as she was, I really don't think she was the girl for you. I'm glad you came on down, anyway," Dr. Clayton replied. "I was a little concerned about the potential genetic combination of Annabelle and yourself. Such couplings should be prohibited under international law," he continued.

"I think I need to get out and celebrate my close brush with matrimony. Maybe I can round up some loose hide over on St. Simons. Why don't we meet at the Coast Cabin at eight?" Jack asked.

"Agreed," was Dr. Clayton's quick response. Jack hung up the phone and settled on the bed with his bourbon for a quick nap prior to getting ready for the evening. The girl in the red bikini with the trout kept running through his head as it touched the crisp down pillow and he dozed off to sleep.

TEN

THE COAST CABIN restaurant had been a fixture just off Frederica Road in St. Simons for many years. It was famous for local seafood and good steaks. As expected, the Coast Cabin was a huge, log structure with a broad green door and high beamed ceilings. The longtime waiters wore white coats and were quick with a serious drink. In the winter there was always a fire in the huge fireplace accelerated by sputtering pine fatwood piled high around the hardwood logs.

In recent years the Coast Cabin had added a dance club in a large room to the side of the restaurant. It was a favorite of the locals throughout Glynn County and the unreconstructed countryside beyond. Ladies drinks were usually a dollar on Friday nights and this greatly increased the crowd. The music was provided by a disc jockey who played favorites from the 70s and 80s along with some South Carolina beach music classics. Most evenings ended with an enthusiastic beach medley after which the house lights were switched on brightly and all exit doors opened wide.

Jack walked through the wide, front entrance door and saw Dr. Clayton seated in an overstuffed leather arm chair near a window overlooking the marsh. He was a little surprised that his friend was engaged in a lively conversation with two attractive women who were seated on one of the ancient leather couches nearby. Usually Howard was quiet and shy and rarely interacted with others, but these girls were laughing loudly at whatever he was saying at the moment. Dr. Clayton looked up and smiled heartily at Jack.

"Jack we were just talking about you. I was telling them the story about when we were Epsilons at Vanderbilt and you picked up that great-looking woman with tattoos at a liquor store. She was trying to make it in music in Nashville. The fraternity hired her as our cook for several months until she got her big break. She then went on to a successful career as a third string country singer. She's probably out there in a motel lounge somewhere, all thanks to you," Dr. Clayton admiringly stated.

"Johnny, you are misleading these girls. You know I was the shy intellectual one, and you were constantly on an ether frolic on your way to medical stardom. That girl bonded with you and wanted to have your baby which would have been born with a tattoo. Luckily, she met that guy from the rodeo and walked out of your life," Jack replied to the laughter of all.

"Jack, this is Cindy Jessup and her friend, Danielle Haaert. Cindy works for the Sheriff's office in Ossabaw County and among her many duties she is the Assistant Homeland Security Director for the Georgia Coastal Region," he said, reading the title from her business card in the dim light. "She was invited to the conference as a local emergency preparedness official. Danielle is in real estate and wants to sell you a condo," Dr. Clayton continued.

"Should there be an Ebola epidemic I would like to be quarantined in a condo with these two," Jack said slowly as he looked straight at Cindy's taut figure and flowing red hair. "Why don't you to join us for dinner?" he continued. With a nod from Jack to the waiter, the group quickly moved to a nearby table. The white coated waiter who had been watching this process and now seeing its expected conclusion, approached and announced the dinner specials which were the usual prime steaks along with freshly caught, local sea trout which only hours before had been lurking on the edge of a nearby oyster bed in the Medway River. It only took a few minutes for fresh drinks and dinners to be ordered and the waiter was on his way.

"Just what are your duties as the Assistant Homeland Security Director for the Georgia Coastal Region?" Jack asked, eyeing Cindy hungrily.

"The Sheriff of Ossabaw County, Roger Odum, is the actual Director of Homeland Security Law Enforcement for the Georgia Coastal Region and that is a Federal appointment. I work for him. We monitor all of the emergency, police and military communications on the rivers and coast in the Georgia Coastal Region. It is our job to know the whereabouts of all these folks and all vessels and aircraft in the region. I also do typing and filing for the Sheriff, so it is not all glamorous," she replied.

"Do you deal with many drug smugglers around here?" Dr. Clayton asked. This question instantly produced a crisp response from Cindy.

"Our job is to notify Washington and the local authorities if there is any suspicious activity which might be terrorist related. But, there is a lot of drug smuggling around here. There are miles and miles of twisting inland waterways which are great places to hide. And there are lots of flat roads and abandoned airfields for planes to land. But it is our job to look out for terrorists, although that does produce some drug smuggling arrests," she replied in almost a mechanical way, as though the response had been rehearsed and memorized. Obviously, this was not a subject which she wished to discuss further.

"Well, our drugs are legal and we will prescribe you some later," Jack said. "Especially if you are nice to us," he continued. "Of course it would be our medical duty to give you a full examination before doing that," he said. Cindy's reticence to discuss the local drug smuggling culture only increased Jack's interest in the subject.

"An Atlanta magazine did an article on the smuggling industry on the Coast a while back. I recall them saying that marijuana and cocaine smuggling were the number three industry down here, right after shrimp and Sea Island. I also remember seeing in a newspaper that the Georgia Attorney General had tried to prosecute a Deputy down here and at the trial called some Sheriff a ... fountain of corruption. Is all of that right? It sounded pretty authoritative," Jack asked, watching Cindy closely.

"That Cindy's Sheriff, Roger Odum all right. He's been down here for years and he is famous. But there are a lot of folks that love him. He is always helping some local charity or making big donations to some politician's campaign fund," was the giggled response of Danielle. "You always hear that there is some big investigation going on and that our local Judge Valentino, the one that did the Georgia Maximum Security Prison case and isn't afraid of the devil himself, will be coming down on them. But for years nothing has happened and Cindy is still not in jail. Of course, some people who might have been witnesses have disappeared sometimes and that may have slowed things down," she continued less gleefully.

Cindy added, "Oh, I see that stuff in the newspapers too. And sometimes we get subpoenas from the Court about our activities. But all we do is arrest drunks, break up domestic fights, give out traffic tickets, and serve divorces and lawsuits. Sometimes some of the shrimpers or high school students get caught with a little marijuana or cocaine, but the Sheriff arrests them and they go to jail with everybody else. I think if this were true the Feds or the Georgia Attorney General would've arrested him years ago like they did in Charleston and Savannah with the big busts they had up there. Anyway, if they were doing stuff like that I don't think they would be including a little file clerk and secretary," she commented, crisply.

Dr. Clayton interjected, "I heard a story once about the drug trade in Key West from a friend of mine at the Georgia Attorney General's office. There was a little State Bank down there with one head cashier. She was an old lady and lived in a trailer with her dog on one of the back Keys. Late one night, the dopers broke into her trailer and gave her the choice of them shooting her and her dog right then, or taking the automatic cash counter they brought with them and processing bags of bills and depositing them in the bank without the proper Treasury paperwork for $10,000 a week. Of course, she and the dog decided not to be shot and when she died of a heart attack two years later they found the cash counter and two million in plastic trash bags in her trailer. Apparently they were able to run about $40 million through that little bank with her help," Dr. Clayton said.

Jack jumped in as Cindy was looking a little irritated. "Gosh, I hope they didn't prosecute the dog. Cindy, we don't mean to imply that you were personally involved. But you do sort of look like a sexy drug babe, and I mean that as a compliment," he continued.

Cindy's expression eased and changed to a faint smile. "Yes, that is right. Like that old lady in the Keys, I have millions of dollars in cash hidden in my luxury trailer in Ossabaw County," she replied with a laugh. At this moment the waiter arrived with their dinners and two bottles of chilled Chardonnay. The music from the disk jockey in the dance room next door picked up and they all had to nearly shout as the subject turned to sea trout and beach music. The seafood was quickly devoured amid laughter with Jack and Cindy moving their chairs a little closer together and Howard and Danielle eyeing each other with smiles. The dinner closed with the waiter flaming a Bananas Foster for four with an elegant flourish along with cognacs for the men and Canadian ice-wine for the ladies. They all moved back and forth to the music which now could not be ignored.

"At least we made it through the dinner like serious professionals. I was a little worried there with all the wine and cognacs that Howie would begin to lose it and embarrass me with his famous Talking Trout Head at dinner, which is a sure sign that he needs to be sent home immediately in a taxi," Jack said as he pushed his chair back from the dinner table in obvious satisfaction.

"Right, Jack. I'm always the one doing the Talking Trout Head. At least the waiter didn't set the tablecloth on fire during his Bananas Foster presentation," Dr. Clayton replied.

"Howie, I do remember that. We were in some restaurant in Nashville the night of our fraternity formal and the idiot nearly burned the entire restaurant down," Jack said.

"And they wouldn't even comp our dinner, but you gave it a good try," Dr. Clayton said.

The girls were beginning to dance seductively in their chairs. South Carolina beach music was now shaking the very rafters of the Coastal Cabin. Jack grabbed Cindy by the hand and motioned to Dr. Clayton.

"We need to get these girls out on the dance floor before they start dancing on the table. Myrtle Beach music is calling," Jack said, gently guiding Cindy toward the dance hall. Dr. Clayton and Danielle were quick to follow.

Once inside, the dance hall could have easily been mistaken for the Illuminated Beer Sign Hall of Fame. The walls were filled with glowing neon slogans. Above the bar were at least ten of the most famous moving beer signs in North America. All night long, the signs worked their magic, hypnotizing several of the regular patrons at their seats at the bar. There was also the required mirrored, rotating ball which hung from the rafters and disseminated the lights from several colored lasers controlled by the DJ. The beer signs and the mirror ball were the only illumination, but it was obvious there was a good crowd on the dance floor with additional onlookers at the bar and at the tables on the edges of the room.

In general, the room was the picture of Friday night partying. But, just for a moment, Jack noticed one serious figure in the crowd. A muscular, thirtyish, black man stood military straight to the right of the front door. He was neatly dressed in dark slacks and a white polo shirt, and in his hand was a red plastic glass which did not seem to be getting much attention. On his hip was a portable radio with a small antenna. Jack turned to talk to Cindy and then glanced back, but the man was gone, and the door where he had been standing was left open.

"Shake your booty, Jack, honey," Cindy said as she danced provocatively in front of him, slightly bent over to give him a full view of her ample and nicely tanned breasts. The man was instantly forgotten by Jack.

"I want to dance!" Jack said, as he moved elegantly toward Cindy. He looked over and saw Dr. Clayton engaged in a stiff, boxlike dance attempt, with an occasional pathetic hand gesture for effect. This sad display of Caucasian dance limitations seemed to have no effect on Danielle who was shaking and dancing hotly enough for both of them. Jack could see the eyes of the rednecks at the bar following each of the girls with close attention. At one point, one of the men began to approach Cindy in an effort to cut in. Jack saw him begin his approach and watched as he stopped and returned to his seat, after a huge man in a Hawaiian shirt, who was obviously the bouncer, tapped him on the shoulder and motioned for him to return to the bar. What Jack did not see was that this activity had been prompted by a slight gesture to the bouncer from the mysterious black man who had somehow materialized near another door on the other side of the room.

After several rousing numbers the music slowed down and Jack knew from Cindy's tight embrace that this night had erotic potential.

"I want to be fucked at the Cloister," Cindy nearly shouted in Jack's ear, but louder than the music, with a slight slur, slightly bumping into other nearby dancers.

"You want to be fucked by an oyster? How kinky," Jack replied, as though he had misunderstood her the first time. He grabbed her by the hand and looked around for Dr. Clayton and Danielle.

"We are heading out now," Jack said to Dr. Clayton and Danielle as he spotted them on the dance floor. They waved as Jack and Cindy went outside. As the door closed behind them it was almost a shock as they left the music behind. The July flies, high in the trees, were the only sounds other than the occasional passing car and the muffled murmurings of the music inside.

Jack kissed Cindy passionately, pressing her tanned body against the cool, white metal of his car, "You can be fucked at the Cloister only if I get to do you in your trailer next time," he said with a laugh.

"I'm going to hold you to that," she said. "I'll be sure and put the best chenille on the bed and dust the velvet picture of Elvis that hangs over it."

The guard at the Sea Island gate took only a few seconds to identify Jack, and with a brief discussion and a slight smile at Jack's newly acquired friend in her truck behind him, the gate was opened and the two vehicles entered Sea Island. No one noticed the tan, unmarked, patrol car with a large antenna on its bumper as it made a U-turn on the road, several hundred yards behind them, but in clear sight of the gate guard house.

ELEVEN

IT WAS SEVEN in the morning the next day when Cindy drove her red truck up to the gate at a remote compound which was at the end of a two mile dirt road into the marshes toward the Doboy Sound. The compound was fenced with nine foot chain-link topped by razor wire. A large metal sign announced that she had arrived at the Ossabaw County Sheriff's Jail Annex and Emergency Preparation Center. The road continued to the right of the compound and the fence on that side was punctuated by a large white metal box with hinged doors which opened with a key lock on both sides of the fence. On the box was a vivid orange warning that it contained hazardous medical waste.

As Cindy pulled into a parking spot directly in front of the gate, a security camera mounted atop the fence swiveled and focused on her vehicle. She waved her hand out the window and the click of the electric lock on the front gate could be heard. Inside the fence was a white, wood frame building with no windows and a thick black metal door which contained a small viewing glass. The building was freshly painted and the grass of its small lawn was meticulously mowed and adorned by rows of flowers. At the side of the building were two huge black metal communications discs and an exotic stainless steel antenna structure from which numerous silver metal discs jutted out, pointed to the sky. The antenna towered sixty feet above the rear of the building. On the left side of the building was a long wooden dock which led out to the Arkola River and the Atlantic Ocean beyond. It was low tide, and a powerful Marine Interceptor boat topped by a large blue light and marked as, "POLICE—SHERIFF OF OSSABAW COUNTY," floated in the brackish water, loosely tethered to the dock. To the right of Cindy's parked vehicle was the Sheriff's personal cruiser, shiny and fresh from daily inmate washings. Several spaces over to her left was the tan, unmarked patrol car which belonged to Major Ross Knowles, who was the Sheriff's second in command and right-hand man.

She pushed open the gate to the fence and let it click back into its original locked position behind her. She walked toward the door to the building and noticed a large pelican had roosted on the stern of the police boat. She tapped her code on the control pad at the door and entered the building.

"Cindy, you're nearly one minute late for the Emergency Preparation Meeting of Ossabaw County," said a tall, heavy set, man with abundant, well styled, gray hair. He wore a crisp police uniform, complete with the shiny accessory of a stainless steel .357 magnum revolver, equipped with custom carved walnut grips of the type used in competition shooting.

"I am sorry, Sheriff. I hope we haven't had an emergency today," she replied. "At least you had Major Knowles to pick up the slack," she continued, looking over at the tall black man who was also dressed in a police uniform, but packing only the standard issue .45 automatic pistol. Knowles shook his head and removed his sunglasses which indicated that he also had just recently arrived.

At that moment, there was a muted clang of metal and curses in Spanish which were coming from the metal door to the lockup area. "It sounds like our guest from last night is ready for his breakfast," Major Knowles observed. "But he will have to wait for our business to be finished," he continued.

"How did last night go? Were there any problems?" Cindy asked the men, a little hesitantly.

"No, no problems at all. Just business as usual. Captain Billy got his boat escorted in here right on time last night. Our only problem is that idiot Mexican in the lockup," the Sheriff replied. "Why don't we go back in the Homeland Security room and take a look?" he continued. The Sheriff then turned to a large windowless metal door and tapped his code into a key pad as he peered into a small retinal scanner mounted to the side of the door. When the click of the locking mechanism was heard, he held the door open and the three of them entered the room. Above the door was a large sign emblazoned with the shield of the United States which warned, "Ossabaw County Emergency Response Control Room-Authorized Personnel Only-Criminal Penalties for Unauthorized Entry—US Department of Homeland Security."

The large room was windowless with cinder block walls painted a light yellow. It was brightly lit and contained four computers, each with two huge flat screen monitors mounted on the yellow walls. There was also a Radar Unit with a large screen that glowed a bright green, even in the well lit room. Four of the computer screens were divided into quarters with each quarter showing a real-time video of some location in the Coastal area via satellite. It was apparent from the captions displayed on the monitors that the videos shown were being taken in daylight but that night vision views are also available. Cindy glanced at the monitors and noticed that they were giving a clear picture of traffic on the Interstate, the town square of Lanier, (the County seat of Ossabaw County), along with a front and rear view of the State Bank of Lanier, and a slightly blurry picture of the State Patrol and GBI headquarters located just off the Interstate. The radar screen tracked the movement of a light plane which had just left the Glynn County Airport and which was now entering the airspace of Ossabaw County. The radar screen also showed a cargo ship on its way to Savannah and two shrimp boats at the mouth of the Medway River on their way into the Atlantic.

The Sheriff looked around expansively at the impressive display of sophisticated surveillance equipment. "It makes me proud to be an American that our Federal Government has been so generous and helpful with equipment and expertise so that even a little rural community like Ossabaw County has the means to fight terrorism and the war on drugs," he said as he clicked on one of the computer keyboards to show a real-time image of the County from space which showed all vehicles moving along the roads and all boats in the rivers or moving along the coast.

"Yeah, but those sorry asses at the State Patrol, the Georgia Attorney General's office and the GBI did everything they could to stop us from getting all this," Major Knowles stated.

"Well, there were those unfounded rumors that our office was somehow involved in the drug trade. Fortunately, our Congressman and local State legislator were able to override the petty concerns of the State bureaucrats," the Sheriff replied with a smile. He zoomed the monitor in with a few clicks on the keyboard to a particular residence where a green car was pulling into the driveway. "Looks like our School Nurse, Judy, is having another early morning pastoral counseling visit with the good Reverend James while his wife is in Atlanta," he said with a laugh.

"God's work never takes a vacation," Cindy said, always amazed at the details of the information now available to them, and thinking back to some of the Reverend's fire and brimstone sermons she had heard on the subject of adultery.

"They say knowledge is power, but I hope no one in this room would abuse the information with which we have been entrusted. It is way too valuable for gossip. And all blackmail must be done with the utmost Southern graciousness and only on approval by me," the Sheriff continued.

"Amen, Boss." Major Knowles said, still looking at the monitor with a smile. "Shall I brief Cindy on last night's take?" he continued. The Sheriff nodded his assent and Major Knowles tapped on one of the other computers and the monitor displayed a history of the radar traffic from the previous night. "The freighter, Cabeza Rioja, previously left Belize a few days ago and then proceeded up the coast to five miles off Cumberland Island. It had a cargo of lumber and rope. It was also suspected of carrying other agricultural commodities of somewhat higher value," the Major said, pointing on the screen with a laser pointer.

"Wasn't it supposed to be boarded by the Coast Guard off Miami?" Cindy asked.

"Yes, and as you can see from the tracking reports, they changed that to board when it was off Savannah," Major. Knowles continued. "So it was important to get some of the more valuable cargo off the boat prior to it being boarded off Savannah. The Captain of the freighter radioed that he had a medical emergency with a crewman who needed to be evacuated immediately. It just so happened that Captain Billy's shrimp boat was nearby for this humanitarian action. Billy made a mid-ocean pick up of the sailor who is now our guest in the lockup. Of course, along with the ill sailor was a clever and compact, submersible torpedo filled with 100 pounds of pure cocaine, neatly packaged into 10 pound waterproof bags which was being towed underwater by the freighter. For some reason, this rendezvous in mid ocean seemed highly suspicious to the authorities in Miami and Savannah who had been tracking this freighter. We offered to intercept Captain Billy's shrimp boat as we just happened to have our Marine Interceptor anchored off Cumberland Island. The Coast Guard ordered us to intercept the shrimp boat and bring it to our dock where they could board it and search it. Of course, we were glad to help out in the defense of

our country," Major Knowles continued, tracking the images of the
events with his pointer on the screen. "An ambulance was dispatched to our dock along with Commander Dalton, the head of
the local Coast Guard station. The medics checked out the sailor
and loaded him into the ambulance. He was clearly ill, suffering
from heart palpitations and probable alcohol overdose. Once the
sailor was secured in the ambulance, Commander Dalton and his
men thoroughly searched Captain Billy's shrimp boat. They found
lots of fresh shrimp and crabs; several, perfectly legal, hunting
rifles, and about ten boxes of cartridges, along with a couple of
shotguns. Commander Dalton declared the shrimp boat free of
contraband and a grateful Captain Billy presented him and each of
his men with a five pound bag of shrimp. While the Coast Guard
was searching the shrimp boat, our men reeled in the little torpedo
which was attached to our Marine Interceptor and put it in the ambulance. The ambulance sped off to the Glynn County Hospital
with Mr. Jorge Cantos, the sick sailor, and the load of cocaine, discreetly covered with a tarp. Mr. Cantos was dropped off at the
hospital in the custody of an Ossabaw Deputy for examination.
The ambulance then made a quick stop at the Glynn County
Airport and exchanged the torpedo and its 100 pounds of cocaine
for $2,500,000 in cash. The cocaine then flew off in a little silver jet
with a false set of FAA numbers to a small airport near Chicago.
As we have done business with these gentlemen many times, I'm
not expecting any problems with the count," he continued.

"Why is the sailor in our jail?" Cindy asked.

Noticing some nervousness on Cindy's part, and anticipating
her difficulty, the Sheriff took over the briefing. "A very good
point, Cindy. Of course, it did not take long at the hospital for him
to be stabilized. However, there may be good reasons that the
Captain of the Cabeza Rioja decided to throw this particular sailor
overboard. He started shooting off his mouth complaining about
his small share in the take and that he did not want to return to the

ship in Savannah. Fortunately he did this when only our Deputy was present so he was immediately taken into custody pending an inquiry into his immigration status. Amazingly, he produced an American passport which unfortunately was noted in his hospital paperwork and commented upon by several of the hospital staff. So we're going to have to let him go now that we have checked his passport and as a citizen he is free to remain in the U.S. But since he won't get back on that ship and he likes to run his mouth, he is a problem," the Sheriff said calmly, leaning back in his chair and looking patiently at the ceiling.

"You're not going to kill him?" Cindy asked fearfully.

"Of course not, Cindy. Despite what the newspapers and the GBI may say, we are a righteous, community oriented, drug smuggling operation. We have to engage in honest graft to protect our people and we do defend ourselves. We have not been in business for over fifteen years by acting like Al Capone and blasting anyone that gives us a problem. This is the South and we need to be nuanced and gracious in dealing with our adversaries. Sometimes they end up being our friends. Most of the time we just need for folks to look the other way, or to have a cloudy memory. Sometimes we need them to do very trivial things without asking questions. Like making a copy of a file somewhere, or retrieving a glass in a restaurant with someone's fingerprints all over it, or placing some small object in a person's house or car which allows us to hear what they really think about us. A lot of these good folks would be horrified if we offered them money. It would make it seem like what they were doing was really wrong. Take Commander Dalton for instance. If I had initially offered him $100,000 for his help with our work he would probably have called the FBI. On the other hand, he well remembers that awful night when his jackass son gave a fatal dose of Ecstasy to that that little 15-year-old runaway before they had sex. It was the middle of the night and the Commander was looking at a dead, underage girl full of drugs and his son's

DNA. Fortunately as this happened in Ossabaw County, Major Knowles was able to take charge of the investigation and he got to use the advanced investigation techniques that the Federal Government had taught him at FBI school in Quantico. Somehow, the DNA sample taken at the morgue, instead of implicating his son, turned out to be the DNA of our local problem child, Billy Purser. Billy had been seen talking to the girl earlier and a half empty glass of rum with his fingerprints all over it was found at the scene of her death. Billy, as usual, was so intoxicated on alcohol and drugs he had no idea where he had been that night. Billy pled guilty to the very reasonable charge of negligent homicide and the girl's body was cremated. I suggested to the Commander that a lengthy, out-of-state drug rehabilitation might help his son get his life back on track. I hear the boy is now in college out West majoring in political science and doing well. Of course, without us rudely mentioning it at all, I am sure the Commander knows that we have enough evidence stashed away to resurrect this problem at any time. And that is why Commander Dalton always takes personal charge of these interceptions and has no problem with receiving his $100,000 now," the Sheriff said.

"Cindy, you know we have to protect ourselves. These drug people are dangerous, but they are a lot less dangerous if you are firm and reliable with them," Major Knowles added.

"I know you're right. We do have to protect ourselves," Cindy said quietly thinking back to some of the unexplained disappearances in the County along with the many inconsistencies in various reports of accidental deaths and shootings which had been investigated by the Sheriff's office. She blinked slightly as a brief memory of her brother smiling and fishing went through her mind. Otherwise, her visage was quiet and thoughtful.

Satisfied with her response, the Sheriff and Major Knowles stood and opened the door to the outer office, "Cindy, we will get out of your way to let you finish up the Homeland Security Report on the interception and our count of the money," the Sheriff said. As he was leaving, the Sheriff reached over and gave Cindy a tight hug. "We aren't going to let anyone hurt you Cindy. You can count on that," he said. Cindy smiled with a little tear in her eye. She did not see the scowl on the face of the Major as he closed the door and pressed the code to lock her inside. She also did not notice the new clock on the wall which contained a small video camera that recorded all her activities through a pinhole disguised by one of the numbers.

Cindy took her key and unlocked the white cabinet above her desk. She removed the two bulging plastic trash bags and placed them on the desk. In a few seconds she had the contents piled before her. She took another key and unlocked another cabinet near the floor. She retrieved the automatic currency counting machine and plugged it into the outlet on the desk. The piles of money in front of her were already sorted into packs of hundreds, fifties and twenties. Carefully, she began feeding the bills from the packets into the counting machine beginning with the hundreds. The machine made a whirring sound as it shuffled and counted the bills with the totals appearing on its digital screen. Once or twice the machine would stop to indicate that a bill was counterfeit. She would then remove the bill and place it aside. She then banded the bills into packets of $5,000 for the hundreds, $2,500 for the fifties and $1,000 for the twenties. She totaled all the packets for grand total of $2,497,000 in genuine bills. She knew that $3,000 of counterfeit bills in a transaction of this size was insignificant to all parties. She placed the counterfeit bills in a separate envelope which she marked, "Destroy—Counterfeit" and placed it in a small metal box in the white cabinet.

Cindy counted out from the packets stacks of bills, totaling $5,000, $50,000, $100,000 and $200,000. She put rubber bands around each of these groups of bills and put them to the side. She then took the packets and arranged them into groups where the total of each group was $9,000. This gave her 238 groups of bill packets. She placed each packet into a large manila envelope and prepared for each envelope a deposit slip which indicated the exact amount of the deposit by using a computer program which randomly selected an account number for each deposit slip from over 400 separate accounts in the State Bank of Lanier. She then placed the deposits in three large, orange plastic bags on which were printed in large letters, "DANGER—HAZARDOUS MEDICAL WASTE."

Cindy then turned her attention to report writing. She clicked on the computer screen and selected "Homeland Security Incident Report." She filled in the blank form based on the incident report worksheets which Major Knowles had used to brief her concerning the rendezvous with the freighter Cabeza Rioja. These clearly set out, with precise times and locations, the radar detection of the meeting in mid ocean between the shrimp boat and the freighter and the transfer of the ill sailor. She succinctly described the request by the Coast Guard and the interception of the shrimp boat by the Sheriff's Marine Interceptor. She went on to discuss the search of the shrimp boat by the Coast Guard and the transfer of the sailor by ambulance to the hospital. The report clearly stated that the shrimp boat was thoroughly searched and no contraband was found. The incident was rated as not a threat to Homeland Security. There was a space for the signature of the Sheriff and the Coast Guard Commander. She printed the report along with a cover letter to Commander Dalton requesting his review of the report and signature for filing with Homeland Security.

Cindy then reached into the pocket of her jacket and produced a small, red plastic thumb drive which she quickly plugged into a port on the computer. She began by downloading the list of account numbers at the State Bank of Lanier. She opened and downloaded another file which showed movement of cash from those accounts to a dozen offshore accounts located in Panama and the Cayman Islands. Finally, she pulled a small crumpled piece of paper from her pocket and typed the password written on it into the security screen of another program. Once the password was typed a list of the usernames and passwords for those accounts appeared. She spent a few more minutes downloading various emails and memos. When she was finished she removed her thumb drive from the computer. She placed the thumb drive back into her pocket and gathered up the packets of cash and the plastic bags. She walked toward the door and pressed the button on the intercom mounted on the wall.

"Sheriff, the count is done and the money is in the medical bags. I have finished the report and it is ready for your signature along with a letter sending it to Commander Dalton. I've also got our quick cash ready in case you need to go shopping and the $5,000 for the sailor," she said. It was now three o'clock. She heard the sound of the Sheriff tapping in his code and stepping up to the retinal scanner. The door clicked and she pushed it open.

"Here's the money you have been waiting for," she said as she handed the stack of bills totaling $200,000 to the Sheriff and the stacks totaling $100,000 and $5,000 to Major Knowles. "I have got my $50,000 right here if either of you would like to count it," she continued. "The Count Report for the deposit of $2,142,000 is also here. It is only $3,000 short from counterfeits."

"We don't need to count your share. Just be sure you don't go and buy anything too flashy. A new Mercedes with jeweled mudflaps attracts a lot of attention down here in South Georgia," the Sheriff said. "You can go on home now and the Major and I will make sure that these hazardous medical wastes get properly deposited in the bank," he continued. As he spoke, Major Knowles retrieved the three orange plastic bags full of money for placement in the white, locked medical waste pickup unit at the fence. He dialed a number on his cell phone and stated that the medical pickup was ready. Soon an ambulance would arrive to transport the bags to the

State Bank of Lanier and discreetly place them in the night deposit bin where they would be deposited separately in each of the 238 accounts with no Treasury Department filings as each deposit was under $10,000.

Cindy was tired as she walked out the front gate to her truck. As she turned the ignition, she checked her purse to make sure she had her pile of bills. She also slipped her hand into her pocket to touch the thumb drive. She pulled her vehicle out of the parking lot and headed for her home. She was looking forward to her evening with Jack and she planned to get a good nap before he picked her up.

Major Knowles carried the orange plastic bags outside and waved to Cindy as she drove away. Using his key, he unlocked the lock to the white metal box which was inside the fence. He walked back toward the door and stood watch for a few minutes. It was not long until an ambulance pulled up to the box outside the fence and retrieved the bags through the hinged door on the other side. Major Knowles waived to the driver and reentered the building.

"Shall we see what she's been up to?" the Sheriff said to Major Knowles as he pressed his eye against the retinal scanner and entered his code on the keypad. They entered the Homeland Security room and the Sheriff removed a memory card from the clock and handed it to Major Knowles. The Major had already booted up the computers and he inserted the card into a slot on one of them. In a few seconds, Cindy could be seen on the computer monitor along with the date and time of the video. The Major fast-forwarded the video through Cindy's workday as the Sheriff watched intently.

"Damn, there she is!" the Sheriff snorted when the video showed her reaching into her jacket and retrieving the thumb drive.

"Back it up and slow it down. We've got to be sure," the Sheriff said tersely, running his hand through his silver hair as he watched the video. There, again, on the huge screen was Cindy, inserting a red thumb drive into the computer, this time in slow motion. The video moved slowly on to show Cindy unfolding a piece of paper and tapping codes into the computer.

"Let me check the keystroke monitor," Major Knowles said as he opened another computer program. The program opened and showed a list of files accessed and downloaded by Cindy that day. It only took a few seconds for both men to scan the entries.

"That damn bitch has downloaded the account numbers at Lanier Bank!" the Sheriff screamed at the monitor. "Shit! She has also somehow gotten into the usernames and passwords for the offshore accounts. She wasn't supposed to have access to those. That is most of our business. We got our own payments to make. If we don't, we will be the shark bait, like her damn brother," he said, nearly spitting as the dangerous reality of the situation became clear.

"At least we caught her today, and the money is still in the accounts," Major Knowles observed dryly, having suspected Cindy for some time.

"She is either going to rob us or rat us out," the Sheriff said in a loud sputter.

"Or both," the Major responded. "She must have figured out about her brother. She is probably working on a deal with Fitz Davis."

"We have to deal with her tonight. Thank God it is the weekend. These offshore banks won't let you change these passwords until they talk to somebody they know personally. But in the meantime, she could move a hell of a lot of money before we could stop her. Also, if the government had these passwords they could freeze the accounts pending an investigation," the Sheriff said, more calmly now, as he prepared their plan of action.

Major Knowles pondered the situation for a moment. "I think we can arrange something very soon, maybe tonight. She has been seeing some drunk doctor from Atlanta over at Sea Island. There could easily be an accident."

"Well, she brought it on herself. Do it, and get that thumb drive. Make sure it looks like that doctor is the cause," the Sheriff said. At that moment there was again clanging of metal and cursing in Spanish coming from lockup. "We also have to deal with that fool. You need to make sure it is obvious we turned him loose since he waved his U.S. passport around the hospital. I would like him back on that damn freighter so he can walk the plank when they get to deep water," the Sheriff continued.

"I have already talked to the Captain of the Cabeza Rioja. They were boarded off Savannah and brought into the harbor. To the great surprise of the DEA no drugs were found and they will be leaving on the tide tomorrow. The Captain is sending some folks to pick up Mr. Cantos. I will make sure he is ready to go with them," Major Knowles said with a slight smile. "Looks like tonight I get to use some of that forensic training Homeland Security gave me up at Quantico."

"He has been screaming all day that he is not going back to that boat," the Sheriff said. "Since he is a US citizen we can't force him. So I will assume that you're going to be subtle about how this is accomplished."

"Of course. It is all arranged. Mr. Cantos' shipmates miss him and there will be a touching reunion. I will make sure it is public and that our hands never move," the Major replied with a smile.

TWELVE

CINDY AWOKE FROM her nap at around 6:30. She was expecting Jack at eight. She stretched and yawned in her bed and enjoyed the chill from the air conditioner in the warmth of her fresh sheets and bed cover. She arose, dressed only in a pair of lime green, thong panties. She admired herself in the gilded full length mirror by her bed and reached for an antique silver hair brush on her dressing table to stroke her mildly disheveled hair. Her dog, a rescue greyhound, had been eagerly waiting for her to awaken. The large gray dog gently pawed at her hand as she stood by the bed.

"Rocco, the race dog, I know I have been ignoring you," she said as she patted the dog's head. "I know you'll forgive me if I give you one of these," she continued as she fished a dog treat from a Delft porcelain canister on her dressing table. The dog took the treat and retreated to a rug on the floor near her bed where he crunched with great enthusiasm. "There is no way you would make it at the track with all the treats you have eaten since I got you," she said, thinking back to years ago when she received Rocco as a Christmas gift. "Maybe I should've stayed with your buddy, officer Tibbs. We both liked him and I think he still misses you. He didn't like that I worked for the Sheriff. He always said that I was going to end up on the chain gang. But what I need is a nice, sexy doctor to take me up to Atlanta," she said, warmly remembering her erotic evening with Jack at the Cloister. "I am going to make sure he keeps coming back for more," she said as she admired her scantily clad figure in the mirror.

Cindy pulled on a red silk robe which lay at the end of the bed and grabbed her jacket she had folded over the arm of a chair. She reached inside the pocket and retrieved the thumb drive. She then reached into her purse which was nearby and retrieved the package of bills. She looked at the thumb drive and placed it on the dresser. She walked out of the bedroom and into the kitchen. She placed the package of bills into a plastic bag and then covered the bag with aluminum foil. She then placed the foil wrapped package into a back compartment of the freezer. This compartment contained ten other similarly wrapped packages with similar contents. The dog followed her into the kitchen and sniffed at the freezer.

"Rocco, I got all kinds of winnings disguised as leftovers, but I don't dare spend much of it," she said to the dog. "I can only buy things that people around here don't know about." Rocco looked up at her as though he understood. She picked up her telephone and dialed a number. It took several rings for the other party to pick up.

"Mr. Davis, it's me, Cindy. I know I am supposed to call on the other number, but I lost it. I thought about what you said about everything and about how this all can't last. I thought about some of those missing people. But especially about the pounds of meat and my brother. He had a big mouth and we didn't get along, but that was no accident, even if nobody can prove it. I did what you asked. I've got everything you need on a thumb drive. But I need some help too. If you can get me out of all this I will even turn over the $100,000 that I have left," she said softly and with hesitation, knowing that her freezer contained an additional $800,000. "I will get you the thumb drive tonight. I will be over at St. Simons and you can tell me where to drop it," she continued.

"I can send a State Trooper over right now to pick it up, or I will come myself," Davis stated with authority. "I can also get you out of here right away to someplace where nobody will find you. I think you are in danger, especially after this call," he continued.

"I wasn't planning on any witness protection plan," she said. "And if you send a State Trooper or you come over here you might as well get on television tonight and tell them all about it," she continued. "They aren't going to get suspicious unless the money starts moving around. I will just drop it off and take my chances for right now."

"Cindy, I think the second you downloaded the thumb drive the game was on. My job now is to keep you safe and get that information. We do want to help you and I am sure we can work something out," he replied. "Look, I know the Sheriff. And you have worked for him for years. I went to High School with him. He can be charming. But he will hurt you if he needs to. I'm also sure you know that about Major Knowles," he continued.

Cindy listened silently, knowing he was correct. "Oh, I don't think they have figured anything out about me at all. They figure I'm in it just as much as they are and everything is going just fine," she said. "I just want it all to stop, because I am scared and because of my brother, even though we didn't get along. I know they will do something else horrible and I'll be right in the middle of it. I know something's going to happen to that sailor, and there have been plenty of others. I just don't know the details. I don't want to know the details. I wish I didn't know about the meat from the slaughterhouse. Maybe I should just disappear with my dog. The Sheriff has made sure we can all disappear at any time," she rambled on.

"Cindy, that's one of the reasons this business has gone on so long. That, and all the Sheriff's good political friends. Anyone else would've tripped up after the first couple of years. But Sheriff Odum has kept this up for over fifteen years, and now the Feds have given him several million dollars worth of sophisticated electronic equipment so he can fight terrorists," Davis replied. "But there are some folks who know what is going on and are willing to do something about it. If I can ever get him indicted and let Judge Valentino's committee get a crack at him, that will do it," he continued, hearing Cindy sigh at his comments.

"I still don't think I need to turn my life upside down right now. I will be over at St. Simons tonight. I know I will be at the Marsh Tide Lounge later in the evening. Why don't I just hand off the thumb drive to one of your undercover guys that hopefully the Sheriff's people don't know. Have him wear a red sweater and ask me if I'm from Alabama. I will have the drive covered up in something and I will stick it in his pocket. After that, I'm sure I will be okay," she said.

"I hope you're not thinking that Atlanta doctor can keep you safe from these people," he replied. "He doesn't have a chance against the Sheriff and the Major."

"And you know about him?" she asked, a little concerned.

"I think that just about anybody who was over at the Coast Cabin the other night, including Major Knowles, would know all about you and your doctor. It really is a pretty small island," he said. "My report said something about you wanting to be fucked by an oyster, and that next time is in your trailer," he continued.

"God damn you! Now you're making me completely paranoid," she said.

"Paranoia is good. It helps you survive. Also, don't think that the getaway identity the Sheriff has provided you will be much use, especially to hide from him. Be looking for my guy in the red sweater who wants to know if you're from Alabama. But it may be a girl and there may be more than one," he said. "And if you feel like you're in trouble you might want to head over their way. They will be armed and dangerous," he continued.

"I will be looking for them. And I will be coming back here tonight. I'm not going to disappear. Nobody's going to run me away from my home, and my dog," she said as she hung up the receiver and stroked the dog's head, a tear in her eye.

"Rocco, I know you will protect me. Maybe I should've just married Tibbs. Then I would be living on a farm in Lester with about five little children and you. Stupid me, I just wanted something better. But this isn't better," she said as she patted the gentle greyhound. Encouraged, he retrieved a squeaky toy and squeaked it several times to arouse her interest. "All right, I will throw Mr. Mouse," she said taking the rubber mouse from the dog's mouth and tossing it back into the bedroom. The dog returned with the mouse and shook his head, hoping for another toss. "I have got to get ready. I've got a big evening planned. We may be moving to Atlanta. You may have a cute poodle as your new girlfriend." The dog was clearly disappointed.

THIRTEEN

JORGE CANTOS SAT in the backseat of Major Knowles' unmarked police van and from time to time slipped his hand into his pocket to make sure the $5,000 package of bills was still there. His other hand clutched a cup of coffee which had been provided by the Major.

"You doing okay back there Jorge?" the Major asked as he turned the ignition to the van. "Don't spill the coffee I gave you. It is expensive. The Sheriff and I insist on fresh ground coffee with spring water. None of this instant crap," he continued. Jorge understood most of what the Major said and continued to sip on the coffee, thinking to himself that it was surprisingly good, but contained some slight aftertaste that he could not quite identify. "I'm going to drop you off at the Bus Station. You've got plenty of money and you can go wherever you want since you are a U.S. citizen. You still have your passport, right?" the Major continued in a friendly manner.

"I don't think $5,000 is enough for being the bait in this game. The Captain knows I have problems with my heart. He took away my medicine and made me get drunk so he could pretend he was helping a sick person. I was really sick though. This business could have killed me. I'm not going back on that boat," Jorge replied. "I bet you got a lot of money for the drugs and I only got $5,000," he continued foolishly.

"That would be something you need to take up with the Captain. We are just doing what was agreed on. You've got your money and we are turning you loose. I'm assuming you don't want to spend any more time in our jail," the Major said as he pulled in front of the Lanier Bus Station. He parked the van and stepped around the back to open the door for his prisoner. "Let's go, Jorge. I'm going to personally escort you into this Bus Station. After that, you're on your own." Jorge scrambled out of the van, tossing his empty coffee cup onto the floor. The Major marched him through the front door of the Bus Station. The cashier and several of the passengers seated on the ancient wooden benches stared at this police escorted arrival. A security camera behind the cashier recorded the scene for posterity.

"Here you are, Jorge. You can go anywhere you want. I would suggest that there are better places for you than Ossabaw County," the Major announced loudly to the onlookers and security camera. Jorge looked up at the bus schedules which were written in chalk on a large blackboard next to the cashier's window. Major Knowles returned to his police van where he completed a report indicating that Inmate Cantos had been released and personally delivered to the Lanier Bus Station. Major Knowles then sat back for a few minutes and waited. The Major smiled as he watched Jorge leave the bus station, survey the street briefly and then head directly toward the "Ossabaw Crab House," which was the only bar in the vicinity. As Jorge entered the bar, the Major dialed a number on his cell phone.

"Jimmy, here's your man. When he starts drinking some alcohol he is going to start feeling mighty sleepy. Some friends of his will be coming to pick him up. Make sure you remember how glad he was to see them. You're also welcome to the $5,000 in his right front pocket," the Major stated.

Inside the bar, the burly, white bartender watched Jorge enter and take his place at a table near the window, waving rudely for immediate service. "I will take care of it," the bartender said softly into his cell phone as he picked up a menu and approached Jorge's table. The bartender nodded as Jorge ordered a double tequila and shrimp fritters. These were soon produced, with Jorge rapidly downing the tequila and demanding another, which was again quickly delivered by the bartender.

The bar was empty at this time of day, except for Jorge and the bartender. Jorge enjoyed his tequila along with the occasional shrimp fritter. Slowly, he felt a warm sleepiness come over him. He took another slug of the tequila and bit off half of a fritter as he settled back into the comfortable chair. The country music of the juke box soothed him. Soon his eyes were closed and he was snoring loudly. He did not notice either the gentle shake by the bartender or the hand slipping into his right pocket and removing the package of bills. The bartender stood briefly at the window and gave a slight wave.

In about two minutes a white sedan pulled in front of the bar and disgorged three large Latino men wearing sunglasses. One of them looked back with a slight nod to the police van parked down the street in front of the bus station. It took only a minute or two for them to enter the bar and to retrieve Jorge, who was picked up by two of the men. They deposited him into the back of the car which then slowly left the town square.

Major Knowles waited until the car had left the square and then turned the ignition to his police van. He listened with interest to the radio which announced a code 10–54, indicating a deer carcass on a nearby road. Without responding by radio, he headed toward the site of the carcass which he found at the side of a quiet residential street. The Major quickly picked up the small, freshly killed fawn which was still slightly twitching and placed it in the back of the van, making sure there were no observers.

The Major drove for about three miles to the highway and turned left on a sandy, dirt road marked by a rusting metal street sign identifying it as, "Marsh View Court." He drove a few hundred yards down the road, past a well-maintained yard with a white picket fence, adorned with flowers and clipped bushes. Under an old oak tree, laden with Spanish moss was a shining and new mobile home which sported a green striped canvas canopy over an enclosed porch overlooking the marsh. He noted that Cindy's truck was parked in the driveway as he took his police van through the roundabout at the end of the street and returned out onto the highway. He then drove toward Sea Island, carefully noting the cross streets and major intersections all the way to within sight of the Sea Island gate. He then turned around and repeated his previous journey in reverse. Once he got to the Ossabaw County line he proceeded more slowly and made some notes as to the cross streets and intersections. Some of these areas he recalled as particularly dangerous. Two of them had curves which were marked with small crosses and artificial flowers in remembrance of persons who had been killed in wrecks at those locations. He stopped his van and pulled over to the side of one of these locations. It was within a mile of Cindy's residence. He recalled one of the fatal wrecks which had occurred when a driver had been going too fast for the curve on a rainy night, lost control and slid into the massive stone outcropping on the side of the road. The Major exited his van and examined the faint skid marks from six months ago. He measured, in paces, the number of his strides from the first skid mark on the road to where the auto had left the road and careened toward the rock. He pulled a small pad from his pocket and made a note of the number of his strides and made a small diagram of the length and number of the skid marks. He then took a broad, careful look around the area and after putting his pad back in his pocket, returned to the van and drove away, satisfied with his calculations.

Major Knowles pulled the van into the parking lot at the Main Jail of Ossabaw County. He took the side entrance to the Administrative Offices in order to avoid the throng of persons who are always waiting at the front entry either to obtain news concerning the incarceration of a family member or friend or to await the imminent release of an inmate. It was a Saturday and the Administrative Offices were officially closed. He opened the door with a key and stepped inside. These offices were fresh and comfortable as compared to the dingy and dilapidated main entrance to the jail. The floor was tan ceramic tile which was waxed to a shiny brightness. In the waiting room was a new and comfortable red leather couch along with two similar arm chairs for visitors. In front of the couch was an intricately carved, mahogany coffee table with numerous local magazines, along with the Sheriff's own glossy publication, "Sheriff's Catch-Ossabaw," which had a picture on its cover of a smiling white Deputy watching over a group of happy black children on a playground. There was a modern, teak desk behind which sat, during office hours, a very pleasant, older black receptionist who had worked for the Sheriff for over ten years. On the wall behind the desk was a large oil portrait of the Sheriff beaming warmly, his ample gray hair preened like a mane. On another wall was a slightly smaller, portrait grade, color photograph of Major Knowles with a somewhat more stern visage.

On one side of the waiting room were the doors to three offices. The middle office had an elaborate double oak door and large gold letters, stating "Sheriff Roger Odum." To the right was an equally impressive oak doorway with its own gold lettering, stating "Major Ross Knowles." The doorway on the left was a more modest, white, wooden door which stated in black letters, "Cindy Jessup, Assistant Director." Major Knowles unlocked his door with a careful glance to make sure he was alone. His desk was strewn with papers and on the far wall was a reinforced black metal door which was marked in large red letters, "Evidence Room, Authorized Persons

Only." He unlocked the door to the evidence room with a key and a few taps on a code pad and walked inside. There was a small desk and computer with numerous locked cabinets taking up most of one wall.

The computer and monitor were on, but locked electronically. Major Knowles entered his user ID and password and the computer unlocked and presented him with an array of programs, one of which was blinking. He clicked on the blinking program to hear a replay of Cindy's recent telephone conversation with Fitz Davis. He clenched his fist slightly as he listened, and then turned to open one of the locked cabinets. In the cabinet was a piece of tire tread about a foot long. On the back of the tread was an adhesive marker identifying the tread by manufacturer, with the date, name and case number of the accident in question. He also removed from the cabinet a stencil of an irregular rectangle which was slightly longer than a foot, and a can of black spray paint. Unlocking another cabinet he pulled out a large yellow rock, about twice as large as a brick. He removed the white adhesive marker which identified the rock as evidence in, "Jodi Simpson fatality, Case 02467, Highway 189" and tossed the marker back into the cabinet. He put all of these items into a large canvas bag and zipped it closed.

The Major then reached for his cell phone and pressed an icon on the small screen. The screen noted, "Confidential Encoded Communication," as he dialed the Sheriff's secure cell phone number and the screen noted, "Confidential Communication Engaged." It only took a few rings for the Sheriff to pick up. "I've got things set up. She is coming back here with that doctor friend of hers tonight. They will be over at Marsh Tide Lounge. She has told Davis she is going to be handing that thumb drive over to one of his folks wearing a red sweater. That will not be happening and I'll pick up the thumb drive from their accident on the way to her trailer. I've got his car tagged for the satellite and you know how many folks slide off the road at the curve on Highway 189 and go into the rocks. It may be a little slick there tonight and I'm sure I'll be able to get pictures of some tire tracks that will show him going mighty fast. The pictures may be a little blurry, but they will be clear enough to show a tire just like the ones on his Mercedes to any expert that looks at it. Since that little stretch of road is scheduled for some emergency pothole work tomorrow my pictures will be the only evidence of those skids, and anything slippery that may have been on the road will be paved over. I also expect the doctor's and Cindy's blood work will show some cocaine and Ecstasy along with plenty of alcohol. In the accident, Cindy's head will also probably come in contact with one of the rocks in that formation, just like that other girl did six months ago," the Major carefully stated.

"Damn Cindy's ass. I wish this weren't necessary. And I can't believe Fitz Davis' superspy drop off with a red sweater in the heat of summer, no less. Why didn't he just send a Trooper over there to pick it up? Or go over there himself? Did he think we would try to stop them?" the Sheriff replied.

"He offered to do just that. And the red sweater nonsense is Cindy's also. Maybe she is snorting our product. But it sounds like Cindy is playing some kind of game with him. I think she's planning on keeping her money and getting some kind of immunity. I imagine she has no intention of turning over that thumb drive tonight. She thinks she is smart enough to play him for a concrete deal. She also doesn't think we're on to her and she may be planning on using some of those passwords to the accounts herself and then disappear. I know she has to have a big pile of cash somewhere because she sure hasn't been spending it," Major Knowles said.

"If Fitz Davis knows about the thumb drive, isn't it going to look pretty suspicious if she has a car accident?" the Sheriff asked.

"Of course, but we really don't have a choice. We know what is on that thing and he doesn't. For all he knows, Cindy could be bullshitting him. Also, when this night is over, even Fitz Davis is going to think that fool doctor croaked her," the Major continued.

"I guess you're right. Just make sure it looks good," the Sheriff said with resignation. "At least it will come down in Ossabaw County."

FOURTEEN

JACK CHECKED HIMSELF briefly in the rearview mirror as he turned the ignition and let down the top of his Mercedes. He nodded slightly with approval at the view of himself and his white dinner jacket and red silk bow tie. A patterned, red silk handkerchief which had been appropriately crumpled peeked out of his jacket pocket. He adjusted his sunglasses and was on his way.

He waved to the guard as he left Sea Island and accelerated out on the causeway toward St. Simons. In a few minutes he was on the new "hurricane proof" bridge which connected St. Simons to the mainland. He looked down at the water a great distance below and thought to himself that it would take quite a hurricane hitting at high tide to get water over this bridge.

Soon he was outside of Brunswick and on his way to the town of Lanier which was the County Seat of Ossabaw County. The road wound around the fabled marshes of Glynn, its curves caused by the road following the natural path of higher ground above the marsh. Jack inhaled the warm salty smell of the marsh and watched groups of pelicans swooping down into the rivers and inlets picking up a fine dinner of shrimp and small mullet. In about thirty minutes he was at the town square of Lanier. He drove slowly past the gray granite Confederate Memorial which was in the center of the square, surrounded by benches and topped by a Confederate flag. There was little traffic around the square with all the businesses except for the Ossabaw Crab House being closed, with most of them boarded up with "For Sale" signs nailed to the plywood. There were five cars in the spaces in front of the Ossabaw Crab House and its several neon signs flashed invitingly. Jack paused for a moment to check the directions Cindy had given him.

Once outside the town Jack speeded up and soon was on Georgia Highway 189 and in the countryside which consisted of marshes interspersed with mounds of higher ground, each of which supported at least one large and ancient oak tree, heavily laden with Spanish moss. At one particularly sharp curve, constructed to take advantage of a ridge of higher ground above the marsh, Jack briefly noticed a small white cross with several weathered plastic flowers attached, planted at the base of a large outcropping of yellow rock. He sped past as Cindy had instructed him that the dirt road which led to her trailer was one mile up the road on the right.

Jack slowed his car as he saw the weathered metal sign for Marsh View Court. He slowly made the turn and began to look for Cindy's trailer. To his surprise, on the left was an attractively manicured lawn with well cultivated flowers and neatly trimmed bushes all surrounded by a freshly painted, white picket fence. The trailer itself was new and shiny and sported a green and white striped canvas awning as part of a screened porch which overlooked the marsh. On each side of the trailer were two huge Magnolia trees. Cindy's red truck was parked near the trailer in the driveway which was made of crushed oyster shells.

As he pulled into the driveway to park behind her truck, the front door opened and Cindy waved to him. "I see you found it," she said. "I was afraid that you would get lost all this way out in the country."

"Cindy, if this is trailer living I'm impressed. What a pretty spot," Jack said as he walked toward the door. Rocco the greyhound shot past her and headed straight to Jack. In just a second the dog had covered the distance between them and was eagerly licking Jack's hand. "So this is Rocco the race dog?" Jack said, patting the dog on the head as they both walked toward the door. "You make me miss my old greyhound, Polly."

Jack looked at Cindy as she stood in the doorway and was again surprised at how gorgeous she looked in her crisp, white, linen dress. "Cindy, you look so great in that dress. And those platform heel knockoffs you must've gotten at the dollar store could fool anybody in Atlanta," he said admiringly.

Cindy tossed her red hair and motioned him into the trailer. "Everything about me is totally genuine, including these shoes," she replied, her authentic and tanned breasts amply filling the top of the linen dress.

"How about that designer solid gold necklace?" Jack said, looking more at the tanned bosoms than the necklace.

"All right. That is genuine costume. I bought it from a street vendor in Savannah. It does look real though," she replied, knowing that she could not admit to owning an eight thousand dollar necklace. "How do you know about all this women's stuff?"

"I have two sisters and have had several very expensive girl-friends," Jack said, thinking to himself about Annabelle's array of treasures, as he and the dog entered the trailer.

"Okay, I'm ready for my drink and the trailer tour," Jack said as he looked around the interior of the trailer. "You know, this is really very nice. It reminds me of a really large boat," he continued as he ran his hand across the green granite countertops in the kitchen.

"This is my kitchen and little dining area. It is like a boat galley, and very efficient," she said as she pointed to the gleaming stainless steel appliances. "I've got two ovens, a cook top, a big refrigerator and freezer, and microwave," she said as she continued to lead the way. "This is my living room. I bought that oriental rug at a garage sale," she continued, fibbing about the origin of the rug.

Jack moved into the living area followed by the dog. A couch tastefully upholstered in light green linen was at the edge of the oriental rug, flanked by a classic armchair. The couch and chair faced a huge plasma television screen mounted on the opposite wall.

"Most people who live in trailers don't have signed Heriz antique oriental rugs," Jack said looking at the rug closely and running his fingers over the weaver's Arabic signature woven into the carpet. "And these Angela Loach oil paintings of the marsh sell for about twelve thousand each, over at the Cloister Gallery," he continued, pointing to the large, detailed oil painting on the wall above the couch.

"I see you're not only an expert on women's accessories, but you also know oriental rugs and art. Angela's brother got into a little trouble several years ago. I mentioned it to the Sheriff, and somehow it all got worked out. She gave me that painting for Christmas three years ago," Cindy said as she opened the door to the porch, continuing the tour.

"Wow, the view of the marsh goes on forever. This kind of view on Sea Island would cost millions," Jack said as he entered the porch and looked out at the expanse of marsh. "Look at those two porpoises out there, running the mullet in the river. No wonder Sidney Lanier used to write poems about this," he continued with a sweeping gesture.

"You make yourself at home and I will get you a nice Planters Punch," Cindy said as Jack sat in one of the white lacquered, antique rattan chairs and continued his enjoyment of the marsh view. Rocco the greyhound nuzzled his head on Jack's lap.

"Cindy, if that necklace were real I would be pretty sure you are in the drug business after having seen the layout of this place," Jack called to her as she headed for the kitchen.

"Well I'm not. Besides, nobody around here knows anything about this stuff. You're the first person I've ever had over here who had a clue," she said as she returned with two potent rum punches in tall, icy, cut crystal glasses.

"You mean the good old boys that you and Danielle ordinarily pick up at the Ossabaw County Sunday combination drag race and tractor pull, don't know a Heriz from their ass?" he asked.

"No, but they can be kind of fun, as long as they don't stick around here too long and don't track in too much mud," she said with a suggestive smile as she handed him his drink.

"To upscale country living!" Jack toasted, clicking his crystal glass to Cindy's.

"Oh look! Here come the porpoises again," Cindy exclaimed as she pointed out to the river which wound its way through the marsh, like a flat, black snake.

Jack looked and saw the two porpoises attacking a school of mullet, causing the fish to jump in all directions. They watched for several minutes as the porpoises devoured their dinner and then headed up the river to the ocean.

"There's one area of the tour I haven't seen and that is your bedroom. With all these quality furnishings, I hope that you will have at least some South Georgia décor in there," Jack said as he sipped on his planters punch.

"I have redecorated it slightly to make sure you would not be disappointed," Cindy said as she took his hand. They walked together back to the master bedroom. On the way, she pointed to a small bedroom which contained a single bed. "That's the guest bedroom you will be occupying if you misbehave," she said, pointing to the tiny single bed. Cindy then flipped the light switch as they entered the master bedroom. "How do you like it?" Cindy asked with a smile.

"Cindy, that is the finest Elvis as an Angel painting I have ever seen. I'm assuming it is painted on genuine black velvet," Jack said, marveling at the large spotlighted painting and its massive gilded frame. "The classic pose without a shirt, and the wings discreetly poking out in the back, definitely put it in the category of rare art. I also like the brass, cat head, belt buckle."

"I got it just for you. I wonder if the apple on the table, and the Bible in his hand have some mystic significance?" she said with a seductive smile as she ran her hand across his back.

"Everything about Elvis is mystic. I also think it goes well with the mirror," Jack said as he noticed the tall gilded mirror mounted on the wall to the left of the bed. Feeling her fingers on his back he began to wonder whether dinner was really necessary. "I think that mirror is perfect and well-positioned," he continued, running his hand across her tanned back. "I also see another shabby Oushak oriental rug on the floor here, and an antique English chest as your dresser. I am going to start attending these garage sales down here," he continued as he turned to kiss her. She returned the kiss passionately and for a moment dinner was forgotten until Cindy lightly pushed him away.

"This is waiting for you Jack. But we don't want to miss our dinner at the Cloister. I have been looking forward to it," she said, running her hands strategically down his chest and back. Rocco the greyhound concurred with a low woof.

"All right. This little bit of foreplay will set the tone for the evening," he said as she gently led him toward the door of the trailer. He glanced back with a smile and a sigh at Elvis and the gilded mirror.

FIFTEEN

"GOOD EVENING AND welcome back," the uniformed doorman said smoothly with an appreciative look at Cindy as he opened the glass door to the Cloister lobby. As they entered, Jack once again noticed the familiar fresh smell and let it stir his happy memories of previous times there. They walked through the lobby directly to the formal dining room. There was a small line of several couples with their well-dressed children. Occasionally, one of the mothers would shake a finger at a slightly rambunctious child and remind the offender to be on his best behavior.

Jack and Cindy stood at the end of the line for a few seconds until the maître d' caught Jack's eye. "Dr. Randolph, we have been expecting you," the maître d' said heartily to make sure those ahead in line were not too offended by his preferential treatment as he waved Jack and Cindy to come forward.

"Robert, I'm so sorry. We were running a little late," Jack announced, also playing the game, as he walked past the line with Cindy and followed the waiter to a quiet table by a window with a good view of the chamber music quartet. "Robert, this is lovely. Here's one of those Presidential Engravings for your collection," Jack said smoothly as he handed the waiter a sealed white envelope which contained a government issued portrait of President Andrew Jackson which was legal tender for all debts public and private.

"Yes Sir!" the maître d' responded, retreating gracefully with the envelope in his pocket. Jack could see one of the frazzled mothers looking back at him with a slight pout as she and her brood were escorted to a side dining room full of parents and well-dressed children.

"I see you got us to the grown-ups section," Cindy said happily as she looked at the elegant couples seated at tables generously spaced around the room.

"I have been in the side room with the mommies and the potted plants many times over many years. And in those days I was pretty likely to disturb dinner by pulling on my sister's hair or something similar. So it is about time I graduated to this room," he replied.

"And it looks like you could have a good long run over here," Cindy said, looking at some of the attractive, older couples nearby who were still obviously enjoying each other's company. "I do hope you won't pull my hair."

"Not until we get back in front of Elvis," Jack replied with a smile. "Of course, eventually, you do have to go back to the side room," he continued as he nodded at another family group in the side room, this time with an elegant older gentleman in a vested pearl gray suit who was gently resisting his middle aged daughter's attempt to tuck a linen napkin into the front of his shirt.

A white coated waiter approached with a substantial wine list. Jack looked at it carefully, finally focusing on the sparkling wine section. "Cindy, you look so lovely I feel like celebrating. Why don't we do a bottle of this California champagne? I hear they serve it at the White House," he said, smiling as he touched her hand, with a slight glance at her tanned and freckled bosoms. The waiter nodded his approval and departed.

"What shall we celebrate?" Cindy asked, returning his smile and lightly tickling the inside of Jack's palm with her finger.

"I think we should celebrate the concept of Elvis in Heaven," Jack replied after a little thought. "We will culminate the evening in your little Shrine in back of the trailer," he continued as the waiter returned and presented the vintage in classical fashion with a crisp white towel draped over his arm. Jack nodded and the waiter uncorked the bottle with a subdued pop and poured a touch for Jack to taste. Jack swirled the golden liquid as he drained his glass. "Perfect!" he pronounced and the waiter proceeded to fill the glasses.

"To Elvis!" Jack toasted.

"To Elvis and Heaven!" Cindy lustily replied, extending her pretty pink tongue into the glass.

"All right. Now I want to know where you got your taste for oriental rugs, antiques, paintings and designer necklaces," he said. "I'm assuming you acquired your taste for Elvis here in South Georgia."

"My grandmother was a fine, small town Virginia lady. My mother, against her wishes, married a Navy guy who moved us down here to the submarine base. I spent a lot of time with my grandmother when things were bad with my parents and brother. She died two years ago," Cindy replied.

"Those little towns in Virginia have a lot of ladies who know their stuff and are in command of their world," Jack said, thinking back to his own elegant Virginia-born grandmother who presided over her small town in Georgia. "What happened to your parents and brother?"

"My dad was killed in a car wreck he caused by driving drunk. My mother died of breast cancer and pain medications. They have both been gone about five years. My brother, Ray, died a year ago in a shark attack while he was fishing. He worked at the bank in Lanier."

"I'm sorry. I can see you are like your grandmother, a quality lady," Jack said as he raised his glass in salute. Cindy's eyes batted back a tiny tear.

"I would like to be," she said softly as the waiter arrived to take their dinner order. "At least I was able to take care of her in her last days and make sure she was comfortable."

"Was that shark attack down here?" Jack asked.

"Yes, he was fishing on a Sunday like he regularly did. He always waded off an oyster bank in a little inlet near his house to catch sea trout. Apparently, he waded into a bunch of big sharks that day," she said.

"That is very unusual. There is so much food for the sharks down here to eat with the trout and mullet and all," Jack responded, touching her hand. "Cindy, you are a fine lady. It seems you have managed to overcome and move on. But I do think we need to be concentrating on our celebration of Elvis in Heaven," Jack said, squeezing her hand lightly and looking into her eyes.

"I am in heaven," she said, looking back at Jack and around the beautiful room. At that moment, the Quartet began to play soft jazz.

"I am going with the Crab Newberg and the blackened local sea bass," Jack said, looking intently at the menu.

"I'm having the sturgeon caviar from Eulonia and the shrimp and grits," she responded. "That Eulonia caviar is from right down the road. The local shrimpers kept catching the big sturgeons in the tidal rivers. Then one of them went to New York to learn from some Iranians how to process the roe into caviar. It's unbelievably good," she said.

"Yes, the Batson family. Every great restaurant and club in Atlanta gets their caviar from them. I have ordered quite a bit of it myself," Jack said.

"You have been down here a lot," Cindy said, slightly surprised at the depth of his local knowledge. The waiter politely nodded as he wrote down their selections and refilled their glasses with champagne.

"Have you ever been married or are you married?" Cindy asked with a laugh. "I should've asked that the other night, but things were moving so fast I forgot," she continued.

"Something about romance with an oyster, as I recall," Jack said with a smile to Cindy. "No, I am not married and never have been. I was recently engaged, but that is now over. How about you?"

"I was engaged and lived with a fellow for two years. He is a correctional officer at the big prison in Lester. He gave me the dog. He was a wonderful, kind man. I just wasn't ready to be a country wife. I know it hurt him when we broke up," she said, as the waiter arrived with dinner. "At least I got to keep Rocco."

"To Rocco, the race dog!" Jack again toasted. "And to my beautiful, sophisticated country lady," he said, leaning over the table to kiss her. She leaned forward to meet him, taking full advantage of the opportunity to show off her breasts at the top of her white linen dress. They kissed delicately and briefly, and Jack could see the smiles and nods of the older couples around them. He also did not miss the glimpse of Cindy's delightful cleavage as each sat back to dinner.

The quartet struck up a gentle version of an old forties favorite as they focused on their dinners. "Are you happy with the Newberg and your sea bass?" Cindy asked.

"Of course, and I love this song. It was my Dad's favorite. He loved to embarrass me by singing along with it," Jack said with a fleeting thought to his father and long ago times at Sea Island. With smiles and laughter they enjoyed their dinner until the slight interruption of the waiter inquiring about dessert and mentioning the evening's specialty, Crepes Suzette.

"Why don't we get the Crepes Suzettes which are my favorite and Edward VII's," Jack said as he looked admiringly at Cindy.

"Yes, and of Suzette, his mistress. The King had his Chef, Escoffier, invent them just for her," Cindy tossed back.

"That does it. There can be no question that you are a quality lady. I suspect that you and I and the Chef at the Cloister are the only people in South Georgia who are aware of that bit of culinary history," he said.

It was not long before the waiter appeared with a brass and crystal cart loaded with the preparations for the classic dessert. With just the right amount of subdued flair, the waiter prepared the orange sauce and gently cooked the crepes in a gleaming brass saucepan. With a deft touch, the crepes were flamed. As always, heads turned around the room in acknowledgment of the creation of the famous dessert.

"More champagne, Sir?" the waiter asked as he divided the dessert equally between two china plates emblazoned with the green Cloister logo.

"Why don't we do one more glass each?" Jack suggested. "We need to take it slow and easy."

"That is a good idea. I want to head over to St. Simons for some dancing. I don't want you going to sleep early," she chided gently.

"Sleep is the last thing on my mind," Jack replied looking at her lustily. His eye caught the finger bowl with its slice of lemon floating sideways. It could have easily been mistaken for some kind of drink. He looked back at Cindy.

"Jack, I'm not going to drink the finger bowl," she said, reading his mind, as she elegantly and correctly dipped her fingers in the bowl and rubbed them on his nose.

"Well then, I will!" he said, as he reached with both hands for his finger bowl and tossed it back, chomping slightly on the lemon slice.

SIXTEEN

THE PARKING LOT at the Marsh Tide Lounge was nearly full. The flashing neon flamingo and blinking, out of season, Christmas lights made it clear the establishment was open for business. Jack eased his car into one of the last remaining spots. As he and Cindy were headed for the door he saw Dr. Clayton and Danielle at the corner of the lot.

"Howie, Danielle, what have you two been up to? I was looking for you earlier at the Cloister," Jack said as he and Cindy waited at the door.

"Danielle wanted to go over to Darien for dinner tonight to get some fresh seafood. It was definitely fresh. The tables are right at the dock with the shrimp boats. You just clean the shrimp yourself and toss the remains down a hole in the center of the table," Dr. Clayton responded enthusiastically.

"I went there a couple of years ago. It was fun. Sometimes the seagulls can get a little annoying," Jack said as the group entered the bar. Jack held the door for Cindy who entered first, followed by Dr. Clayton. Danielle dropped her purse and Jack stopped to pick it up. They cracked their heads together as each bent over to retrieve it. After a bit of laughter and apologies, Jack and Danielle entered the bar together.

When Cindy and Dr. Clayton had entered the smoke-filled room, Cindy immediately looked up at the bartender. "Jimmy, I see you have a night job over here at the Lounge. It must be a long day after working at the Ossabaw Crab House," she said in a crisp tone that conveyed a touch of dislike for the bartender.

"I fill in here sometimes. Might as well get my share of these Atlanta tips." The bartender then looked at Dr. Clayton and surmised he was Cindy's date for the evening. The group made their way to a table on the edge of the dance floor as Jack excused himself to go to the restroom.

The waitress returned to the bar with an order for three drinks. "These for the two girls and the guy?" the bartender asked.

"A bourbon and cola is for the guy. The beer is for the lady on the left, and a planter's punch for your friend, Cindy," the waitress replied.

"Yeah, my friend, Cindy. I will get them fixed up," the bartender said, as the waitress walked away toward another table of customers. He reached in his pocket and palmed two small vials of clear liquid, each with a rubber stopper. He poured the drinks and before he placed them on the bar, he deftly popped the top of each vial and poured the contents into the bourbon and the planter's punch. He carefully stirred each drink with a swizzle stick as the waitress returned and picked up the drinks.

The bartender watched the waitress deliver the drinks just as Jack arrived from the restroom. The bartender watched as Jack put his arm around Cindy and sat in the chair next to her. He quietly hit his fist on the bar, now realizing that Jack was Cindy's date. He fumbled into his pocket again and was relieved when he found another vial. He had brought another vial, as some recipients needed an extra dose if they were especially large. Looking at Jack's slight frame he knew that one dose would be more than sufficient.

"I need a brandy and soda for table six," the waitress said as she returned to the bar. She pointed to Jack who now had his arm around Cindy. The bartender nodded and began preparation of the drink, again adding the contents of the vial, making sure the waitress did not notice.

"There you go honey. I bet those folks will be having a good time tonight," the bartender said, smiling grimly. The waitress flashed a fake smile, and was gone with the drink.

The band was slowly assembling on the small wooden platform in front of the dance floor. An ancient upright piano was on the platform as a permanent fixture. The musicians slowly unpacked their instruments and amplifiers, all of which showed the wear and tear of many years of low-level Saturday night entertainments.

Cindy glanced around the room several times, looking for the red sweater. "Are you expecting a friend?" Jack asked on her third visual tour of the room.

"Well, yes. I always see people I know here. I just want to show you off a little," she replied as she spotted a small middle-aged man across the room wearing a red cardigan sweater. She then noticed an athletic young woman in a tight red sweater take a seat at a table across the dance floor.

"Danielle, have you sold Howie a condo down here yet?" Jack said with a broad smile, now suddenly feeling witty and bright as he sipped his drink. He also noticed the unusual glowing smile on Dr. Clayton's face as he sipped his half full bourbon and cola.

"I am ready to buy the whole island!" Dr. Clayton responded happily, putting his arm around Danielle.

"And I will sell it to him," Danielle replied.

The band settled into place, making the usual instrument checking sounds which indicated that the music was about to begin. A tall, thin, older white man positioned himself at the piano. He wore a white polo shirt and a yellowing white linen jacket which looked as though it had spent most of its years crumpled in a ball. The man pecked at some of the higher keys of the keyboard, apparently testing them. Jack noticed that Cindy was carefully watching the entrance of a college aged couple who were both wearing red University of Georgia sweaters. Jack watched as she then moved her glance to the middle-aged man and the young woman.

"It looks like there are quite a few University of Georgia folks wearing their red and blacks tonight," Jack commented.

"You're right. I really didn't think of that. On any night there are usually a lot of Georgia fans wearing red. Maybe green would have been better. But you know, right now, I am feeling happy and sweet and not really caring," Cindy replied with a slight slur and a broad smile. "I've got my Dr. Jack and everything is just right," she said, giving Jack a hug, as she felt in her pocket to check to make sure she still had the thumb drive. She felt relieved when she touched the small ball of the drive wrapped carefully in tissue. "But maybe I will just talk to all of them until I find the right one," she rambled on, as she briefly thought to herself that she was feeling odd.

"What do you mean green?" Jack asked as the band suddenly began to play with a roar of music that drowned out his words. Jack turned and saw that the piano player had exploded into action. His wrinkled white coat now flashed from the glare of the one spotlight which hung precariously from a rafter in the ceiling. The light also lit up the green and red glass gems which endowed the several rings on his slender fingers which were now moving rapidly across the keyboard. Jack watched as the man stood and kicked away the piano bench, all the while continuing to hammer the keyboard as he tossed back his yellow mane of hair.

"Let's party!" Dr. Clayton yelled as he waved his arms wildly. Danielle smiled at him and sang along demurely. Jack squinted at his friend, surprised at such enthusiasm, and looked over at Cindy who was also singing loudly and waving her arms in the air. He took a long pull on his drink and settled back into his chair. In a

few seconds he began to have a feeling that the music was personally talking to him. As a doctor, there was a fleeting logical thought
that this reaction was something more than mere alcohol. But this
thought was like a brief flash of lightning in the face of a warm,
happy rising storm.

"More piano!" Dr. Clayton now shouted as the band switched
into another old favorite. He grabbed Danielle by the hand and was
out on the dance floor. Dr. Clayton then proceeded to perform a
medley of ancient dances beginning with the funky chicken which
culminated with a somewhat jerky shag, with unsettling tango in-
fluences. Danielle appeared to be having a good time, but was
having difficulty keeping up with her deranged partner.

Jack watched his friend with approval as he felt a great cloud
of cosmic happiness and universal communion rising up inside
him. These glorious feelings were interrupted by the hot and erotic
intervention of Cindy passionately kissing him and running her
hands through his hair. Again, a distant and tiny rational voice
warned him that there was a problem with this behavior in a public
place. However, this voice soon faded in the face of Cindy's
amorous attentions. The thought entered his mind that now would
be a fine time to pull down the top of Cindy's dress and get a really
good look at her tanned and freckled breasts when the band
stopped playing. Dr. Clayton, Jack and Cindy all winced at the sudden cessation of the music with which they were all reverberating.
They stared quietly as the band walked off the stage for their break.
The upright piano sat empty, still illuminated by the harsh light of
the spotlight.

Even in his highly amplified state, Jack was surprised to see
Dr. Clayton stride up to the stage and after retrieving the bench,
position himself in front of the upright piano. The microphone was
still on and attached to the amplifier, so when Dr. Clayton reached
over and announced, "Ladies and gentlemen, the Flight of the

Bumblebee," his words boomed out across the establishment. Everyone, including the bartender, bouncer and waitresses watched and waited. At once, Dr. Clayton with a great flourish began to play the difficult classical masterpiece. He played it perfectly and its substantial power was only increased by the amplification provided. Cindy became swept up in the music and played an imaginary air piano with rapidly moving fingertips as she accompanied Dr. Clayton. Jack also felt the power of the music and shook his head in time with the ringing notes from the piano.

When Dr. Clayton was finished, everyone in the audience jumped to their feet and applauded. "Classical, baby, classical!" Cindy shouted almost incoherently while she gave Jack a fierce hug. Danielle watched and clapped, amazed at her date's proficiency on the piano. Dr. Clayton strode in triumph back to the table to the applause of the entire room. "You were so good!" Cindy said. "Where did you learn to play like that?"

"My mother made me take piano lessons from elementary school through high school. I took a few of my own when I was in college and medical school. I play for myself and I rarely play in public, except for recitals over the years. Today I just wanted to get the music out," Dr. Clayton said as he returned to his seat. "Usually I am too shy to play in front of other people. I think Danielle has put something in my drink, but I'm not complaining," he said smiling at Danielle.

Jack finished his drink as he laughed out loud. "Howie, I assure you, that's the first and last time that Rimsky-Korsakov has been played at the Marsh Tide Lounge," he said. "I feel so good if I could play an instrument I would've been up there with you," he continued. Cindy was now groping him enthusiastically under the table as she delicately pushed the tip of her tongue into his right ear. Suddenly she stopped, her eyes fixed on a figure across the room.

"What the hell is Major Knowles doing over here on St. Simons?" Cindy said excitedly. Jack turned to look in the direction indicated by Cindy but saw no one.

"Cindy, who is Major Knowles?" Jack asked as he continued to scan the room. "What does he look like?"

"Oh it doesn't matter. He is my boss at the Sheriff's office," she said. "Let's get on out of here. But I don't want to go straight home. I know a place where we can chase ghosts," she continued, again groping Jack under the table as she spoke her words wildly into Jack's ear with an occasional tongue poke for extra emphasis.

"What will we do if we catch a ghost?" Jack asked as he took her hand and they headed for the door.

"We will fuck them, of course. And I get to go first," she explained, with a wicked laugh.

SEVENTEEN

CHRIST CHURCH HAS been ministering to the inhabitants of St. Simons Island since 1736. The Church was rebuilt after its malicious destruction by Union troops in the Civil War. It is now a fresh white structure with a grey roof, surrounded by old oaks heavily laden with Spanish moss. Behind the church and enclosed within a wrought iron fence is the church graveyard with the oldest tombstone dating from the early nineteenth century.

General Oglethorpe, the founder of Georgia, appointed his Secretary for Indian affairs, Charles Wesley as Chaplain of nearby Fort Frederica, succeeded by his brother, James Wesley. The Wesley brothers later left the Church of England to become the founders of the Methodist Church. Charles Wesley returned to England abruptly, after only a few months of service on St Simons, with no explanation. There had been well known arguments with his brother and many rumors of sexual adventures to add mystery to Charles' sudden departure to England.

It was whispered among the locals that the graveyard was haunted and it had been a favorite late night trysting place until the Church restored the wrought iron fence and installed a formidable gate which was padlocked daily by the Church Sexton. However, these defenses could be breached.

"Pull right up to the gate," Cindy instructed as Jack pulled his car from Frederica Road into the Church compound. Cindy got out of the car with her purse and walked up to the gate. Jack watched her lustily as his headlights revealed the delicious tightness of her dress and the fact that several of her top buttons had been undone in their journey to the church.

"Cindy, look at that chain and padlock. There is no way we are getting in there," Jack shouted.

"Jack, do I have to remind you that I am the Assistant Homeland Security Director for the Georgia Coastal Region and that Christ Church is a Hurricane Evacuation Center under my jurisdiction? That would be why I have the key," she said, waving a large key ring she retrieved from her purse. In an instant, she had unlocked the padlock and was removing the chain.

"Now, I'm going to show you how the local wenches had their way with the Right Reverend Charles Wesley. They say some of them still haunt the graveyard as naked ghosts," Cindy said as she kicked off her shoes and proceeded to remove her dress. Jack watched in amazement as she undressed and stood totally nude in the glare of his headlights.

"You have to catch me now if you want some!" she said giddily as she turned and ran off into the graveyard. Jack got out of the car and followed her past the ancient headstones. Once inside the gate, he looked around in the darkness, but he could not see her anywhere. He walked down a cobblestone path which turned past a large magnolia tree, all the while, peering into the darkness. He stopped and stood by the tree for a second, looking back toward the car and listening for any sound. All was quiet and he continued down the path, past the tree. The second he was past the tree, Cindy jumped out and, waving her fingernails in a ghostly fashion, said, "Who goes there, mortal? What is the password?"

Jack looked at her lovely tanned body and puzzled for a second. "My guess is Wesley," he said.

"Wesley will do!" she said as she ran forward to embrace him. At that moment, from the other side of the graveyard and down the road was the sound of a car starting and then its lights illuminated the path near where they were standing. The car was some distance away on a side road leading to the Church. It would take a few minutes for it to wind around to where their car was parked.

"Time to go now, Ms. Ghost. I hope they didn't see us," Jack said as he pulled at Cindy's hand. They scampered back up the path, stopping quickly to retrieve Cindy's clothes and lock the gate. Jack could see the car's lights as it backed up and turned to get to their side of the Church. Cindy wriggled halfway back into her dress as Jack threw the car into reverse and without turning on his lights, headed down the blacktop toward St. Simons village.

"I'm going to pull in to a side street up here in case they are following us," Jack said as he accelerated the car down the narrow road. He could see in his rearview mirror that the other car had now arrived at the Church gate and was continuing behind them. As Jack topped a hill he sped up quickly and then turned into a small subdivision. He waited for the car to pass. In a few seconds the other car sped past the entrance to the subdivision.

"Glynn County Sheriff's Department," Jack said softly as he read the lettering on the car as it drove past.

"Can we go back now and get naked in the cemetery again?" Cindy said laughing. "They will never expect us to return to the scene of the crime."

"We are getting you back to trailer trash heaven. We have a date with Elvis and your gold framed mirror," Jack replied, now feeling a wave of excitement at the thought of getting Cindy into a bed. His heart was racing and he felt especially happy and in control. Again, a small flash of a message from some part of his rational medical persona warned that things were not quite right, and that the amount of alcohol they had consumed should not be producing this sort of wildness. But the message faded as he watched

Cindy glide her flowered silk panties up her long legs and back onto her tight bottom while he sped across the bridge toward the mainland, Ossabaw County and Cindy's trailer.

In his euphoria, Jack didn't say a word as Cindy reached into her pocket and pulled out a pack of chewing gum and a small wad of tissue paper. He watched her chew several sticks of gum briefly and then retrieve a small red plastic object from the paper. She then covered the red object with the chewed gum and pushed it up under the dashboard in front of her. "The red sweater people from Alabama won't be getting this tonight," she said dreamily. At the time, this seemed quite fine and normal to Jack. "I hate it when girls chew gum," was his only comment as he grabbed the pack of gum from Cindy's hand and put it in his pocket.

EIGHTEEN

MAJOR KNOWLES SAT in his tan unmarked van and stared at the glowing screen of his laptop. The van was parked unobtrusively off the side of Highway 189 behind some scrub palmettos and a small magnolia tree. It was not visible from the roadway. Only the bar of blue lights on the roof identified it as a police vehicle. His position was approximately two hundred feet from the rock outcropping which had been the scene of other crashes. The computer screen showed a map of the local area within twenty miles. Major Knowles watched the glowing green dot which was Jack's car, as the map showed it moving rapidly across the causeway bridge.

"You better slow down, son. You're speeding. I don't want you to get caught just yet," he thought to himself with a smile as he analyzed the trajectory of the bright dot headed toward his location. The Major then clicked to open another program which showed a night vision satellite view of his location within a two mile radius. He noted the headlights of an oncoming truck on the screen, and within a few seconds the actual headlights appeared on the road behind him as shown on the computer in real time. He switched back to the tracking program and with a few additional clicks he was given an estimated time of arrival for the car represented by the glowing dot to arrive at his exact location.

The Major activated the security icon on his cell phone and speed dialed a number. "Yes," the Sheriff answered. "It appears we are on target for contact," the Major responded quietly. "Good, let me know after," the Sheriff said without further comment. Again, the Major clicked back to the tracking program to make sure that Jack was still on course and then clicked to a full screen version of the two mile area satellite view. Satisfied, the Major placed the laptop sideways in the passenger seat so that the screen could be easily seen from the outside of the vehicle through the driver's window. He then reached around his seat and retrieved his canvas bag from the cargo area of the van.

The Major exited the van and walked over to the rock outcropping and carefully paced twenty nine full strides to a point on the blacktop approximately four feet from the faded skid marks left from the previous fatality. He placed the rectangular shaped stencil on the road. It would make sure any inadvertent paint droplets were not deposited on the road surface. He then removed the piece of rubber tire and a can of black spray paint from the canvas bag. He sprayed the rubber track with paint until it glistened black. He then carefully placed the tread on the rectangle in the stencil and then removed it quickly, creating a realistic impression of a tire track skid on the road. Pulling a retractable measuring tape from the bag he carefully measured the width of a Mercedes such as Jack's and then re-sprayed the tread and laid down another painted skid mark to the left of the first one, simulating a skid of the left tire. In the warm evening air the black paint began to dry immediately.

The Major then returned to the van and placed the canvas bag which contained the tire tread, stencil and spray paint in the cargo area. Sliding the cargo door open he picked up one of two five gallon cans of liquid and carried it to a location fifteen feet in front of the skid marks. He poured the glistening liquid soap on the right side of the road so that it covered the blacktop with slickness for a distance of about ten feet. He then returned to the empty can to the van, being careful not to disturb the painted skid marks or the slippery liquid.

The Major then grabbed the dead fawn's tiny legs, picked the little carcass up easily and took it to a spot about ten feet in front of the soap slick. The Major carefully placed it with about two feet of the deer's head protruding across the center line on to the right side of the road.

The Major stepped back to review his work. A driver coming down this road at high speed would see the deer carcass and naturally move his car slightly to the right to avoid running over the deer's head. This would put the car careening into the slick at an angle which would send it sliding directly into the rock outcropping. There would be a crash with the passenger side of the car having massive impact with the rock as had happened in the previous fatal car wrecks at that location. The painted skid marks would make it appear that the car was traveling at a much higher speed when the brakes were hit to avoid the deer carcass. There would be no skid marks from the actual auto as the soap would quickly slide the auto off the road.

Satisfied with his work, the Major then walked back to the van and settled into the driver's seat. He clicked on the tracking program and saw that Jack was about three minutes away from being viewable on the two mile satellite program. The two mile view showed no other traffic on Highway 189. The Major took one long look around the scene and settled back to wait.

Jack was now happily cruising his top down Mercedes through the center of Lanier with music blaring and Cindy dancing in her seat and waving her arms. There was no traffic at this time of night and their merry travel went unnoticed until they sped past the Waffles N' Grits, at the city limits of Lanier and its posted speed limits of 25MPH. Inside, coming off his evening shift was Georgia State Trooper, Doug King. He had just settled into his late-night dinner of country ham, grits and coffee when he happened to look up and out the window toward the highway as Jack and Cindy went speeding by. He could even hear the music as a customer opened the glass door to the restaurant.

"Dammit, I thought I was done for today. Lilly, keep my plate warm. I've got to intercept some drunk perpetrators. I'll be back," he said to the waitress, pointing to his food as he moved through the door. By the time he had his patrol car back on the highway, Jack and Cindy were miles ahead.

Jack was going about 65 when he saw the deer in the highway. "Oh no! He's dead," Cindy said as she also saw the deer. Jack braked slightly as there appeared to be plenty of room on the right to avoid running over the carcass. Jack was calm and now that he had spotted the situation, it was just a matter of avoidance as he approached. But as he drove closer something seem to be wrong. The road just ahead was shining and reflecting in the bright moonlight. Jack had no time to respond as the car slid off the slippery road and careened directly toward the rocky outcropping. "Jack stop!" Cindy screamed as the car hit the rocks. The impact crushed her door with the most jagged part of the rocks. A piece of the yellow rock hit Jack in the head just as his airbag exploded.

Major Knowles watched the collision and its aftermath silently for a few seconds and listened to the hissing of broken radiator hoses over the sounds of the still audible music. He turned on the blue lights and moved the van from its hidden position and parked it directly over the soap slick. Exiting the van, he pulled open the cargo door and retrieved the second five gallon can, filled with water which he poured under the van to wash away the soap. He returned the empty can to the van and groped around for the canvas bag and retrieved the brick sized yellow rock from the previous accident. He put on his leather gloves as he approached the wrecked vehicle.

Jack was unconscious and still strapped into his seat belt. Blood poured from the gash made by the rock down the side of his face. Major Knowles could see that Cindy was still alive even though the door on her side was penetrated by a piece of the rock formation. It was clear she had been pelted by several large rocks that had been slammed loose like cannonballs from the impact. She appeared to be unconscious and was making only low moaning noises. Major Knowles stepped around to her side of the car and positioned himself with the rock in both hands to break her extended neck as she slumped forward. There would be no way to show that this blow was any different from the others. As he pulled back to strike, he took a quick glance around to make sure his actions would be unwitnessed. Suddenly, in the corner of his eye, he saw the flash of a blue light about a thousand yards away and behind a distant hill on the highway.

"Damn, they must've picked up a Trooper," he said as he tossed the rock to the ground. He removed his gloves, placing them in his pocket and took his radio from his belt. "Two-zero here. We have an accident with two injuries. Highway 189 at the rocks. Send an ambulance," he said loudly into the radio, continuing with the car tag information and vehicle description. It was only a few seconds before the State Trooper pulled quickly around the blinking van and off the road to within a few feet from the crash site. Major Knowles stepped forward as the door to the State Patrol cruiser door opened. Trooper King emerged from the car and walked quickly over to the wrecked vehicle.

"So here they are. They blew right past the Waffles N' Grits just as I was starting dinner," the Trooper said, looking at the smashed car and its bleeding occupants, wondering how Major Knowles had arrived so quickly at the scene.

"I have already called for an ambulance," Major Knowles said calmly. "The girl is in bad shape. The guy looks better, maybe just a head laceration."

The Trooper looked out to the highway as the blue lights from both the Trooper car and Major Knowles' van whirled about them both. "Looks like they hit a deer and swerved," the Trooper said, looking at the carcass. "They sure were flying. I wish I had caught them. How did you get here so fast?" he asked, always suspicious of anything involving Major Knowles or the Ossabaw Sheriff.

"I was just on the way to the Waffle N' Grits myself when I saw them on the side," Major Knowles said smoothly.

"Do we have any ID on these folks? Have you called in the tag?" the Trooper continued.

"I called in the tag when I called for the ambulance. I didn't want to move them to look for an ID until the ambulance arrived," the Major responded. At that moment they both heard the wail of a siren and they turned to see the flashing red lights of the ambulance approach. It pulled off the highway and flashed a spotlight on the wreck as it pulled alongside. The driver, a thin, twentyish, white boy with long blond hair and the EMT, a tall, middle-aged black man with a beard, jumped out of the ambulance and walked quickly to the wrecked vehicle.

"Look at the passenger first. She is the worst off," the Trooper instructed as they approached the car. The EMT opened the rear door of the ambulance and pulled out two stretchers which he placed upon the sandy ground. He then dragged one of the stretchers near the door to the passenger side of the car and looked at Cindy's crumpled form in the light of a flashlight.

"Well, at least, she had her seatbelt on and the side airbag activated. But that didn't do her much good with these rocks," he said as he unlatched the seatbelt and continued to examine her with the flashlight. On the other side of the car the ambulance driver was performing the same maneuver with Jack. The EMT flashed his light briefly on Jack.

"I think we can safely lift them," the EMT pronounced as he put on a pair of gray rubber gloves and a face mask. "Come over here and give me a hand with the girl," he said to the driver. The driver, who had also donned his gloves and mask, walked quickly to Cindy's side of the car.

"I'm going to lift her out from under her shoulders. You get her feet and we will put her on the stretcher," the EMT ordered. He then gently put his arms around Cindy and slowly pulled her over the side of the car. As he did so, several large rocks fell to the floor of the car. The driver caught her legs and they deposited her on the stretcher. Cindy's face and dress was now a mass of blood and the gold necklace which had survived the impact was painted with blobs of red mixed with the yellow dirt of the rocks. The EMT snapped the straps of the stretcher around Cindy and then he and the driver carried her to the back of the ambulance. In a few seconds they returned for Jack. Again, the EMT gently pulled Jack's limp form from the car seat and the driver grabbed his legs as they lowered him onto the stretcher.

Major Knowles and the Trooper watched as Jack was carried on the stretcher to the ambulance. The Major reached over and picked up Cindy's purse from the floor of the car and retrieved her driver's license. "Damm! This is our girl, Cindy Jessup. I didn't recognize her with all the blood. This must be that doctor from Atlanta she talked to us about," the Major said convincingly. "Why don't you escort the ambulance and I will finish up here. I want to make sure we get this guy that fucked Cindy up. I will be right behind you," the Major suggested to the Trooper.

"I'll look after her!" the Trooper responded with a wave, as he bounded back into his cruiser. In a few seconds the ambulance containing Jack and Cindy was speeding toward the Glynn County

Hospital preceded by the State Patrol cruiser with sirens and lights at full alert.

After their departure, Major Knowles continued to examine the contents of Cindy's purse, and the interior of the car, hoping to find the thumb drive. He then walked back to the van where he tossed the purse into the cargo area. He picked up his cell phone, again activated the security icon and speed dialed a number.

"Yes," was the Sheriff's response.

"We are not quite done. They are headed for the hospital. I've arranged for the County to be doing some repaving here tomorrow," Major Knowles said softly.

"So she is still alive?" the Sheriff asked. "Did you get that thumb drive?"

"Negative," Major Knowles replied. There was no response from the Sheriff and the call was disconnected.

The Major pulled his digital camera from his pocket and took several pictures of the car, the skid marks, and the deer carcass. He was careful that the pictures of the road did not include the now disappearing slick.

NINETEEN

IT WAS ABOUT ten the next morning when Jack finally woke up. His head throbbed. He touched his face where it was tightly bandaged. His tongue felt fat and his mouth was very dry. He was lying on a metal bed with side rails as in a hospital. But it did not seem quite like a hospital. It took him a few seconds to focus as he blinked his crusted eyes to look around. He felt too weak to sit up, so he moved his head slightly to look around. Even this gentle movement greatly increased the undulating pain in his head. He could see that he was wearing an orange uniform of some type and that his right wrist was attached the bed rail by some sort of plastic bracelet. He tugged on it, but it was impervious to his efforts. Slowly, as he flicked his eyelids, the details of the room became more apparent. He saw that the whole room was painted stark, shiny white. The floor was a dull gray concrete. There was a black metal table on the opposite wall and the room had a small window which was glazed with translucent glass bricks which allowed light to enter, but provided no view of the outside. Focusing on the window, he saw it was buttressed by white metal bars. Jack looked up at the ceiling which contained a large fluorescent panel which gave off a white, flat, light. It was encased in a heavy white metal frame, secured by a key lock. A question dimly occurred to him about why a light on the ceiling would need to be so secure. The answer became evident when he painfully turned his head to the door of the room. Where the door should have been was a white steel gate made of bars about an inch and a quarter thick. At the handle was a locking device in a metal box which appeared to have an electric component and a brass manual lock. He could see people in white medical dress moving outside the gate, along with others in his same orange outfit.

As he watched the gate, an Asian nurse and a large black man in a police uniform stood outside. Jack heard a metallic click, and saw the officer push the metal gate open. "It's about time you woke up," the man stated loudly. "Although with your blood tests it could have taken a week," he continued harshly. The nurse followed the officer into the room and began to take Jack's pulse and temperature.

"Where am I?" he asked, fearing the answer.

"You are in the custody of the Sheriff of Ossabaw County, in the jail infirmary. I am Major Knowles. We picked you up last night from the Glynn County Hospital emergency room in Brunswick. Your friend Cindy is not so lucky," Major Knowles responded.

"Where is she?" Jack asked, thinking back to last night with great difficulty.

"She is still in intensive care. She is in bad shape," the Major responded.

"What happened?" Jack asked slowly.

"Real simple. You were drunk and on drugs and lost control of your vehicle. It hit some rocks and she got the worst of it. A State Trooper witnessed you blowing through town, past the Waffle N' Grits," Major Knowles said.

"I think there was a deer," Jack said slowly, dimly remembering.

"Your skid marks show you going off the road at about 90. You have been charged with driving under the influence of alcohol and drugs and reckless driving. If she dies you will be charged with involuntary manslaughter," he said curtly. "Sign here," the Major said, thrusting a paper in front of Jack's face.

"What am I signing?" Jack asked, peering at the paper.

"Just that we have your clothes and your personal property, like your wallet. You will get them back when you get out," the Major responded.

Jack peered at the paper briefly and signed. "Do I get to talk to a lawyer?" he asked.

"Of course. We have most of the major Constitutional Rights down here in Ossabaw County. And if you can't afford one, which I doubt, from looking at what's left of your Mercedes, and the cards in your wallet, the Court will appoint you one for free," Major Knowles said briskly, articulating the usual language of incarceration.

"The nurse will give you a portable phone. There is a phone directory in the drawer to the table," he continued crisply.

"What about my car? And when do I get out of here?" Jack asked softly while putting his hand on his throbbing forehead.

"Your lawyer will be the one to talk about your bonding out, if that is possible. Your car, what is left of it, has been impounded as evidence for testing," was the Major's terse response. "You can also tell your lawyer that Cindy works for the Sheriff and is a friend of mine and many of the other staff. If he is concerned about us treating you unfairly we will be glad to have you transferred to the Atlanta or Savannah jail," he continued with a smirk.

"Thank you for your concern, but somehow I think I might be better off here. And could you please take this off my wrist?" Jack replied, knowing full well he would be a major target for abuse in the Atlanta or Savannah jail.

"We didn't want you waking up and falling on the floor," the Major said, nodding to the nurse to undo the plastic cuff as he turned and left.

The nurse continued her examination, removing a metal scope from the pocket of her uniform along with a portable telephone. She handed Jack the telephone and undid the plastic bracelet with a small specialized tool which popped the plastic rivet on the bracelet.

"Sit up. I check your pupils now," she ordered. Jack did as commanded, although for a second he thought he might be sick. She peered with the scope into his pupils and then shuffled over to the metal table and scribbled something in his chart. She reached into the drawer and retrieved the small phonebook. "You okay, better than Miss Cindy. Here, make your call," she said, tossing the book on the bed beside him. She then turned and left, closing the metal gate with a hard clang.

Jack squinted and flipped through the book to the section for Sea Island residences. It took him a minute, but he found the listing he was looking for, Hiram Keller on Sea Island Drive. Jack dialed the number slowly and waited as the phone rang. "Hello, Keller residence," a hardy male voice answered.

"Mr. Keller, this is Jack Randolph. You may remember me, you were my father's law partner before he died," Jack began.

"Jack, I know about the accident and that you are in jail. It was on the news and in the local paper. Don't say anything else on that jail phone. I want you to call a lawyer friend of mine. His name is Fitz Davis. Call him at his house. He lives on St. Simons. I know he is there. I just talked to him," Mr. Keller interrupted.

"Yes Sir," Jack replied politely, with relief that his father's partner seemed to be on his side.

"Son, you be careful in there and from now on. You haven't been too careful in the past. But I still remember when my daughter cracked her head and you hovered over her at Piedmont Hospital until she woke up, after I called your Dad."

"Yes Sir," Jack said, thinking back years before when he had been an intern. He remembered the pretty teenage girl who had been in a coma for three weeks after a bicycle accident.

"You talk to Fitz Davis and let's see how this shakes out. He is the fellow to be representing you. You need someone who is local and knows the system," Mr. Keller said before he hung up. Jack again thumbed through the phone book to find the St. Simons residence of Fitz Davis. He dialed the number and waited.

"Fitz Davis here," the voice said.

"Sir, my name is Jack Randolph and I'm calling from the Ossabaw County jail. I understand you are a lawyer and I need your help. Hiram Keller suggested that I call you," Jack said quickly.

"Yes, I just talked to him. I will be over shortly to see if we can't get you turned loose. In the meantime, don't you be talking to anyone about anything in that jail. Do you understand?" the lawyer instructed.

"I understand. But I think I was trying to avoid a deer on the road," Jack responded.

"Let me say this again. Don't be talking at all in that jail about the deer or anything," he ordered firmly. "You just wait for me."

"Yes Sir," Jack said as the phone disconnected. Jack put down the phone and lay back on the metal bed. It was only a few seconds before he was again asleep with his mind giving up confused flashes of Cindy, the deer, and Christ Church cemetery, as he tried to recollect the events of the previous night. It did not seem like he had been asleep for long before a Deputy was shaking him back to consciousness.

"Come on. Your lawyer has gotten you bailed out," the Deputy yelled as Jack sat up, startled. "You can pick up your clothes and your wallet on the way out," the Deputy said as he held the gate open and Jack shuffled painfully out into the hallway. At the end of the hallway, standing next to a metal desk and talking to the female booking Deputy was a sixtyish man with close cropped, slightly gray hair wearing khaki pants and a white polo shirt. He was holding a large brown paper bag which had "Jack Randolph" written in wide, black, marker ink. Jack followed the Deputy and

approached. "Here's your man, Mr. Fitz," the Deputy said, turning
to leave. The lawyer reached out and shook Jack's hand.

"Here are your clothes and personal items in this bag. I've
also brought you a clean shirt which I hope will fit. I figured the
one from last night might be kind of nasty. Here's a list of your
property. Step in there and change and let me know if there's anything missing," the lawyer said as he handed Jack the bag and clean
shirt and pointed to the men's restroom to the side of the desk.

"I appreciate your being here so fast," Jack said slowly, still
feeling the pain in his head as he opened the door to the restroom.
In a few moments he returned wearing his tuxedo pants and the
clean plaid shirt the lawyer had provided. "Everything seems to be
here," he said, looking at the inventory sheet.

"Then sign it and we will get you out of here," the lawyer said.

"But what about booking, fingerprints and having my picture
taken and all?" Jack asked, surprised at the simplicity of his release.

"Oh, they did all that last night when you were released from
the hospital. Your booking picture is a gem. I take it you don't remember?" the lawyer asked, not waiting for the answer. "I got you
out on bond with the amount to be determined tomorrow by the
Judge. Sometimes we skip the formalities a little down here since
we all know each other," he continued.

Jack followed the attorney out to the parking lot. The bright
sunlight hit Jack like a punch. The lawyer looked at Jack squinting
with pain and said, "I thought we would go by the hospital to see
Cindy. Maybe she is conscious by now. Also, I would like to drive
by the scene of the accident. There could be something out there
that could help us," the lawyer said as they walked to Davis' car.

"I would like to see Cindy. But probably all we will see at
those rocks is the dead deer," Jack said as he held his throbbing
head and got into the car.

It took only a few minutes for them to arrive at the site of the
accident. Fitz Davis pulled his car to the side of the road across

from the rocks. On the opposite side of the road at about one half a mile away was an Ossabaw County paving crew which consisted of an asphalt truck and a small steamroller. As Jack and the lawyer crossed the highway it was apparent that the stretch of road had been repaved with new blacktop only a few hours before. The blacktop gave way slightly as they walked across it and the acrid smell of tar lingered as they neared the rocks.

"This is where it happened, I think. The deer was lying in the highway," Jack said, pointing to a portion of the highway.

"It is interesting that the County needed to get out here on a Sunday to pave this particular patch of road. But I'm sure that the good Sheriff will have a work order dated several weeks ago in a file somewhere," Davis said as he stopped to examine a patch of dirt full of fresh footprints from the recent paving to the side of the new pavement. "I'm sure they have all the photos of skid marks and vehicle damage printed and carefully filed also," he continued, stopping to put his fingers in the slightly sticky dirt as they walked to the rock outcropping. "This is just about the only pile of rocks beside a road in the whole County. Mostly there is just marsh, sand and trees. But this is the third big wreck here in the last two years. When a car hits the rock it shakes loose big sharp chunks of rock. That is what makes it dangerous. They need to blow it up."

"I don't see the deer anywhere." Jack said, surveying the scene.

"Don't worry. If they took the trouble to pave out here, they picked up that dead deer. I'm sure they have pictures of him too," the lawyer said.

"I don't see how I could have slid this far off the road. I wasn't going that much over sixty-five and there was plenty of room to get around the deer. Next thing I know we are headed for the rocks," Jack said as he slowly began remembering more details of the previous evening.

"Did Cindy mention anything about meeting somebody last night?" Davis asked, looking intently at Jack.

"She said something about a red sweater, which seemed odd. It turned out that a lot of people were wearing red. She seemed to forget about it and just started getting wild. I guess we both did," Jack responded. "I just don't know. I remember feeling really high. I also remember wondering why I felt that way. We had some drinks, but not to that level. Also, Cindy seemed way ahead of me."

"What do you mean?" the lawyer asked.

"Well, I was a little surprised, even with the drinks that we had, when she insisted on going to the cemetery and then proceeded to get naked," Jack replied.

"Did you all take any drugs or smoke anything?" the lawyer asked.

"No, but you sure would have thought so. Even my quiet friend, Dr. Clayton, was putting on quite a show. That was not like him at all," Jack said.

The lawyer thought for a moment and then asked, "Did Cindy know any of the staff at the bar?"

"Well yes, now that you mention it. I was behind her when she and Dr. Clayton walked into the restaurant together. She said something to the bartender. He didn't seem to be too friendly," Jack responded.

"Jack, did Cindy ever say anything to you about being involved in any drug business?" Davis asked, looking squarely at Jack.

"I teased her about that, and about working for Sheriff Odum. I told her she must be dealing drugs when I saw the kind of furnishings in her trailer, not to mention her clothes and jewelry. She denied she was doing anything like that. She said the jewelry was fake and that she got the oriental rugs at a local yard sale," Jack replied.

"I see. So it wouldn't surprise you if she was deeply involved in the drug business?" the lawyer asked.

"Not really. She may have been trying to keep a low profile by living in a trailer and driving an inexpensive truck, but you would have a hard time owning the stuff I saw on a County salary. But I'm a doctor, not a detective. She was pretty and fun and we were having a good time. I didn't see any need to investigate her life," Jack said.

"Son, I think we both know that Cindy was very much involved in drug smuggling. She was in way over her head. Recently, she had become an informant. She wanted to get out, but she was scared and cocky at the same time. She really didn't think the Sheriff could figure her out and she was real cagy with us as to her deal. And it came down to last night. She was finally going to give me the evidence I needed to pull down the Sheriff. If she could do that she would get full immunity. On top of that, there would have been a little winking by the government about the money she had piled up for herself. She told me it was all on a thumb drive she was supposed to deliver last night. But that never happened, and she ended up out here somehow. The people that did this still want that little piece of plastic and they want Cindy dead," Davis said.

"What do you mean ... people that did this? My car went off the road because of a deer, didn't it?" Jack said.

"That is certainly the appearance. But you and the deer may not be the only actors in this play. Maybe Cindy can help us out, if she can talk," Davis continued as they returned to the car.

It took them about twenty minutes to reach the Glynn County Hospital in Brunswick. Once inside, Jack felt more in his comfort zone as he walked past orderlies and nurses and into the waiting area of the ICU.

"We are here to see Cindy Jessup," Davis said with authority to the nurse at the glass-enclosed counter. Jack started to explain he was a doctor, but thought the better of it when Davis gave him a stern look.

"She is still unconscious, and you can go inside. But you should speak to the officer outside her door first," the nurse said, pointing to the entrance door to the ICU. Jack and Davis pushed through the door and saw a uniformed officer seated in a chair beside the door to the brightly lit, glass encased ICU unit.

"They are guarding her?" Jack asked, eyeing the officer.

"This is not a guard. He is a friend," Davis replied, as he stretched out his hand to the officer. "Jason, I'm glad you could make it over so quickly from the prison," Davis said as he shook the officer's hand.

"I am always ready to watch over Cindy," officer Tibbs said, ignoring Jack.

"Is she doing any better?" Davis asked as he peered into the glass wall of the unit. As he looked inside, he noticed Cindy's chart in a plastic pocket attached to the door of the unit. "Has anyone else been by to see her?" Davis continued as he handed Cindy's chart to Jack. Jack began to scan it quickly.

"Major Knowles came by, but I asked him to leave. This must be the doctor that was driving the car," officer Tibbs continued with a flash of hostility in his voice.

"I don't think we need Major Knowles around here. Yes, this is my client, Dr. Jack Randolph. Jack, this is officer Jason Tibbs from Georgia Maximum Security Prison," Davis stated flatly.

"You must be the one that gave Cindy the greyhound," Jack said in a kindly way.

"That would be me," Tibbs replied with a note of sadness in his voice as he turned and looked at Cindy lying motionless on the bed and connected to numerous tubes and monitors. Davis touched Tibbs' shoulder gently, and said, "Jason, there may be more to this than just a car wreck. You keep an eye on Cindy and her trailer and let me know if you hear anything. I need to get my client back to the hotel. He has a rough day in Court ahead of him tomorrow."

TWENTY

JACK WAS NOT surprised when Fitz Davis pulled up to the front door of the Cloister at precisely eight in the morning as agreed. The ride off Sea Island, across the causeway and into Brunswick felt like it was happening in slow motion as Jack looked down at the expanse of marsh below the causeway.

"What exactly are we doing today? Except for a DUI four years ago, I really haven't been to Court much," Jack said as they approached the center of Brunswick. "I haven't even had a speeding ticket for the last two years."

"Today is your arraignment. You will be pleading not guilty and the Judge will set your bond. I understand from his Clerk that it will probably be thirty thousand dollars, based on what the Judge has done in similar cases," Davis said.

"But I don't have thirty thousand dollars! Especially after I pay you," Jack said quickly.

"Our local bondsman will handle that for you. You just need to pay him one thousand today and another thousand later and sign a bunch of papers that basically say that if you were to skip he could take your property. But you won't skip, because if you did, you'd be found very quickly and put in a gunnysack to be delivered to the Courthouse by his Geechee bounty hunter, Polonius Starr.

Very few people have been able to evade Polonius for long," Davis continued.

"Of course, I'm not going to skip," Jack said with irritation. "What else will we be doing?"

"I expect that there will be a little dog and pony show concerning the accident by the Sheriff and the District Attorney in opposition to your bond and a request to have you kept in the Ossabaw jail until your trial in about six months," Davis explained.

"So what is the difference with this DUI? For the previous one, I paid a big fine and did community service, usually working weekends at Grady Hospital in Atlanta," Jack asked.

"The difference is that we are dealing with a serious injury along with reckless driving involving drugs and alcohol. You could get two years for those. And that is assuming that Cindy lives. If she were to die, you would certainly be looking at involuntary manslaughter which could be ten years," Davis replied.

"So I could be looking at years in prison either way? Even though you seem to think there is something strange going on with this accident? And even though I know for certain I didn't take any drugs?" Jack said, now understanding the seriousness of his situation.

"Thinking something is not quite right about this accident and proving it are two different things. But at least we have Judge Valentino. He is under no illusions about the Sheriff, and he will take the time to get to the bottom of things. Also, there has been a development over at Georgia Maximum Security Prison in Lester. The prison is under a bunch of Court Orders from Judge Valentino that cover everything that goes on in the prison. Some of the Orders involve medical care and order the State to provide adequate medical care for the inmates. Recently, the prison doctor was murdered. So they need a doctor over there, at least temporarily. It takes a while to find a decent doctor who'll work in a prison like G-MAX," Davis continued.

"I'm not going to work at Georgia Maximum Security Prison! I have a job waiting for me in Atlanta. Besides, I don't know anything about inmates and their medical problems," Jack stated, somewhat loudly for emphasis.

"We will see. You may find Judge Valentino to be quite persuasive. And inmates get sick just like anybody else," Davis replied with a slightly knowing smile. "Also, the State has a history of being creative in providing doctors at G-MAX. Years ago, a Board Certified internist from Macon got into a bunch of trouble with drugs. Everyone agreed he was a good doctor. The State Medical Board decided to give him a limited license to practice medicine at the prison. The Warden made him a trusty and gave him a white coat and a State house on the prison grounds. After he completed his sentence he continued to work for the Department and did a good job. I think you will find Judge Valentino to be quite imaginative and flexible in the way he handles things."

"Most patients don't generally murder their doctors," Jack replied sharply.

They pulled into a parking spot on the side of the Courthouse. The Courthouse took up an entire block in the center of Brunswick. It was a white columned, classical stone structure, placed in the center of a manicured green lawn and surrounded by palm trees and huge oaks laden with Spanish moss. A work detail of three inmates in orange jumpsuits was lightly supervised by an older Deputy as they picked up the few pieces of trash that had accumulated from the previous day. The Deputy waved at Davis as he and Jack walked up the granite steps and into the building. Davis looked at the Deputy manning the metal detector at the entrance and stated, "He's with me." The Deputy nodded and they walked directly through the metal detector which buzzed loudly. Jack followed meekly as Davis moved quickly across the polished tiles of the Courthouse rotunda, stopping to pull open a huge mahogany door with a brass handle. Above the door, large brass letters announced, "Superior Court, State of Georgia."

The few people in the Courtroom were milling about, preparing for the arrival of the Judge. Two deputies on each side of the Courtroom looked out toward the entrance and carefully scanned the Courtroom for any potential security problems. The Judge's long time Clerk, Albert Rogers, was at his seat below the bench, sorting through a sheaf of papers. In front of the Judge's bench were two varnished wooden tables for counsel. Beyond the bar of the Court were twenty rows of pews divided into two parts by a red carpeted path which led to the Judge's bench. Seated on one of the front rows was Major Knowles and beside him was the District Attorney, Dewey Lawson, an ancient, white haired, attorney in a rumpled seersucker suit who seemed to be somewhat nervous as he took his glasses off and on while looking at the file in his lap. Arnold O'Berne, the attorney for the inmates at Georgia Maximum Security Prison, was seated at the counsel table on the right side of the Courtroom. From time to time, he would make a comment to the Clerk which the Clerk seemed to generally ignore.

Davis moved toward the empty counsel table with nods and waves to the Clerk, the Major, the District Attorney, the Deputies and Arnold O'Berne. Jack followed him, comforted somewhat by the fact that his attorney seemed to know everyone in the Courtroom. Once they arrived at the counsel table Davis signaled for Jack to take a seat while he walked over to speak to Arnold O'Berne who rose to shake his hand.

"I see you brought the new prison doctor with you," lawyer O'Berne said to his opponent, very quietly so that Jack could not possibly hear. "He's certainly got great credentials from the checking I have done."

"You know, Arnold, we need to get a good doctor in there right away. This could be a good opportunity for my man if the Judge is willing. I am sure he would be delighted to serve the community over at Lester," Davis said, just as quietly with a sly smile.

"Fitz, we have been litigating this Class Action on the conditions of confinement at G-MAX for the last five years. We both wrote the Judge's Order that sets out the qualifications of the prison doctor. We also both know that the Judge is going to make sure that there is no medical lapse over there because of Dr. Bridge's death. So my question is, how long did it take to get that Vanderbilt, Buckhead doctor of yours to agree to this?" attorney O'Berne asked.

"I have talked to him about it. But I may just let the Judge explain it to him. Judge Valentino can be so persuasive," Davis replied quietly as he returned to his seat next to Jack.

"What is going on? Is there some other case on here today?" Jack asked. Before his attorney could answer, the Deputies stood at attention and the Deputy on the right side of the Courtroom announced in a booming voice, "All rise, the Superior Court of the State of Georgia is now in session. God bless this Honorable Court and the United States of America."

A tall, broad faced, portly man with graying brown hair, who appeared to be in his early seventies appeared from the door behind the bench. He was wearing a black robe and hanging around his neck was a pair of bifocals. He sat down and adjusted the glasses as he picked up a file. "Please be seated," he quietly announced and all persons in the Courtroom took their seats.

"Mr. Davis and Mr. O'Berne, I understand we have a problem with the G-MAX case?" the Judge asked, looking out at the two lawyers over his spectacles.

Fitz Davis rose and addressed the courtroom. "Your honor, sadly, Dr. Amy Bridge, the prison doctor, was murdered recently. She was a Board Certified physician in internal medicine and had devoted her life to helping inmates. I think the Court and Mr. O'Berne would agree that she was doing a wonderful job as the prison physician at Lester. The State has set up a national search committee to try to replace her. But finding a doctor of her caliber will take some time. She was one of those doctors who are devoted to the public health. Most doctors with her experience and credentials tend to practice outside the prison system. The Department is making every effort and I'm sure we will have acceptable candidates soon," he said.

Attorney O'Berne then rose to address the court. "Judge, I am also saddened at the death of Dr. Bridge. Mr. Davis is correct that she was a large part of the solution to medical problems at Georgia Maximum Security Prison. It was very unusual for the State to find someone of her caliber for the job. I also know that the tragic circumstances of her death will add to the difficulty of finding a replacement. Warden Hammond has assured me that security in the medical area has been tightened. Even so, a lot of female doctors are going to be very afraid of working at Lester. I hope that in the long run a suitable replacement can be found. But as your honor is aware, your Court Order requires the State to employ a full-time, Board Certified physician at Georgia Maximum Security Prison. Your Order also sets out experience and qualification criteria which, thankfully, are quite high. But until she is replaced, the work at G-MAX must go on. I would like to hear from Mr. Davis the State's plan for the months it will take to find another Dr. Bridge."

Judge Valentino peered over the edge of his glasses directly at Fitz Davis with a slight side glance at Jack. "Mr. Davis, losing Dr. Bridge created a huge hole in the health-care system at Lester. We have all worked hard to get healthcare for inmates at Georgia Maximum Security Prison up to a reasonable level. How exactly does the State plan on providing high-level physician services to Georgia Maximum Security Prison while you look for a new doctor?" the Judge asked in a crisp voice as he leaned slightly over the bench.

Fitz Davis again rose and addressed the court. "Judge, the State understands that we are under your Order to keep a full-time doctor at G-MAX. The Order also requires that this doctor must be Board Certified in internal medicine and also meet the experience requirements as set out in your Order. We may need a temporary modification during the search period. We plan on bringing contract doctors from Brunswick and from other institutions while there is a vacancy. We will also transport inmates to the Augusta Correctional Medical Institution as necessary."

"Mr. Davis, the inmates are still going to get sick and now Dr. Bridge is gone and Augusta is a long way away. You're free to bring a formal modification request, but so far I'm not hearing anything to incline me to modify my Order. You know we need a full-time, experienced doctor at a big prison like G-MAX," the Judge responded briskly.

"Yes, but under the circumstances ..." Davis began as Arnold O'Berne quietly smiled, looking at the Judge.

Mr. O'Berne stood and again addressed the court. "Your Honor, I believe there is another case on the calendar today. Perhaps if you went ahead with that case it would give Mr. Davis and I time to review this issue," he said, looking directly at Jack.

The Judge smiled and looked around the courtroom. "That is a good idea. I will call the next case, State of Georgia versus Jack Randolph. It is my understanding this is on the calendar for an arraignment and a bond hearing," the Judge said.

After the Judge spoke, Mr. O'Berne picked up his file and was replaced at the counsel table by Major Knowles and the District Attorney. Jack and Fitz Davis stayed in their seats, and Davis again addressed the Court. "Your Honor, I represent Dr. Randolph in this matter and we have requested a bond of thirty thousand dollars. He was released by the Sheriff pending this hearing."

The Judge looked at Jack over his spectacles and asked, "Dr. Randolph, you are charged with driving under the influence of alcohol and drugs and for reckless driving. How do you plead, Dr. Randolph?"

Jack stood and faced the Judge. "I am not guilty," Jack said firmly. "I would like to explain," he began until he was interrupted by Fitz Davis who was on his feet in a flash. "Your honor, my client has pled not guilty. I believe that is all he has to say today," Davis stated in a tone of authority as he motioned for Jack to sit down immediately. The Judge smiled slightly.

The District Attorney rose to address the court. "Your Honor, the Sheriff and I have an objection to this bond. We would like to present evidence on that issue," he said, pointing to Major Knowles.

"You may do so," the Judge ruled. Major Knowles rose, carrying a file and a laptop computer, took the witness stand, and was duly sworn. It was apparent he had testified many times as he calmly opened the file in his lap and booted the laptop.

"Major Knowles, could you identify yourself for the record and tell the Court the circumstances of this accident?" the District Attorney asked in a slightly halting voice, giving the Major and open ended invitation to testify at length. Fitz Davis sat back in his chair, rolled his eyes slightly and prepared to listen.

"Your Honor, for the record, my name is Major Ross Knowles and I work for the Sheriff of Ossabaw County. This accident is upsetting to all of us at the Sheriff's office, as I'm sure it is to this Court. Cindy Jessup is a longtime employee of Sheriff Odum and she is the Assistant Homeland Security Director for the Georgia Coastal Region. She is a wonderful person we all know and love. This is what she looks like now, because of Dr. Randolph," Major Knowles said forcefully as he clicked a key on the laptop. On a large flat-panel screen, directly across from the jury box and visible throughout the Courtroom flashed a huge picture of Cindy in her bed in the ICU unit, connected to numerous machines by an assortment of tubes. "This is the Cindy we used to know, prior to Dr. Randolph," he continued, clicking forward to a picture of Cindy in a crisp blue dress making a presentation to a group of Deputies. "Dr. Randolph's blood-alcohol level, taken at some time after the accident was a .09, which is above the legal presumption of intoxication at .08. Also, Dr. Randolph's blood showed a significant concentration of the drugs Ecstasy and cocaine. As such, looking at the combination of these, we feel we have a strong case for driving under the influence of drugs and alcohol," Major Knowles said firmly, clicking again on the computer to show a printout of the blood analysis with the alcohol and drug findings highlighted and enlarged on the screen.

The Judge looked at the screen intently and then asked, "Do you have anything to show how the accident happened?"

Major Knowles clicked on his laptop again to show a blowup of the tire tracks at the scene. "Judge, here are photos of the skid marks at the scene. I took these myself. We expect to be using a professional accident reconstruction expert to analyze the skid marks, but I have done a primary analysis and they show that this car was traveling around 90 mph. This supports the reckless driving charge."

"What about your satellite, the 'eye in the sky,' that the Homeland Security Agency has so generously provided Sheriff Odum? Was it tuned into that stretch of road at the time of the accident? It would be able to give us a completely accurate reading of the speed, would it not?" the Judge interrupted in a slightly con-frontational tone.

"It would, Your Honor. But there are a lot of roads, rivers, and seacoast in our territory and we weren't looking at this highway at precisely the time of the accident," Major Knowles smoothly continued, confident in his handling of the satellite data. "But the speed was great enough to cause this damage to the vehicle," he said as he clicked through several photos showing Jack's demol-ished car. "Also, we expect that at any trial, Trooper Doug King would testify that he witnessed Dr. Randolph driving through Lanier at a high rate of speed just prior to the accident. Such a high speed that Trooper King left his dinner to go after them. He arrived right after the crash."

"Are there any other factors which could have contributed to this accident?" the Judge asked.

"There was a deer carcass on the road. It appeared to have been freshly killed and Dr. Randolph may have been avoiding running over the carcass. That would be in line with the location of the skid marks," Major Knowles said, clicking to a picture of the deer on the highway which also included a view of the skid marks.

"Anything else, Major Knowles?" the Judge asked sternly.

"Yes, Judge. Dr. Randolph was driving ninety miles per hour under the influence of drugs and alcohol. Of course, if Cindy were to die we would be looking at involuntary manslaughter which carries a potential ten year sentence. We just don't think a thirty thousand dollar bond is appropriate in this situation," Major Knowles continued.

"Mr. Davis, I'm sure you have some comments," the Judge said, looking over to Jack and his attorney.

"Judge, we don't know how this accident happened, and we are just beginning our investigation. I do know that the stretch of road has for some reason just recently been repaved, so it appears that the Major's photos are the primary evidence in the case so far. I would note that Dr. Randolph strongly denies taking any drugs and his alcohol level was very close to the legal limit. He had a DUI four years ago. He has been two years without even a speeding ticket. Also, there was a deer involved, which is something that could happen to anyone. Dr. Randolph is a well-respected doctor in Atlanta and is Board Certified in internal medicine. He has worked at the CDC and did his internship at Piedmont Hospital and residency at Grady hospital in Atlanta. It would not be right to keep him behind bars while the Court deals with this matter."

"Did you say he is Board Certified in internal medicine?" the Judge asked, looking over at Arnold O'Berne.

"That is correct your honor. He is also a graduate of Vanderbilt medical school and worked on infectious diseases when he was at the CDC," Davis replied, pointing proudly at Jack. Jack straightened in his chair, listening closely to these arguments concerning his future.

"Mr. Davis, does your client have any interest in community service?" the Judge asked in a kindly tone.

"Certainly, your Honor. Under the proper circumstances of course," Davis replied smoothly as Jack looked at him with concern.

"Well, it is obvious that we have a temporary opening for a physician at G-MAX. Dr. Randolph seems to fit the profile in terms of his qualifications and experience. Is there any objection to him serving as the prison doctor until the replacement for Dr. Bridge can be found?" the Judge asked with a sweeping look at the lawyers and parties before him. "I do remember that years ago the State obtained a fine doctor for the inmates when one of Macon's respected physicians had a problem with drugs. So there is some precedent on this."

Arnold O'Berne stood and stated with a flourish, "Judge, counsel for the inmates has no objection. We have researched Dr. Randolph and feel that he would be more than adequate to fill Dr. Bridge's shoes temporarily."

After a slight prodding from Major Knowles, the District Attorney was on his feet. "Your Honor, Dr. Randolph is the cause of a serious accident involving grave injuries. He has a prior DUI. All of this reflects poorly on his judgment in general. Dr. Randolph should be an inmate in Georgia Maximum Security Prison rather than the prison doctor," he said loudly.

"Do you have any further suggestions as to how this vacancy at G-MAX gets covered while a Board Certified doctor sits in Sheriff Odum's jail?" the Judge asked crisply.

"No I don't," the District Attorney said meekly, sitting down.

Jack was at the same time whispering to his attorney and shaking his head. Finally, he jumped to his feet despite a strong tug on his coat from Fitz Davis. "Judge, I am a Board Certified physician, no doubt. And I have worked at Grady and Piedmont hospitals in Atlanta. Sometimes inmates from the Atlanta jail would end up as my patients at Grady. But that is about all my experience with medicine for inmates. Also, I have just accepted a position in Atlanta and that is where I should be practicing," Jack said strongly, looking at the Judge and Fitz Davis. Davis looked away and Arnold O'Berne rolled his eyes and looked up at the ornate ceiling in the Courtroom.

The Judge leaned forward and peered over the top of his spectacles at Jack as though he were an unruly schoolchild. "Doctor, here are your choices. You don't have to be the doctor at Georgia Maximum Security Prison. You have pled not guilty. You have rights. You can stay in the Ossabaw County jail, under the supervision of Major Knowles while this case is investigated and is ready for trial. We have a pretty heavy caseload down here, but that could be as quick as six months. Then you could have a trial in front of a jury and they might let you go. On the other hand, they might convict you of driving under the influence and reckless driving. If you are convicted this Court will have to sentence you. This case involves a catastrophic wreck with serious injury. The last three similar cases which involved catastrophic wrecks with serious injury in my Court were each sentenced to two years in prison. Another possibility is that you could change your plea from not guilty to guilty. That means you would be convicted and again the Court would have to sentence you. I might add that the Defendant in one of those three similar cases that I sentenced to two years in prison also pled guilty. So, if you are convicted, it may be that you will be going to Georgia Maximum Security Prison, not as a doctor, but as an inmate. Of course, I will consider your case on the merits as it is heard. Perhaps your situation is very different. But, if you were to accept this temporary position at G-MAX it would give you and your counsel the opportunity to fully investigate this accident. With both of you focused on this there might be something that Major Knowles overlooked which could be very helpful to you. You would also be receiving whatever Dr. Bridge's salary was at the prison. I am sure that this is already budgeted by the State and I see no reason it should not continue. Also, in the final resolution of this matter, the Court would be inclined to take favorable judicial notice of your gracious and voluntary community service to the inmates at Georgia Maximum Security Prison. I would add that this would be conditional on Cindy surviving this accident. Were she to die you would be looking at a charge of involuntary manslaughter and we would have to revisit this whole matter. These are your choices. We need to know your decision today."

Jack's mouth was open as the reality of the Judge's words sunk in. "Judge, nobody has quite explained it to me like that," Jack said quietly.

"So you will be reporting to Lester as the temporary physician for Georgia Maximum Security Prison, I assume?"

"Yes, your Honor," Jack said, looking at his attorney.

"Motion for bond granted with conditions as noted and agreed to by Defendant. The Court is in recess," the Judge ordered and adjudicated with a crack of his gavel.

TWENTY-ONE

JACK ARRIVED AT Georgia Maximum Security Prison at 7:35 a.m. the next day. He was driving a rented, white, compact sedan which badly needed washing, and appeared in general to have suffered some hard use in its brief life span. It had taken Jack three visits to local car rental companies to find one willing to risk renting a car to the holder of a driver's license which consisted of his bonding document for the offenses of DUI and Reckless Driving. Even then, it had taken a seven hundred and fifty dollar deposit to work the deal. Listening to the clanking of the engine as he drove under the guard tower, Jack was not sure that the auto was actually worth seven hundred and fifty dollars. Before he could press the button on the communications box, a voice crackled out loudly from the metal speaker.

"Turn off your engine and state your business," an authoritative voice commanded. He looked up and saw peering from the guard tower window the frowning round face of a black female officer, critically surveying him and his suspect vehicle. The metal bar in front of his auto remained firmly positioned as he turned off his engine.

"I have an appointment with Warden Hammond at eight o'clock," he responded to the communications box while also looking up at the officer in the tower.

"You must be the new doctor that Judge Valentino sent over," the voice said crisply.

"I am here of my own free will to serve the people of Georgia," Jack replied, now knowing that his situation was common knowledge throughout the prison.

"I bet that's right!" the guard replied with a slight laugh as she caused the metal bar in front of Jack's car to lift. "Park in the lot on the left," she continued.

Jack started his car and slowly drove into the parking lot and found a spot directly in front of the metal gate. As he exited his car and began to walk toward the gate he heard a loud buzz which indicated that the tower officer had unlocked the gate. He pushed the gate open, and as the gate closed behind him he heard a second buzzing which indicated that it had now been re-locked. As he walked down the sidewalk toward the entrance to the prison, he noticed that the fiftyish, white, inmate trusty had stopped his sweeping to leer at him lustily, which made Jack feel somewhat like the new girl at the strip club. The officer who was supposedly supervising his inmate stood slouched by the fence reading a newspaper. As Jack approached the door the officer gave no sign that he was in any way aware of Jack's existence. Jack pressed the black communications button to the side of the metal door and peered through the thick glass down the long concrete corridor.

"May I help you?" the voice on the communications box boomed in a tone that did not convey helpfulness.

"I have an appointment with the Warden," Jack said once again, trying to be polite.

"Right," the voice said curtly as Jack heard the click of the metal door unlocking. He pushed the heavy door open and began his walk down the long corridor. As the door behind him closed he heard again the now familiar click of the door relocking. It seemed like a long walk before he arrived at the second metal door of the sally port at the end of the concrete corridor. The officer behind the second door could clearly see him through the glass. However, while looking directly at Jack, the officer picked up the telephone on his desk and dialed a number. Jack watched the officer for what seemed like quite a long time, no doubt because he was locked in a concrete and steel tunnel. When the officer again looked directly at him while hanging up the phone and picking up a file on his desk, Jack decided to press the communications button on the device at the side of the metal door.

"Officer, I need to get in to see the Warden. He is expecting me," Jack said curtly. He could see the officer press the button on the communications device on his desk.

"Sir, I know that. We are at the end of the morning count. The entire institution is on lockdown with no movement allowed," the officer stated flatly, showing no intention of unlocking the sally port door. However, in a few seconds, there was an announcement on the public address system which was so loud that it actually startled Jack.

"Morning count is clear. Return to normal movement," the voice commanded. The officer then, in a very leisurely fashion, reached over and pressed the button which caused the door in front of Jack to unlock. Jack pushed through the door and entered the rotunda of the prison.

"The Warden's office is on your right," the officer stated slowly, barely looking up from his file. Jack walked briskly into the Warden's outer office.

"Warden Hammond will be with you in a minute, Dr. Randolph. Please have a seat on the couch," Darla Cooper, the Warden's secretary instructed, the second he was within the office. Jack sat on the couch and proceeded to thumb through the small stack of year-old magazines which were scattered on the top of the coffee table in front of the couch. He selected a worn issue of an outdoor magazine and settled back on the couch. Over the course of half an hour Mrs. Cooper came and went from the Warden's inner office, each time carrying a stack of documents. From time to time an inmate trusty would drop by to ask her if she needed any assistance.

Jack had resigned himself to a long wait when suddenly the Warden's door opened and Warden Hammond rushed out clutching a walkie-talkie.

"Come on Doc. We got two stabbings in the courtyard. One of them is hurt bad. They are bringing them up to medical right now. Darla, call the ambulance. One of them is going to the hospital in a hurry," the Warden almost shouted as he grabbed Jack by the arm and the two of them headed for the Medical Unit. The Warden used his radio to quickly command the opening of the two sally port doors between his office and the Medical Unit. The Warden then quickly unlocked the shiny white metal door to the Medical Unit with a large stainless steel override key instead of waiting for the usual electric lock procedure. He held the door open for Jack and they both stepped into the Medical Unit.

Jack blinked in horror at the scene before him. Floating in a pool of blood on the floor was a metal and canvas stretcher on which a large white inmate was lying with what appeared to be a small hand saw protruding from his chest. A nurse was cutting away the remains of his shirt and attempting to stop the massive bleeding. Also visible were numerous other stab wounds of a smaller nature.

Seated on a metal chair at the side of the room in his own pool of blood was a middle aged, black inmate with a large gash across his face which left his nose hanging at an angle from the cut. A blonde nurse attended him and was in the process of cleaning and bandaging his wound.

"Warden, that son of a bitch attacked me with a damn saw knife he made. He tried to cut my head off. But I stabbed him back and got it away from him. You know, I was just defending myself," the inmate on the chair screamed at the Warden.

"Okay Jerome, let's get everybody fixed up here now," the Warden—calmly replied.

Jack took off his jacket and knelt beside the stretcher as the nurse continued to work on the inmate. "I'm Dr. Randolph, the new prison doctor. We're going to get you to the hospital and get that saw out of you. We need to keep it in right now because if we take it out you could bleed too much. We will give you some pain medicine and some fluid to make up for the blood you've lost to get you to the hospital," Jack said to his new patient who blinked and grimaced in response. Jack was surprised that the man was still conscious. The nurse returned with a vial of morphine and a saline solution transfusion bag on a rolling cart. Jack nodded as she loaded the syringe and injected the inmate with morphine, while he found a vein to connect the saline transfusion. Jack watched the inmate's eyes follow their actions and saw his lips move slightly.

"I need some of that shit! I'm in pain too," the black inmate yelled.

"You're next, so be quiet," Jack said, looking at him with a scowl. At that moment an officer with two EMTs from the ambulance arrived. They were carrying an oxygen tank and another stretcher. "Use the stretcher he is on and get him some oxygen. We just gave him morphine and take the fluid with you," Jack instructed. The EMTs proceeded to take over and within a few seconds the inmate was on his way out of the Medical Unit with an oxygen mask over his face and a bag of fluid on his chest.

"We have a loading dock for the Medical Unit which gives quick access for the ambulance," the Warden explained as the inmate was carried out a side door to the waiting ambulance.

Jack then walked over to the other inmate. He looked at the inmate's face carefully. "We need to get you a pain shot and get you to the hospital for some stitches. But you will be fine," Jack said as the nurse prepared another morphine shot.

"What about my face! He tried to cut my head off," the inmate screamed.

"Do you want this pain shot? I think you are the winner of this fight," Jack said firmly. The inmate took the threat of withholding the pain shot to heart and meekly held out his arm. The nurse then gave him the injection.

"Get the inmate orderlies to clean up this blood. Make sure they follow the blood spill protocol in the Court Order and use plenty of bleach," the Warden directed the nurses. Jack turned to a sink to remove his gloves and wash his hands.

"Now might be a good time to formally introduce me to everyone," Jack said, exhaling fully, with the situation under control. The Warden smiled and looked around the room.

"Ladies and gentlemen, I would like you to meet our new doctor at G-MAX, Dr. Jack Randolph. Dr. Randolph is Board Certified in internal medicine and has previously worked at the CDC and Grady Hospital in Atlanta. He will be working with us until we find a doctor to replace Dr. Bridge, which could be quite some time," the Warden announced in a grand manner. "Dr. Randolph, I would like you to meet Thelma Griggs, our new Chief Nurse," he said, pointing to the large black nurse now seated at the rear of the Medical Unit. "I believe you have already met Mr. Jerome Quinton, who is a valued frequent customer of the Medical Unit," the Warden continued, pointing to the inmate who was now slumped in his chair with his mouth open and snoring heavily due to the pain shot. "And finally, we have nurse Tacy Crandall who has been with us almost a year and is a former Miss Lester," he said, pointing to the blonde nurse standing next to the snoring inmate. "I will leave you all now. Hopefully, this is the last excitement for today. Tacy, I would appreciate if you could show the doctor around the prison and keep him out of trouble," the Warden directed as he turned to exit the Medical Unit.

Jack looked over at the sleeping inmate and nodded politely to nurse Griggs. He looked up at Tacy Crandall with a start as her green eyes synchronized with his across the room. In the confusion he had hardly noticed her. But now, as she smiled at him, he nearly had to brace himself as he involuntarily responded to her beauty, even though she was some distance away. Jack took a deep breath, as this was a very unusual response for man who considered himself a jaded Atlanta bachelor. With some effort, he was able to apply his usual, cold rationality.

"I'm glad to meet all of you, including inmate Jerome," Jack stammered. "This is quite an introduction to correctional medicine even for an old Grady Hospital hand. If we could get the inmate to the hospital and I could get a tour and your medical protocols to review, including this Court Order I always hear about, that would be very helpful," he said.

"Tacy, you take him around with an officer. I will round up the Court Order book and the Protocols and get Jerome to the hospital," Nurse Griggs directed with authority as she pressed a button on the communications box. "This is medical. We need an escort officer to take Dr. Randolph around the prison," she instructed.

"Yes ma'am," was the immediate response.

TWENTY-TWO

IN A FEW minutes a tall, middle aged, white officer arrived. In his hand was a six inch stainless steel hoop which had about thirty keys of various types attached.

"Captain Jamison, this is Dr. Randolph, our new doctor," Nurse Crandall said to the officer. "I would like to start the tour from the courtyard and end up back in medical. I would like him to see how the inmates live and work and how they get up here to medical from different parts of the prison. I would also like to show him that it isn't all stabbings every day," Nurse Crandall said as she smiled at Jack. "Captain Jamison is our Senior Security Officer. He has access to all areas of the prison. He also has all the keys," she continued.

"That would be me, Nurse Tacy. I will give you the full tour," the officer said with a sheepish smile as he shook the massive key ring.

Jack took a few seconds as he thought back to his public health days at Grady Hospital and the CDC. "I am interested in the entire layout of the prison. I'm interested in how sick call is conducted and how an injured or sick inmate gets to medical on a daily basis and also in an emergency. I also want to understand how we get to the inmates in an emergency, and how we get to them if they are in a remote part of the prison. I want to see the food areas and see how special diets are dealt with. I want to see how we handle inmates with chronic diseases like diabetes and high blood pressure. I also want to understand how you deal with sexually active inmates with infectious diseases like HIV," Jack responded thoughtfully.

In a few minutes, after passing through numerous gates and sally ports they arrived at a large grassed courtyard in the center of the prison. It was boxed in by numerous three-story concrete block buildings each of which was freshly painted with a shiny coat of whitewash. Captain Jamison speeded their movement with the judicious use of his key ring and numerous directions on his walkie-talkie to various Control Officers to electronically unlock gates. Jack marveled at how quickly they moved through the prison with the guidance of this officer.

The three of them stood at the top of the concrete steps to one of the buildings. Around the courtyard were several officers watching the passing inmates and surrounding buildings. There were at least thirty inmates in clean, white uniforms, each with a blue stripe on each pant leg, moving around the courtyard at any given time. Occasionally, an inmate would stop to talk to an officer or to another inmate. Jack noticed two inmates playing catch with baseball gloves and a yellow tennis ball. To Jack, it seemed almost like school with the continuous movement of people, the occasional ringing of a bell, and the frequent public address announcements.

"I see you let them play baseball out here," Jack said.

"We do have a baseball field outside the fence and some teams for those inmates with the lowest security. We don't allow any bats or baseballs inside the prison, but they can keep their gloves and practice with tennis balls," Captain Jamison replied.

"What are all these buildings?" Jack asked.

"These three buildings are the cellblocks. Most of the inmates at G-MAX are maximum-security, but the ones in these buildings live in dorms and are generally considered to be lower security. Over there are the L and M buildings which house High Max security inmates. We don't have any death penalty inmates anymore, but those guys are as bad as any on Death Row. They will kill you if you give them a chance," Captain Jamison stated, looking over at L and M buildings.

"Where are the death penalty inmates?" Jack asked.

"They are over at Jackson Correctional Institution. That is where Death Row is now. They use lethal injection now but they had the electric chair until a few years ago. We have Lester's old electric chair in a museum for the prison, out back," he continued.

"Does anyone ever escape? It looks like it would be pretty hard," Jack asked, surveying the scene with its imposing fences, topped with razor wire, under the watch of several guard towers.

"They do get loose from time to time, usually because somebody makes a mistake. Nobody gets out over the fence. The ladies in the guard towers will shoot them. After a verbal warning as required by the Court Order, of course. The inmates know that. We did have two boys make some clever bulletproof vests in the machine shop and take a run at the fence a while ago," the officer replied.

"What happened to them?" Jack asked.

"They forgot about their legs and that they needed some padding in the vests when the shotgun pellets hit. When the ladies blasted them, it didn't kill them. But they were off the fence and on the ground in a hurry," Captain Jamison said.

"So how do they get out?" Jack asked.

"Lots of ways. They make or steal a correctional officer uniform and trick someone into letting them through the gates. Or they intimidate a trusty to swap places with them and then they escape from the trusty dorm which is outside the walls. Sometimes they hide in a load of something going out of the prison," the Captain continued.

"Don't forget to tell him about faking illness to get to the hospital," Tacy reminded the officer.

"You're right Tacy. That is a favorite. You medical folks are warm and wonderful and are trying to help them. The inmate will hurt himself just enough so he needs to go to the hospital or a specialist. Once he gets there it is a lot easier to escape. A long while back we had one that got sent to a specialist doctor in Savannah. The inmate had tossed a shank over the fence near the transport van. When nobody was looking he picked it up before he got in the van. Then when he got to the doctor's office he pulled it out and kidnapped the doctor and took his car. But he wasn't such a bad guy. He just tied the doctor to a tree a few miles up the road. They picked up the inmate at his mother's house the next day," the officer said.

"I imagine that doctor has dropped out of the specialty consulting program," Jack said with a laugh.

"Yes, he is no longer with us. These days we take them over to the medical prison in Augusta," Tacy said. "That was way before my time," she continued, looking directly at Jack.

Again, Jack had to take a breath as her blonde hair tossed in the light breeze and he admired the fit of her nurse's uniform on her beauty queen figure.

"Let's take a look inside one of these dorms," Captain Jamison said, noting the interaction between the two and smiling slightly. With a quick call on his walkie-talkie they entered the nearest building. Inside was a glassed Control Room staffed by two officers which overlooked a large dormitory with numerous double bunks. Captain Jamison signaled the Control Officers and with a few clicks of the locks they were inside the Control Room.

Jack looked around and noticed that two of the inmates were waving at him. A tall, white inmate, with his head wrapped in a towel, turban fashion, was blowing him an extended kiss. Each of the inmates' uniforms was crisp and neatly pressed with the white cuffs of the pants carefully rolled up. Jack noticed that several inmates were wearing sandals. The turbaned inmate's sandals were gold and shiny.

"As you may have guessed, this is the Sissy Dorm. These guys are active and aggressive homosexuals. We keep them segregated in here. If these ladies were mixed in with the general population they would be causing all kinds of fights and trouble," the Captain explained.

"Just like real women," Jack said with a smile aimed at Tacy as he peered out from the Control Room window. The inmate in the turban had now stripped down to his jockstrap and sandals and was swaying back and forth with his hands in the air. His athletic and ripped body glistened with sweat. The other inmates watched with delight and clapped.

"I think he likes you," Tacy said to Jack, nudging him slightly.

"All right Harris, that is enough striptease for you today," the Control Officer announced over the loudspeaker. The inmate sulkily put back on his pants and shirt.

"We try to keep an extra watch on them to cut down on sexual activity and to keep them from being victimized. But as you can see, they present a little bit of a management problem," Captain Jamison explained.

Another inmate approached the Control Room with a piece of paper in his hand. He placed it in a metal slot and then looked up at the Control Officer.

"I need to go to medical. Ask Nurse Tacy to let me go back with her. My foot is swelling up," he said, holding his uncovered foot up to the window for Tacy's examination.

"Thomas, you were just in yesterday for your foot. It looks about the same. You need to keep putting that antibiotic salve I gave you on it and we will see you tomorrow," Tacy said as she peered through the glass and spoke through the microphone. The inmate frowned and walked back toward his bunk. Tacy picked up the paper the inmate had provided and handed it to Jack.

"This is a Sick Call Request Form. Blank forms are in the dormitories. The inmates can turn one in at any time to any officer. The officers collect them every day and give them to medical. We look at the forms and make a sick call list for the next day. We send the list every day to the Warden's office. The Warden then sends an order that the inmates on the list be brought to the Medical Unit that day," Tacy said.

"What about emergencies and chronic care for things like diabetes and high blood pressure? And how do they get their medicines?" Jack asked, as he looked at the form.

"Sick call is for day-to-day problems. Colds, flu, migraine headaches, small cuts and bruises, stomach aches, whatever. We deliver the prescriptions with a Pill Call run by a nurse every day. She takes the pill cart into the dorm with an officer and gives out the pills. Sometimes, we make the inmates swallow the pill in front of us and then stick out their tongues if the medicine is something they could sell, like pain pills. The Pill Call nurse then notes that they got their medicine on the Medicine Administration Chart for each inmate. That chart is part of the Court Order. That way, if an inmate writes the Judge and says he is not getting his medicine, we can pull the chart and show that he has gotten it," Tacy replied.

"Or show that he hasn't gotten it," Jack said, thinking back to his days at Grady where sometimes everything did not always go as planned.

"That is probably why we are still under the Court Order," Captain Jamison added. "It is one thing to write this stuff in Atlanta for the Judge to sign, and another to get it done behind six locked gates."

"I'm sure that is right," Jack said as the Captain escorted them back into the courtyard.

"Let's take a look at the law library," Captain Jamison suggested, pointing at another building. Again, with his assistance, it only took a few minutes for the group to enter the building. Jack commented on the metal garage door type device at the top of the doors, similar to protective metal curtains on liquor stores in tough neighborhoods. "That is to give officers in the courtyard a safe haven if something kicks off in the courtyard. They can get inside the law library and it will take the inmates a while to bust through that metal curtain which can only be let down from the inside," Captain Jamison explained. Once inside the building, the room appeared much like an ordinary library in a school, with rows of bookshelves and several tables. There were also two wooden desks. Behind one desk was a large, powerfully built, white man with thinning gray hair, wearing a rumpled plaid sport coat over a wrinkled white shirt. He appeared to be in his sixties and his tanned skin with red splotches had the appearance of a man who had spent his entire life working outdoors. A pair of inexpensive reading glasses perched on the end of his nose. His massive hands cradled a book which he was reading intently. Jack noticed the title, which was *The Count of Monte Cristo*. The man looked up as he noticed the group's arrival.

"Folks, this here is Chester Thomas, our librarian. He retired from farming and has been with us for ten years. He has probably read every book in this library," Captain Jamison said as the big man stood up behind the desk and smiled, taking the time to push back the few gray hairs on his forehead to ensure his maximum best appearance. He held out his huge hand to Jack.

"You must be the new doctor. I'm pleased to meet you. We usually have a few medical books down here. Usually anatomy or internal medicine text books which have been donated. But we mostly have the classics in the regular library along with a bunch of westerns and mysteries. Of course, under the Court Order, we also have a first-rate law library. When lawyers come through, they often say it is better than the one at the County Courthouse. And that may be true, as we have a lot more Federal books than they do," he said proudly.

"Do the medical books get used much? And does anybody understand these law books?" Jack said, pulling a Federal Reporter off the shelf and perusing its intense, jargon filled contents.

"We have quite a few that understand these law books very well," the librarian said, pointing over to the two inmates at the desk on the other side of the room and also to one inmate seated at a table with a stack of papers and law books. "On the medical books, we don't get quite as many takers, but sometimes legal cases have medical issues and there are also those inmates that like to try to diagnose themselves when they are sick," he said as he led the group over to the other desk. As they walked across the room Jack noticed that the inmate at the table appeared to be working on some type of government forms. When they arrived at the other desk, the two inmates stood and smiled pleasantly. The inmates had a similar look as each was black, slightly built and equipped with thick wire rimmed glasses. Each had a stack of law books before him and each was working on some type of handwritten pleading.

"Jimmy Richards and Albert Sams are some of our law library clerks. They help the inmates find the law books they are interested in and keep up with the procedures for the Court Order on the law library," Chester stated with a smile. The two inmates beamed in response.

"How did you learn about law books? I don't think I would have a clue," Jack asked the inmates as he looked at the rows of similar looking law books.

"The State has a training program for law library clerks. It lasts three days and covers all sorts of legal subjects and the law library," one of the inmates offered. "It is part of the Court Orders."

"They had the first training program years ago and even brought in a professor who went on to be the Dean of the Georgia law school. They videotaped his presentations and we still use it. It is on the Georgia Court System," Chester added. "Lawyer Fitz Davis and a paralegal from the Attorney General's office in Atlanta do the training now," he continued.

"Yes, I know Mr. Davis well," Jack said with a slight frown. "How do you pick the inmates who get trained to be law library clerks?" he continued as he looked at some of the pleadings on the desk and wondered how many inmates could really understand these legal terms.

"Well, they need to be smart and read well. They also need to be somebody we think will follow the Court Orders. And, they need to have a really long sentence because it costs a lot to train them," Chester replied. Jack looked at the very pleasant clerks in front of him and wondered what crimes they had committed to allow them to qualify.

Captain Jamison interrupted and pointed to a side door, "I think we need to move on to the kitchen. I'm getting hungry and pork chops are on the menu." In a few minutes they were inside the huge kitchen of the prison.

Jack looked out at the large space with surprise at the cleanliness of the operation. Even though the room was filled with inmates working on the noon meal, the floors were shiny and spotless and the rows of stainless steel ranges and metal cooking vats gleamed in the bright lights. A small, bald, portly man in a cook's apron, worn over a maroon jacket with a thin black tie approached them. Captain Jamison reached out and shook his hand enthusiastically.

"Harold, this is the new doctor, Dr. Randolph," the Captain said. Then he said to Jack, "Harold Timmons is the Kitchen Manager and he keeps things right."

"I've never seen such a clean kitchen. This is much cleaner than the kitchen at the CDC," Jack said as he shook the man's hand.

"Well, we have got a lot of really good help and we put them to work," Harold replied modestly. "Years ago, before the Court Order, things weren't like this. The kitchen and the whole prison were filthy and the inmates' lawyers were complaining that they were idle. After looking at the problem, somebody in Central Office figured that if you had enough officers to supervise, there wasn't any reason these prisons couldn't be spotless. The cleaning supplies don't cost much and cleaning gives the inmates something to do," he continued.

"So now we have ten inmates assigned just to keep the floors cleaned and waxed in the kitchen. We have another ten to take apart the grills and hoods and clean and shine them on a weekly basis. We have another five for general cleaning and sanitation," Captain Jamison added.

"I don't think that would be possible in the private sector," Jack said.

"A lot of officers bucked at first because it meant more work for them. But now, I think everybody can see the benefit of using all the manpower we have," Captain Jamison said.

"Is it hard to get the inmates to work?" Jack asked as he observed the vigorous activity around him.

"There are a few slackers, but they get moved out in a hurry. For most inmates, prison is boring and they are looking for something to do," Captain Jamison replied as they walked through the kitchen. "Also, the kitchen is a prize job assignment."

Jack noticed one inmate at work at a stainless steel table, rolling and cutting fresh dough while two inmate assistants filled his creations with fresh blueberries from a large metal tub.

"That's Henry Jansen. He used to be the pastry chef at a big hotel in Atlanta. It seems there was an unfortunate confrontation with his wife one evening. Now we get the benefit of Henry's artistry," Harold said quietly as they admired the inmate's technique with flour and dough.

"It doesn't hurt to have these fresh blueberries that we grow here at the institution by the ton, either," Captain Jamison said as he scooped up a handful of the glistening berries, tossed them into his mouth and directed the group towards several large grills which were loaded with fresh, pink, pork chops. "We raise our own hogs, so pork chops are often on the menu. I like the breaded ones best," he continued.

"We also have a non-pork menu every day for the Muslim inmates," Harold added as he pointed to another grill on which hamburgers were being prepared.

"I really wasn't expecting a kosher dining room," Jack said, looking at the burgers steaming on the grill. The group walked over to a section of the kitchen where masses of fresh collard greens and carrots were being prepared for cooking in several large stainless steel vats.

"Again, we grow all the vegetables at the institution. And we don't use any pork products when we cook them," Harold said as the inmates looked at them without expression and continued their work. One of the inmates busily slicing the collards with a large knife had a huge scar running sideways across his face. On his muscular arm was a tattoo of the Virgin Mary.

"Is there a problem sometimes, with these knives?" Jack asked as he watched the inmate makes short work of mounds of collards with the knife.

"We have a lot fewer problems than we used to. Now the Classification Committee at the prison makes sure that the inmates they put down here are people they are pretty sure won't cause a problem. Generally, the officers on the committee know all the inmates well and we haven't had much trouble. I guess it is sort of like high school teachers knowing who the troublemakers are. Also, we are real careful now with tool control since it is part of the Court Orders," Harold said as he pointed to a large board on the wall of the kitchen. On the board, each knife, cleaver, and other piece of edged equipment was depicted in black shadow form on the board. Below each shadow were hooks on which the tool was to be placed to match up with the shadow. Most of the shadow tools were empty, but there were a few in place, neatly matching up with their shadow outline.

"The Court Order requires us to keep the shadow boards anywhere in the prison that tools are used. The Judge had a security expert go around the prison and make recommendations. Now it is rare for us to lose a tool since we have the shadow boards and do a daily Missing Tool Report," Harold said.

"I can see it would be easy to detect if something is missing," Jack said as he looked at the board.

"When the Judge first ordered this, some of the older officers groused that we really didn't need it as we always got the tools back after few days. Of course, a lot of times they were sticking out of the back of somebody when we found them," Captain Jamison said, as Harold shook his head at this remark and announced, "Is everyone ready for lunch?"

They moved to the Staff Dining Room which was a large, brightly lit room directly off the kitchen. Food was served cafeteria style and there was a salad bar off to one side. It was only eleven, so the room was almost empty except for one officer and a maintenance technician wearing a tan jumpsuit.

"You go first, Dr. Randolph. Today your lunch is on us. But don't get to too impressed as it is only a dollar," Harold said, handing Jack a tray.

"I take it that the staff eats the same food as the inmates," Jack said as he looked across the assortment of food.

"That is right. Except maybe a few times a year there might be something special for the staff," Harold replied.

"That way, they can't poison us as easy if they don't know whether they will be eating it or not," Captain Jamison pragmatically added.

Jack and the others loaded their plates with pork chops, steamed vegetables and cornbread muffins and then sat at a table at the rear of the room. Jack made sure that he got two of the blueberry pastries.

"Did you have any questions about anything you have seen so far?" Tacy asked with a quick smile.

"I do have one question. That one inmate in the law library seemed to be working on some government forms. Are they tax forms?" Jack asked.

"Oh that's Quentin Schubert. But those are probably not tax forms. The inmates used to do a lot of tax returns for the officers and for each other. But the Commissioner and the Judge cracked down on that. Mail to and from the IRS is logged and under certain circumstances can be opened. Outgoing mail to the IRS is stamped as coming from the prison. Now the new game is immigration forms, green cards and the occasional passport application from a dead person. We have also had a few problems with them refinancing somebody's mortgage in Atlanta and having their mother or somebody show up at the closing to pick up the money. Also, I would be real careful about what you put in the trash or else you may find that your credit cards are buying all sorts of interesting stuff. We confiscate their materials if it is blatant, but we have to be careful not to be messing with their legal papers," Jamison said with a laugh.

"I'm sure that is all good business these days," Jack said as he took a bite of the blueberry pastry. "This tart is so good I'm worried your baker may never make parole," he continued, enjoying the warm flakiness of the pastry.

"Tacy, where else should we take the good doctor today?" Captain Jamison asked.

"I think we should go to the school and gym and end up with the dogs and the State house he's been assigned," she said.

"Aren't we missing L and M buildings?" the Captain asked.

"I'm not going into M building as long as Henry Kirk is here at the prison," Tacy said with a shudder.

"I got you," Captain Jamison replied. "We can follow up with the bad boys another day."

After lunch was finished the group moved to a large cinder block building on the courtyard. Once inside, it was clear from the ringing bells and the numerous bustling classrooms that the school was an integral part of the prison. Indeed, it could have been a school anywhere except for the numerous roaming correctional officers and the uniformed inmates that made up the student body.

"The Corrections Department is the largest provider of adult education in the State. We've got everything being taught from remedial reading on up. We used to have college courses, but they got canceled because of politics. Folks didn't like paying for their children to go to college and inmates getting a free college education. So now we pretty much concentrate on the fundamentals. An inmate can get a High School Certificate if he works at it," Captain Jamison explained as the group peeked inside a classroom. The class was American History and a formidable, middle-aged black woman was in charge. She was lecturing about America's involvement in the Spanish-American war. Occasionally, she would direct a question to a particular student to make sure everyone was following along. Looking at the faces of the inmates, Jack saw the healthy level of disinterest in such faraway events that could be expected of any high school student.

"Are there any classes on trades? Or do they just make license plates?" Jack asked.

"Oh yes. There is lots of vocational training, plumbing, carpentry, electrical and such," Captain Jamison said as he moved down the hall toward a double door. Once past these doors, Jack could see a large room where several instructors and small groups of inmates were working on projects of various types. Near each group there was the shadow board for tools similar to those he had seen in the kitchen.

They stopped at an area where two inmates were constructing brick walls and brick mailboxes. The sand mortar was designed for practice and tear down. Jack was surprised at the quality of the brick structures and the interest of the inmates as they worked, compared to the group studying the Spanish-American war.

"Can they get jobs when they get out of here?" Jack asked.

"The construction trades don't care what you did as long as you show up sober and know what you're doing. But the best training we got is down the hall. The folks that learn how to do it make decent money when they get out. And they always get a job right away," the Captain said as he moved the group to another room across the hall.

In this room the instructor was a fortyish black man wearing a white coat. At two tables beside him were four inmates working away on various dental appliances.

"Mr. Jackson, why don't you tell our guest, the new doctor, about your false teeth class," Captain Jamison said. The instructor looked up with a look of slight irritation to the reference to false teeth.

"Doctor, this is our dental appliance workshop. I teach the inmates to make bridges, mouth bits, and yes, some false teeth. Once they have certified here they can work for any dentist in the State," the instructor said.

Jack looked at the devices being created by each of the four inmates along with the models and tools on display. "I have heard from my dentist friends how hard it is to find techs that can carry out their designs. I'm sure there's a lot of demand for this work," he said, picking up a device and examining its wires and intricate plastic construction, as the inmate artisan smiled with pride.

"All right, doctor, you can refer Billy to your dentist friends when he gets out. But Ms. Tacy wants to go look at the musclemen," Captain Jamison said.

"Yes I do!" Tacy said with a bawdy toss of her blonde hair.

"I am sure the musclemen will also be looking back," Jack said, as he looked at her lean figure.

The gym was at the back of the compound, just inside the fence, and directly under a guard tower. It was a large structure made of brick with a new metal roof. Inside was a basketball court and in the corner was a weight area. There were two inmates on the basketball court shooting hoops under the bored watch of an older white officer. In the weight area was a large collection of free weights and several weightlifting benches. In this area were three inmates who were hard at work with weights. Occasionally, the gym officer would glance over to check the activities in the weight area.

Captain Jamison led the group around the edge of the basketball court to the weight area. Two of the inmates were twentyish, black males with athletic builds that could have passed for well exercised college linebackers. The third inmate was something different. He stood six foot four with close cropped blond hair. In each hand was a dumbbell which weighed twenty five pounds. He lifted them over his head from a standing position, butterfly style, as though they were made of paper. His chest heaved under his shirt which appeared to be pasted to his body. On one bicep was a bright green tattoo of an alligator. Jack could see that the knuckles of his massive right-hand had the word "Mom" brightly tattooed in red ink. The left-hand had the word "Dad" brightly tattooed in blue ink. The tattooed alligator shined with sweat and appeared to slither slightly on the inmate's arm. Jack noticed that Tacy was enjoying the show, including the bulge on the inmate's sweatpants which had enlarged exponentially upon her arrival.

"We are the only prison in the State that still has free weights. The inmates at Milledgeville tore up their prison and used the free weights to bust out the Control Room glass. The Commissioner took the weights out of the other prisons. He left them at Lester since they were in the Court Order. Judge Valentino said he wasn't going to punish the guys at Lester for foolishness at Milledgeville. Joey, here, spends all the time he can with the weights and it shows. When he arrived here five years ago, the meth had him down to 140 pounds. But he is feeling better now," Captain Jamison said as the inmate exhaled deeply and sat on the metal weight bench. Jack noticed that Tacy was breathing a little deeper also.

Jack smiled as he watched Tacy lustily admiringly the inmate, her hands on her hips. "You know, President Carter said that lust in your heart is a sin, Tacy," Jack said quietly.

"I am a sinner, then," she responded in a very low sexy voice as she shifted her heels to slightly widen her stance.

"We need to show the doctor the dogs and his State house," Captain Jamison said, as he also observed Tacy's enjoyment of the scene. Jack could see the inmates' disappointment as the group started to leave.

TWENTY-THREE

THE SOUND OF barking dogs was very loud once they got through the sally port of the back gate. Jack watched as a delivery van was searched prior to being allowed into the prison. One officer opened the cargo doors and poked around the boxes of canned goods with a flashlight and a stick. Another officer looked under the truck with a mirror which was attached to a metal retractable pole.

"There is no way we can keep all the drugs, cell phones, liquor, marijuana and cigarettes out, but at least we can raise the bar a little. Now and then, they get sloppy and we catch somebody," Captain Jamison said as they observed the process. "We confiscated over a hundred cell phones last year."

"I imagine that stuff is mighty valuable inside these walls," Jack said, thinking that even with a search there were numerous possibilities for concealment.

"Yeah, it's all gold inside here. But unfortunately a lot of it comes through with the officers and staff. We get a bunch fired every year. Every once and a while somebody gets prosecuted," Captain Jamison said. "It's bad enough when they bring in a little dope or something, but sometimes inmates get real tricky. There was an incident, years ago, where some cans of beans in a

Christmas package turned out to contain a .25 caliber automatic and some bullets. That caused a real bad day in the neighborhood."

"I am amazed that could happen," Jack stated.

"Oh, a lot of times it starts out real innocent. Please sneak in a package of snacks from my Mama. Then it turns out that they aren't snacks and they aren't from Mama," Captain Jamison replied. "Also, once an employee breaks the rules for an inmate then the inmate can threaten to turn them in and can get the upper hand."

"Don't forget that love and romance sometimes cause problems," Tacy interjected.

"Oh yes! Love has been known to throw open the gates many times. My favorite is a great con artist named Jim Tabor who is now staying with us. He is a slick talking, good-looking fellow. They had him working in the kitchen at a prison in Milledgeville. He seduced the dietitian who was a big, lonesome, white lady. She actually brought him a loaded gun and he was out of there in a flash and on his way to Florida where they caught him a year later. She was heartbroken he didn't take her with him. Fortunately, if you had to give a gun to an inmate, he would be the one. So nobody got hurt. Once he was recaptured the Department decided he needed a little higher security environment so he will be with us for the next fifteen years," Captain Jamison responded.

Once outside the gate, they approached the kennel. It was a small, brick building with a tin roof, surrounded by a chain-link fence. Inside were numerous dog runs and a large yard of swept, red Georgia clay. The gate was unlocked and they entered the kennel to the great excitement of the numerous bloodhounds, who barked and howled mournfully. Jack was surprised that the usual kennel smells seemed to be at a minimum. Several of the dogs rushed up to greet Captain Jamison and lick his hands.

"Dogs, dogs! You're supposed to be ferocious bloodhounds. All you want to do is lick me to death and be petted," Captain Jamison said as he patted each dog on the head. Jack and Tacy followed his lead and also petted the dogs that had now approached them.

On the yard was an older man with frazzled white hair who was wearing a plaid cotton shirt with overalls, and an equally ancient black inmate. They were surrounded by five bloodhound puppies that played and nipped at their feet under the watch of their mother, a large black and tan bloodhound who sat at the edge of the yard in the shade. The two men were seated on the ground and from time to time gave one of the puppies a treat. Beside them on the ground were several rolls of toilet paper.

"Folks, this is Hiram White our Dog Handler and his assistant, Bo Lankford. They run the kennel and train these ferocious bloodhounds," Captain Jamison said, pointing to the two men who waved at the group. "Why don't you show the folks how you train them to track."

The men nodded and the man in overalls picked up a reddish puppy and held his nose to the chest of the black inmate. The inmate popped a treat into the dog's mouth which produced yelps of jealousy from the pups below. The inmate then took a roll of toilet paper and secured the end under a large rock. He handed the pup to the other man who put the pup's head inside his overalls to block the dog's view. The inmate then began to move away, slowly unrolling the paper as he went, making sure the paper was well handled by his weathered black hands. Soon the inmate was at the other side of the yard and hidden behind a large tree. A trail of toilet paper clearly showed the way to the hidden inmate.

The pup was then placed on the ground near the beginning of the toilet paper trail. "Treat, Fluffy, treat!" the man in overalls said as the puppy began a serious sniff of the paper. "That's it boy! Treat, treat!" he encouraged, as the little dog moved his nose slowly along the paper and crossed the yard. In a few seconds, the dog had followed the paper trail and went around the tree to the inmate.

"You got me! Treat time!" the inmate said as he stepped out from behind the tree with the pup in his hands. The pup was happily chomping on his treat and licking the inmate in hopes of another.

"We do these toilet paper trails to get them started with tracking. Then we make the pieces of toilet paper further apart. Finally, we get rid of the paper completely. Sometimes we put patches of pepper or water in the gaps so they can figure out how to handle that and get back on the trail. To the dogs, it is a game for treats," the Dog Handler explained to the group.

"So it is not exactly the Killer Bloodhounds from the movies?" Jack asked as an older dog continued to lick his hand.

"No, they might lick you to death when they find you, especially if they're wondering where you have hidden their treat," the Dog Handler responded.

"And did I hear you call that little pup, Fluffy?" Jack asked. "What sort of a chain gang name for a dog is that?"

"Yeah, we used to have names for them all like, Killer and Chainsaw, but with the Court Order and all, lawyers came down from the Attorney General's office in Atlanta and gave them all new names. That hound licking you is Happy, formerly known as Gator."

Jack noticed that each of the dog houses at the end of each run had a freshly painted name over the entrance. He also noticed a small dog graveyard just outside the fence. Near the fence were two fresh graves each with a small white wooden cross with the deceased dog's name neatly stenciled in black. "It looks like you have lost two recently," Jack said pointing at the fresh mounds of earth.

The Dog Handler looked over at the graves with sadness. "Those two fools broke away on a training exercise and decided to go after some wild hog babies. Unfortunately for them, Momma Hog was close by. The experienced dogs know better than to take on these giant wild hogs, which are about the size of a car with razor tusks. And just because they're gentle dogs doesn't mean they aren't effective. The experienced hounds can track an inmate across creeks and highways, through swamps and ignore pepper and other smelly stuff that gets tossed out. They might slow down for a minute for some meat, but then they will head right on," the Dog Handler continued.

Tacy picked up one of the pups which was scrambling around her feet. "I think 'Stinky' might be a good name for you," she said, looking at the small pile of dog poo at her feet.

"Stinky it is, ma'am," the Dog Handler replied. "Doc, if you would like to keep one of the older dogs over at your house for a pet, that would be fine. They are good company and Lester can be kind of lonesome at night for a young man."

"Which dogs are you talking about?" Jack asked as he basked in the canine affection all around him and thought happily about his long deceased greyhound, Polly.

"That one right next to you with a white spot on its head that makes him look bald. His name is Slick after one of our Commissioners that had a shiny bald head. He is a prize tracker but we have now retired him. We still use him for stud. All these rascal puppies are his," the Dog Handler replied.

Jack looked down at the dog in question who returned his attention with a happy gaze and vigorous tail wagging. "I guess I do need a watchdog will all these criminals around," he said, patting the dog on the head.

"The only way that dog is going to bite anyone is if he sees somebody he likes being attacked. Otherwise, it's only licks and tail wagging," the Dog Handler said. The dog seemed to understand he was being discussed and wagged his tail excitedly in response. "I will get you a leash and some dog food. You can just let him loose in your yard in the daytime. It is fenced and he won't go anywhere but just lie in the sun."

As the group headed to his new State house, Jack found himself in possession of a new friend tugging at the end of his leash and a large bag of dry dog food. The dog would occasionally bark at a squirrel or chipmunk, but otherwise trotted happily along. "I really wasn't expecting a hound dog as part of the perks of this job," Jack said as they walked across a newly mowed field toward his new residence. "I do miss my long departed greyhound, Polly. So I guess I'm just a complete pushover for such a fine dog." The hound barked slightly as if in affirmation.

At the edge of the field was a small, wood framed house surrounded by a white picket fence. It had a tin roof and a red brick chimney. The house and the fence were shiny and crisp with a fresh coat of white paint. To the left of the house was a well tended vegetable garden which contained tomato plants, squash, lettuce and several large eggplants. Behind the house, the yard sloped gently down to the river which was edged by several large oak trees laden with moss. Beside the river was a concrete bench with a view of the slow-moving black water. A rickety looking, wooden dock jutted a short way into the water. The grass was freshly cut and there were numerous hydrangeas blooming throughout the property. The dog sniffed carefully as they entered the gate.

"He can smell a lot of folks coming and going since we moved Dr. Bridge's stuff out," Captain Jamison remarked as they watched the dog explore the area with his sensitive nose.

"What a wonderful house!" Jack said, truly surprised at his accommodations. "It is perfect, with a view of the river and even a growing vegetable garden.

"Dr. Bridge loved her garden. We have been keeping it up since she died," Tacy said fondly.

Captain Jamison took a key from his massive key ring and opened the door. "It ain't the Cloister, but it's clean and comfortable."

Jack and Tacy stepped inside at his invitation. The house had shiny, dark red, varnished, hardwood floors across the large living room and dining area. There was a freshly upholstered sofa with two wing chairs which were similar to the ones Jack had seen in offices throughout the prison. On the floor was a multi colored, oval, handmade braided rug. Over the mantle was a large framed portrait of Robert E Lee. Beside the fireplace was a dented but shiny copper pot which was full of fatwood for kindling.

"The furniture is mostly from the shop and made by the inmates. The Ladies Association did the rug and the Warden bought it at their auction. We had to move the General out of the Lester elementary school since he is no longer politically correct. Since this is a private residence we thought it was okay to have his picture over the fireplace. You can move him out if you want," Captain Jamison said.

"I am glad to have General Lee. Do you think I'm a Yankee?" Jack said with a laugh.

"With all the folks moving to Atlanta these days you can never tell," Captain Jamison replied.

The small kitchen was spotless with a new patterned linoleum floor. The window over the sink looked out over the river. "Tacy, you're going to have to instruct me in cooking up some local favorites," Jack said as he peeked into some of the cabinets.

"I'll show you the mysteries of smoked mullet and gumbo any time," Tacy said with a smile. "I might even throw in some shrimp hush puppies."

They moved to the bedroom which was dominated by a king-size bed covered with a handmade quilt. Over the bed was a large oil painting which Jack recognized as the view of the river out back, accurate down to the concrete bench. The small unfinished pine chest was topped with a tall, blue, ceramic light with matching shade completed the room's furnishings.

"Dr. Bridge did that painting of the river," Tacy said. "Some of these other paintings in the house are hers also. But she gave most of them away to the folks at the institution."

"She was obviously a very talented lady," Jack said as he admired the detail in the painting. "I will be very comfortable here," he said as he pushed his hand on the firm mattress. "This place has everything I need and more." As he looked at the huge bed, he could not help imagining occupying it with Tacy, who stood directly across from him, looking gorgeous in her crisp nurse's uniform. Looking out the window, Jack could see the dog chasing a squirrel down to the river and up one of the big oak trees.

"Doc, I think this completes the tour. Is there anything else you would like to see?" Captain Jamison said with a glance over to Tacy.

"No, I think this has given me a good overview. I'm sure there are still many mysteries to be uncovered but I think Tacy and I need to get back before medical gets overwhelmed," Jack said. Tacy smiled and glanced at the bed herself for a sweet instant, recalling her comment to her friends that, "… if I do find somebody good, you can be sure I will give them both barrels."

TWENTY-FOUR

WHEN JACK AND Tacy arrived back in the Medical Unit it was a little after two and the waiting area had fifteen inmates in various stages of distress. Nurse Griggs had already situated one inmate in an examination room and was taking his vitals. She had pulled the files of all waiting inmates for Jack's review. They formed a neat pile on his metal desk in his small office. Tacy took over from Nurse Griggs who followed him as he closed the door to the office.

"Things are pretty quiet now, mostly cuts and diarrhea. Of course, we do have our usual visit from inmate Thompkins. I would suggest you have a nurse present during his examination as he does like to file complaints," Nurse Griggs said.

Jack correctly assumed that inmate Thompkins was the short, black, inmate with slicked back hair, gold hoop earrings, a red bandanna and sunglasses who he had observed quietly singing to himself as he rocked back and forth on the metal chair in the waiting room. Jack sat at the desk and quickly reviewed the fifteen medical files and their attached medical requests while the nurse waited. "Let's start with inmate Thompkins. I assume he is the fellow with a red bandanna," Jack said, picking up the file. Nurse Griggs nodded her agreement and they both proceeded to the waiting room.

"Mr. Thompkins, Dr. Randolph will see you now. I'm going to take your vital signs and see how you're doing," Nurse Griggs said with authority as she opened the door to an examination room and directed the inmate inside. Mr. Thompkins rose and padded into the room with his handcuffed hands held out before him.

"Doctor, I wish you would take these off so I can show you my problems," the inmate said, gesturing with the handcuffs.

"I think the doctor can examine you just fine with the hand-cuffs on," Nurse Griggs quickly responded, not wanting to give the new doctor a chance to make the mistake of removing the cuffs.

"I think Nurse Griggs is correct. Let's start with your vital signs and then check on your problems," Jack said as he closed the door to the examining room.

Nurse Griggs briskly placed the thermometer in the inmate's mouth and proceeded with the blood pressure cuff. As she worked, the inmate somehow managed to pull down his pants revealing a striking pair of red thong underwear. Despite his claims of illness, the inmate was well enough to be quite aroused which caused his undergarments to bulge accordingly.

"I got the jock itch again, Doc. Nurse Griggs gave me some stuff but it never works," the inmate said, proudly displaying the inner part of his thigh.

Jack put on a pair of examination gloves and examined the area with a small flashlight. "It does look like you have a fungus infection down there. I'm going to prescribe some antifungal oint-ment. I'm also going to suggest some non-binding, white cotton boxers might help with the situation," Jack said as Nurse Griggs nodded her approval.

"So you not going to let me be pretty, back in the back," the inmate complained.

"Mr. Thompkins, I'm trying to get you well, not help you be pretty. I might add, so far you are negative for HIV. I hope you understand the importance of staying that way. Maybe some cotton boxers could help both situations," Jack continued.

"In Atlanta, the Habershams go right across Paces Ferry where the Governor lives. When I get out that is where I'm going," the inmate replied, his eyes wild with irritation. "Maybe the Governor will talk to me this time."

"Yes, and let's put you down for another mental health evaluation. Are you doing okay on your medicine?" Jack responded, looking at the inmate carefully.

"Old Governor Maddox said that if he knew how many people thought inmates volunteered to retrieve ducks from the swamp for the officers he would tell you how many fools there were in Georgia," Thompkins commented, somewhat more calmly.

"You know, Mr. Thompkins, I do remember when Governor Maddox said that. And he was right. You will probably remember he also said we needed a better class of inmates in the system. I want you to be that better class of inmate!" Jack said with a broad smile to Thompkins.

"That will be me! You can count on it, Doc. No more red underpants," Thompkins replied with a smirk, delighted that someone in authority had finally agreed with one of his statements. He pulled up his pants as Jack finished writing the prescription and handed it to the nurse.

"This ointment will be on the next pill call, Mr. Thompkins," Nurse Griggs said as she directed him out to the waiting area.

"Mr. Thomkins is quite a character. What is he in prison for?" Jack asked, certain that Mr. Thompkins' criminal biography would be an interesting one.

Nurse Griggs smiled and laughed. "Mr. Thompkins does have a curious history. Previously he was at G-MAX on a fifteen year sentence for armed robbery of a gas station. Since he was just the getaway driver and no one was hurt, the Parole Board paroled him after five years. He was free as long as he reported to his Parole

Officer and didn't get into any trouble. When he was in prison he filed a lawsuit against the Warden claiming a constitutional right to practice witchcraft as his religion and a First Amendment claim for cable television, which he was handling without a lawyer, but probably with the help of the law library clerks. He had one hearing before Judge Valentino, and the Warden was represented at the hearing by an attractive, Assistant Attorney General from Atlanta, named Alex Hibbs. Apparently, Thompkins became infatuated with Mr. Hibbs, and Thompkins would file all kinds of strange pleadings in the case which were just short of love notes to Hibbs. Hibbs, as a seasoned AG, ignored these as mere general craziness and probably helpful to eventually get the case dismissed. However, when Thompkins was paroled and back on the street, Thompkins continued to file pleadings in the case. Finally, Hibbs got a pleading that was over the top. He noticed it was slightly stained as he read through the pages. On the last page was a large, shiny, oily spot on which Thompkins proclaimed his love for Hibbs and explained that since he would never be able to consummate his love whose name cannot be spoken, he had ejaculated his essence on the page to proclaim his eternal devotion. That did it for Hibbs, and the pleading was sent to the crime lab where the stains were identified as human semen which matched Thompkins' DNA. Of course, after that, it didn't take long for Mr. Thompkins to have his parole revoked. So now he is back at G-MAX serving the remaining ten years on his sentence," Nurse Griggs said.

"Perhaps that is just as well. I am not sure Mr. Thompkins is quite ready to take his place in lawful society," Jack replied with a laugh.

"Your next patient is in the exam room," Nurse Griggs said, handing him the medical file as she walked to the storage room. Jack perused it as he opened the door to the neighboring exam room. A middle-aged black inmate with numerous tattoos was seated on the examination table with the thermometer in his mouth. Nurse Tacy was busily pumping the bulb on the blood pressure cuff. The inmate had a large cut over his left eye. It looked like it had been there several days. Jack closed the door and put on a pair of exam gloves.

"I believe you are Jonas Sims and you said on your Medical Request that you got this cut three days ago playing basketball," Jack said carefully as he examined the cut and doubting it had any sports origin.

"It got to be red and hurting, so I did a sick call request," the inmate said in a flat voice.

"You sure you didn't get in a fight or something?" Jack said delicately, wanting to give the inmate opportunity for explanation.

"Nah, just basketball. You get in trouble round here for fighting," the inmate replied as Jack continued to review the file.

"Mr. Sims, I see you have been in here every week for five weeks with a sports injury like this. I'm sure basketball is a contact sport at G-MAX, but maybe I could see about moving you to another dorm where you could make some new friends," Jack said, flipping back though the documentation of the other numerous cuts and injuries.

The inmate's eyes brightened immediately. "That would be real good Doc. I would like to move around a little. I have been in that dorm a whole year. Some of those other dorms got more of my Augusta homeboys," the inmate said enthusiastically.

"Tacy, if I requested Mr. Sims be moved, what will happen?" Jack asked.

"Your request would go to the Classification Committee. It is their decision, but they always worked with Dr. Bridge in the past," Tacy said.

"Well, Mr. Sims, you heard the lady. I will make the request to get you moved. We will get this cut cleaned up and hopefully you will be playing in a little gentler league," Jack said as he watched Tacy bandage the wound.

"Thank you Doc. I don't want to be ratting anybody out. I just live my own business," the inmate said thankfully as he walked out to the waiting room.

"You seem to be a lot more street smart than I would have expected from a silk stocking, Buckhead doctor," Tacy said, impressed with Jack's insight into the personalities and problems of the inmates.

"Remember, I worked three years in Atlanta. I've had gang members try to get into my operating room to finish off the person I was operating on. So it was not all Mint Juleps on the veranda at the Club," Jack replied.

Jack and Tacy worked through the remaining inmates in less than two hours. Jack was beginning to feel tired and after the last inmate he was glad to retire to his office to complete the paperwork of the day.

Nurse Tacy opened the door to Jack's office carrying two large stacks of files. Several of the files were large accordion folders. "We have loaded your desk with a bunch more medical files. In general, these are the folks we see most often. We thought you would want to take a close look at some of these. It won't be long until they are here in person. Also, if you would like to get some good barbecue for dinner, there is a really good place in Lester that is owned by a former inmate," she continued.

"After I have looked at all these files I will be very ready for some good barbecue," Jack replied.

"I will meet you there at six thirty. It is right across street from the Courthouse. Look for the Maximum Pig. You can't miss it," she said as she closed the door.

Jack picked up the first file on top of one of the stacks. Opening it, he saw what was to be a recurring pattern. An inmate with minor ailments, presenting again and again to medical, often without any compliance with the treatments given and accompanied by numerous official Medical Grievances and the occasional lawsuit. Putting down this file, he looked through the stack for another file with more medical than correctional challenges. His eye landed on a thick accordion folder with numerous notations on the outside of the file.

Jack picked it up and looked at the label which stated in bold typed letters, "Henry Judson Kirk." It only took a few pages for Jack to realize this was the inmate who had murdered his predecessor. This was apparent from the HIV testing Notice and memo which were among the most recent medical attentions given to Mr. Kirk. The Notice, a copy of which had been delivered to Mr. Kirk, stated that because of his being charged with a sexual assault and murder of Dr. Bridge, he was required under Georgia law to be tested for the HIV virus. A memo with an attached Use of Force report described in precise detail the steps and amount of reasonable force which was required to get Mr. Kirk to submit to such a test. The memo also indicated that due to the difficulty in obtaining samples that three samples in three separate vials were taken instead of the usual one. Two samples had been sent to the testing laboratory and one remained under refrigeration in the Medical Unit should further tests be necessary. The most recent document in the file was the returned Lab Report which clearly announced that Mr. Kirk was negative for the HIV virus.

His attention focused, Jack began to carefully review the file in chronological order starting from the back of the file. The record showed Kirk arriving at Georgia Maximum Security Prison from the Fulton County jail in Atlanta, over four years ago. The paperwork from Fulton County showed that Mr. Kirk had remained in the Fulton County jail from the time of his arrest through his trial and conviction for a period of one year and sixty days. Attached to the paperwork were the lab results from Grady Hospital of another HIV test done under similar circumstances one month after his arrest. As Jack looked at the familiar form from Grady Hospital, he had to stop and read it again. The Grady lab work from over five years ago clearly showed Kirk as positive for the HIV virus a full year before he entered the Georgia prison system.

Jack moved ahead in the file to the documentation of Kirk's transfer from the Fulton County jail to Georgia Maximum Security Prison after his conviction. After twenty four days in the Georgia prison system he was again given an HIV test along with a full physical. Again, the lab report in the State system showed the same positive HIV result as the Fulton County jail. Mr. Kirk's physical exam noted only mild flulike symptoms which had gone away quickly.

Jack then read through Kirk's records showing ordinary medical problems such as occasional diarrhea, cold symptoms and lacerations. He stopped at a series of records from ten months ago. Mr. Kirk had committed a vicious sexual attack on another inmate. His prey had been a slightly built, twenty-two year old white inmate whom he had raped and nearly beaten to death. The procedures by the State were the same as followed after his attack on Dr. Bridge. Again, Kirk had been served with a Notice that he was required to be tested for the HIV virus, which he had refused to sign. Then there was the Use of Force Report and Incident Report which described the manhandling necessary to obtain a blood sample from Mr. Kirk. Again, the report used the magic legal phrases, numerous times, that the "minimum amount of force was used to maintain positive control of the inmate." In this particular situation, this minimum amount of force had involved the use of an electric shock device and night sticks by three officers in riot gear. Again, care had been taken to retrieve a sufficient amount of blood for three samples in order that the procedure would not have to be repeated.

Jack blinked when he flipped the page to observe the result. The lab results had come back negative for HIV. Jack saw a handwritten order from Dr. Bridge to have another of the samples sent to the lab for retesting. On the margin of the first lab report she had written in garbled handwriting, "HIV test on initial entry to GMAX positive. Maybe, false-negative? Send another sample to the lab."

The file showed the return of the second lab test to the institution a week later. It also came back negative for HIV. On this report a question mark was again scribbled in what appeared to be Dr. Bridge's handwriting. Jack went back and forth through these documents and looked on the backs of each to see if there were any further notations or explanations. His eye then caught an entry of a name with which he was familiar. On this Notice of Results of HIV test, where Kirk once again refused to sign, his refusal was noted by the signature of Nurse Tacy Crandall on the form.

He then saw another notation in Dr. Bridge's handwriting in the medical narrative. The note stated, "Call to CDC," and the illegible name of the doctor to whom she had spoken. Jack looked at the name carefully and thought it easily could be a scribbling of the name of his friend at the CDC, Dr. Clayton. "Will send sample," the note continued. The next note in the same handwriting stated, "remaining blood sample lost." The records then continued in ordinary fashion to document the minor medical problems of Kirk as a healthy, fifty year-old male until the legally required tests for HIV caused by the rape and murder of Dr. Bridge.

Jack went over the file again to make sure that he had not been mistaken, or had missed something in his review. But the results were the same. Kirk had been found positive for HIV in two separate tests. The first, at the Fulton County Jail in Atlanta, and the second when he entered the Georgia prison system a year later. Then, ten months ago he had tested negative for HIV, and was retested, again with negative results. Dr Bridge had talked to a doctor at the CDC and was going to send them an additional sample but remaining sample had been lost. Now, after the murder of Dr. Bridge, Kirk had been tested again and the results were still negative. Somehow, over a period of years Kirk's body had purged itself of the HIV virus. If this was correct, then Kirk was exactly the Elite HIV Controller the CDC and Dr. Clayton had been seeking for years. The Blood Cleaner.

Jack looked again at the scribbled notes by Dr. Bridge about her questions and call to the CDC. Could this have been a call to his friend, Dr. Clayton? The handwriting was abominable. He closed the file and looked at his watch. He was already late for dinner.

TWENTY-FIVE

TACY WAS WAITING patiently, seated in a booth, when Jack pulled into the gravel parking lot of the fabled, Maximum Pig restaurant in Lester. There was no missing the Maximum Pig with its rows of white light bulbs strung across the roof and the signature Maximum Pig, which was a twenty five foot tall, pink metal structure in the likeness of a large smiling pig, with broad horizontal prison stripes depicting a prison uniform and sporting a black mask painted on the face. The pig appeared to have been constructed from cast-off metal military parts such as airplane gas tanks and the like. Tacy watched Jack's speeding vehicle kick up a cloud of dust from the dry gravel in the parking lot. She smiled when he exited his car looking at his watch. He seemed relieved when she waved at him through the plate glass window.

Jack entered the restaurant and noticed that the porcine décor continued inside. Each table had a ceramic pink pig light and on the walls were several large blowup photographs of hunters standing over huge hogs. Jack noticed that on one picture where the immense hog had especially large tusks, there appeared to be a dead dog to the side, apparently a victim of those tusks. Jack approached the wooden booth where Tacy was seated. "I'm sorry to be so late, Tacy. I just got interested in one of those files and forgot about the time," he said, somewhat breathlessly. As he spoke, Jack noticed a large print of a painting showing a group of hogs killing a rattlesnake which hung on the wall by the booth, but did not comment on it.

"You're only twenty minutes late. Besides, I was going to eat here anyway. I would have just ordered for myself after half an hour," she said pleasantly as Jack took his seat across from her in the booth.

"So you are the new doctor that Nurse Tacy has been waiting for?" asked a tall, fortyish, black man who had just appeared next to their booth, wearing a red apron emblazoned with "MAXIMUM PIG" in large black letters. His smile revealed a magnificent gold front tooth with a small diamond insert, no doubt a sign of new-found prosperity.

"Jack, this is Ray Pitts. He owns the Maximum Pig and makes the best barbecue in the South," Tacy said as the man smiled proudly.

"What would you to like to drink?" Mr. Pitts continued with a slight lisp in his soft voice as Jack looked quickly at the menu.

"What kind of beer you have?" Jack asked as he searched the menu.

"We are BYOB. I don't have any beer or liquor. Couldn't get a license, since I had some convictions. Tacy may have told you I had a little problem with the law a few years back," he said with a wink to Tacy. "But Miss Tacy always has her own, back in the locker."

"Ray, I think we will have two of my lite beers from the back," she quickly replied. Jack looked at her quizzically and nodded his agreement.

"So what files had you so fascinated that you were late for your big night out in Lester?" Tacy asked.

"The one that got my attention was Henry Kirk," Jack said, noticing the pained look in Tacy's eyes at the mention of Kirk's name. "He tested positive for HIV years ago at the Fulton County Jail in Atlanta and then again when he arrived in the State prison system. In the last year he has now had two separate negative HIV tests. There was one when he raped that white inmate ten months ago. Dr. Bridge sent another sample back for a second test which was also negative. The latest negative test was done when he murdered Dr. Bridge," Jack replied.

"I hate to even think about that man. He's so evil. I do remember Dr. Bridge saying something about HIV with him. But I don't remember anything else other than the horror of that day," Tacy said.

"The medical notes show her reviewing the two previous negative HIV tests and calling a doctor at the CDC. She may have called someone I know. She looked for the third blood sample to send to the CDC, but it was missing. You signed the Notice that was delivered to Kirk about the results of the HIV test," Jack replied.

"I remember now. We both looked in the refrigerator for the other sample. It was gone. Dr. Bridge said that the results were very unusual. But about that time, we had a mini riot between two gangs. There were about fifteen inmates stabbed and two officers seriously injured. The prison was on lockdown for three days. Medical was packed. I know she meant to follow up, but I don't think it ever happened," Tacy said. "Dr. Bridge did mention it may have been just as well the sample was lost since it would have been ethically and legally dicey for her to send the sample to the CDC without his permission, since the required legal testing had been done and was completed with the forms and all," she continued.

"She may have a point there. The Georgia HIV testing law was upheld in Federal Court. But once you have an accurate test you're supposed to destroy the remaining samples," Jack replied.

"And you can forget about Henry Kirk agreeing to anything. You probably saw the Use of Force Report on what it took to get the samples after he killed Dr. Bridge. The samples we got from his attack on Dr. Bridge are long gone. I destroyed them myself, once we got the results of the first one back."

"Still, this is a very unusual situation. The CDC and a bunch of other research groups have been looking for a Blood Cleaner like this for years. They call them Elite HIV controllers. They are usually white men and they are extremely rare. Usually, it turns out that the first test was a false positive or the second test is a false negative. And even on the ones that test out there is no one yet that totally cured themselves down to a zero viral load of HIV virus. But with Kirk, there are two clear positives and then a negative test years later with a second sample resubmitted and now a recent negative test," Jack said.

"It does look like his body cured itself, somehow," Tacy replied.

"No kidding. But I hope we don't have to wait for him to rape or murder someone else again to get another sample for the CDC," Jack said.

"Well, considering how well liked Dr. Bridge was by the inmates and staff, it wouldn't surprise me if some day we were treated to his entire blood supply courtesy of one of the inmates or officers Kirk has messed with over the years," she said.

"I do know that my friend at the CDC, Dr. Clayton, has worked on this for years and has counseled on something called the National HIV Controllers Panel. The people that can stop the virus from replicating on its own are called controllers and the best of them are called Elite Controllers. These Elite Controllers are extremely rare, but I think Mr. Kirk is in a class by himself. Apparently, these Elite Controllers have some connection to something called major histocompatibility complex, MHC for short. They are still trying to figure it out," Jack said.

"If they do, will it lead to a vaccine for AIDS?" Tacy asked.

"Exactly. But it would be more than just preventative. It would be a shot that could be given to people who are sick with the virus now, to train their blood to stop the virus from replicating and make them well," Jack said.

"And a jerk like Kirk could be the key to stopping AIDS all over the world?" Tacy asked.

"The Lord does work in mysterious ways," Jack replied. As he spoke, Mr. Pitts reappeared with two large frosty glasses.

"Your beers from Miss Tacy's special stash have arrived," he announced.

Jack looked at the white froth at the top of his icy blue glass and gave his drink a taste. "Tacy, do you really have a locker back there loaded with cold beer?" Jack asked. "And since you're the homeboy here I'm going let you order my dinner," Jack continued.

"Ray, I think we will have two orders of your ribs, two bowls of Brunswick stew and two sides of your homemade creamed corn," Tacy quickly announced and Mr. Pitts was off with their order.

"Ray can't get a beer or liquor license but no one seems to mind this faux BYOB setup. He has a secret recipe for barbecue sauce on the ribs. We all know it has something to do with honey and bourbon, but he won't tell. His Brunswick stew is full of local okra and tomatoes and is a little spicy. The creamed corn is fresh corn with thick cream and butter sauce topped with black pepper. It is probably a hundred calories an ounce," Tacy explained.

"Are the ribs from these giant hogs I see on the walls? I remember seeing that painting of the hogs killing the snake at the Chicago Art Institute. And aside from barbecue and chain gang, what else is there to do around here?" Jack asked with a smile as he looked directly at Tacy while pointing at the print and one of the faded hunting photographs.

"No, the pork is just good old farm fresh. These woods hogs are too hard to hunt for any steady supply and they are really dangerous. They are huge because long ago the wild hogs mated with domestic stock to produce these monsters. They have killed lots of dogs and hunters and they are especially aggressive when their piglets are around. You can see from that picture, hogs can even kill rattlesnakes. But for entertainment, there is gambling and fishing on the river. Most of the men and a lot of the women hunt deer during the season," she replied slyly.

"What do you mean, gambling?" he replied, taking the bait.

"I will take you gambling sometime soon," she replied mysteriously. Jack's mind conjured up images of rural dog fighting and back room poker games.

"Will I need my pistol?" he asked.

"No, I think you will find it very genteel," she said mysteriously, erasing the poker and dog fighting images from his mind immediately.

"Tell me about the fishing on the river. I love to fish," he said.

"The big river is the Altamaha. That is where I fish. You can catch bass, sea trout, catfish and mullet. There are also lots of alligators. Everyone has their own secret recipe for smoking the mullet," she said happily.

"Any time you want to get your boat out, I am ready," Jack responded as Mr. Pitts arrived with their dinner. After setting the plates before them, with a grand gesture and a flash of his gold and diamond tooth, Mr. Pitts presented Jack with a keychain which had attached a plump plastic pig, complete with prison stripes and mask like the model outside.

"With my compliments to the new doctor," Mr. Pitts said as he squeezed the plastic pig. A loud squeal could be heard throughout the restaurant as the light in the plastic pig's mouth sent a beam of light toward the ribs on Jack's plate.

"Wow, that thing is loud. It really sounds like a piggy in distress," Jack said, examining his new present. "The flashlight will come in handy also."

"I hope it will remind you to come back to the Maximum Pig. Just don't be squeaking it in the woods or you might be looking at some angry tusks," Mr. Pitts said as he made his exit.

"You are now officially part of Lester society. We all have several of these," Tacy said as she reached in her purse and pulled out an identical striped piglet with her keys attached. "So if you are serious about fishing, could you come by at seven on Saturday? We can get the boat launched and have a mess of fish before noon," she continued.

"Do you mean seven in the morning?" Jack asked, knowing full well that all serious fishing began early in the morning.

"Of course, you Atlanta slugabed. By noon all the fish will have eaten a pound of bugs and will be happily sleeping in the bottom of the river instead of being in our boat," she said.

"All right, I will be there," he assured her, picking up a well roasted rib and gesturing for effect.

She smiled and turned her attention to her dinner, starting with a ladylike poke at the creamed corn with her fork. "There is one restriction. I don't want any discussions about Henry Kirk. I want to enjoy our day on the river," she said seriously, looking directly at Jack.

"Yes ma'am," Jack said obediently as he bit into the succulent rib. "These are really good," he said, a little surprised with the quality of the country cuisine. "I think he must have some kind of secret sauce, maybe just a trace of Spanish moss or something in here. What do you want me to bring to the boat and what sort of attire should I wear?" Jack asked.

"You can bring a cooler and some drinks. I will take care of lunch, bait and everything else. Bring your bathing suit. For fishing and the boat, jeans, tee shirt and a windbreaker with tennis shoes," she said.

"And when we do the gambling, are you sure I won't need my pistol?" he asked.

"I am sure there will be several of those in the parking lot, along with some assault rifles. That would be standard South Georgia," she said.

"And exactly where do you live?" Jack asked.

"Take a left at the Courthouse and go a mile. Then take a left at the sign for Altamaha Marsh Road. It is the third house on the left. You will see my green truck in the driveway. Remember, you bring the drinks, and no Henry Kirk."

TWENTY-SIX

IT WAS ABOUT ten in the morning when the two young, white officers arrived with inmate Kirk for his monthly visit to the law library. As it was a Saturday, the officers escorting Kirk were two of the more junior and inexperienced staff at the prison. One officer, Jesse Orland, was from a well respected Lester family, known for staffing the prison. He eyed Kirk nervously as they entered the law library. The other officer, John Saxon, a newly trained recruit from Macon, seemed more relaxed, viewing Kirk as just another inmate.

Inside the law library was a lone law library clerk, Jimmy Richards, seated at a desk with a typewriter and numerous law books. The only other inmate in the law library was inmate Thompkins who sat at a table with a stack of papers and several law books.

The officers escorted Kirk into the law library handcuffed and with a belly chain. In his hands was a sheaf of legal papers. "I need these cuffs off so I can do legal work," Kirk demanded loudly. The two officers looked at each other, not sure what to do.

"Usually they take his cuffs off. He really can't do law work with them on," clerk Richards commented calmly. Officer Saxon nodded and proceeded to uncuff Kirk. Officer Orland stood nearby, his hand on his nightstick.

Kirk walked over and sat in a chair in front of the inmate law clerk's desk. "I need to be able to talk to him so you can't hear. That's my right," Kirk snarled. The officers looked at each other and then took seats at the other end of the room near inmate Thompkins.

Satisfied the officers were out of earshot, Kirk handed the clerk some papers and leaned over the desk. "Have you finished the Transfer Order and the fax?" Kirk softly asked the clerk. The clerk pushed two typewritten documents across the desk for Kirk to examine. The first document was an official looking, "Order Of Transfer For Hearing" which ordered the Warden to produce inmates, Henry Kirk, Jimmy Richards and Nurse Tacy Crandall for a hearing at the Courthouse in Brunswick, Georgia. The signature of Judge Valentino had been carefully forged. The second document was a fax cover sheet of the Central Office in Atlanta of the Georgia Department of Corrections. It was complete with the Seal of the State of Georgia and instructions to the Warden of Georgia Maximum Security Prison to transport the inmates and Nurse Crandall to the hearing as required by the Order of Judge Valentino attached. "These are perfect. Now what about the tools for today's ruckus?" Kirk asked.

The Clerk pulled up the side of a stack of papers to reveal a screwdriver with its end sharpened to a point and a box of matches. "You get these faxed from the Librarian's office and I will start giving them some problems. I want to be sure when this fax hits the Warden's office everyone will be busy and not be noticing it arriving," Kirk said.

The clerk took the fax cover sheet and Order and folded them inside a law book. He stood with the law book in his hand and asked the officers, "I need to get into the Librarian's office to retrieve some materials for Kirk. Mr. Thomas keeps some of the most requested materials in his office so they won't get stolen," the clerk said calmly, pointing to the door to the Librarian's office which was just around the corner from the library stacks.

Officer Saxon reached in his pocket and retrieved the key to the Librarian's office. "Come with me," he ordered as he led the clerk to the door of the office. The officer unlocked the door and watched as the clerk entered. At that moment, Kirk could be heard talking loudly to officer Orland. Officer Saxon stepped back into the law library to see Kirk standing and arguing with officer Orland.

Clerk Richards quickly dialed the Warden's fax number and inserted the two documents into the fax machine in the Librarian's office as he listened carefully to the arguments nearby. He picked up several law books from the Librarian's desk just as the fax machine printed out the confirmation that the fax had been received in the Warden's office upstairs. He picked up the confirmation and folded it into one of the books.

At that moment, officer Saxon returned and looked carefully around the office. "That damned Kirk is always causing problems. You get out of here and I will lock up," he said loudly, as he took a quick look at the books retrieved by the clerk from the office.

After locking the office, officer Saxon followed clerk Richards back to the library. Clerk Richards returned to his seat in front of Kirk and pushed the law books toward him. "Kirk, there's no need to get excited. What you need is right here," the clerk said calmly. Inmate Thompkins looked up from his work and around the room nervously. The officers returned to their seats across the room, satisfied that Kirk's agitation had ended.

Kirk leaned across the desk and asked softly, "Did the fax go through?" Clerk Richards smiled and showed Kirk the printed fax confirmation which he retrieved from the law book. The clerk then pushed toward Kirk the stack of papers under which the screwdriver and matches were hidden.

"In a minute I will take everyone's minds off the fax in the Warden's office. Jimmy, you know I will have to rough you up a little, so they don't think we are friends," Kirk said softly, fingering the screwdriver.

"Whatever it takes to get out of here. I got two life sentences. Maybe I shouldn't have shot both my wife and my mother in law," the clerk replied with an emphasis on "mother in law." He then stood up and walked toward a cart loaded with law books. "I will be back in the stacks re-shelving these law books," he announced.

The officers nodded, then stepped outside for an against-the-rules-smoke, both keeping an eye on Kirk through the glass doors. Kirk watched and smiled, looking at the metal curtain over the doors and the unprotected activation switch at the side of the door. Once he closed the metal curtain he would have the few minutes he needed to create a first rate disruption. He also looked forward to a few moments alone with inmate Thompkins.

TWENTY-SEVEN

IT WAS 6:30 a.m. when Jack pulled onto Highway 189 headed for Lester. In the backseat was a plastic cooler loaded with beer and sodas. The South Georgia sun was already beginning to heat the thick air as he accelerated down the blacktop through the forest of tall thin pines. It took only a few minutes to reach the center of Lester. He smiled as he drove by the Hi Max Beauty Salon and the Chain Gang Car Wash. He glanced at the stately Courthouse which shone in the morning sun and turned left as he had been directed.

It did not take much of the mile down that road to be in the countryside with few houses and great expanses of pine trees with an occasional smattering of scrub palmetto. Jack slowed his car as he read the slightly rusted metal sign which announced that this particular gravel road was the "Altamaha Marsh Road" he was looking for. He turned left and proceeded slowly, looking for the third house on the left. Each of the houses on the street was set back on a lot of over two acres, land not being at a particular premium in Lester, Georgia. He passed the first house which was a prefabricated cottage with white aluminum siding which gleamed imperviously to the Georgia sun and salt air. A green concrete birdbath gave a touch of contrasting color to the white aluminum.

The second house was a new looking mobile home which sported a red canvas awning and a large vegetable garden to the right side. Down the road about a sixteenth of a mile he saw his destination. It was a simple, one-story, white frame house set back from the road by a long green yard. The house was accented by neatly trimmed shrubbery, and was flanked by two large magnolia trees on each end of the house. Jack could see Tacy loading her green truck which was parked in the driveway beside the house. Tethered to the truck was a shiny, electric green, fiberglass fishing boat, securely attached to its trailer. Jack slowly pulled into the driveway which was solidly constructed of oyster shell tabby.

Tacy watched as he exited his car and removed the cooler. "You are actually early, and you remembered the drinks and the cooler," she said happily as he approached. Placing the cooler on the ground, he gave her a hug and the obligatory light kiss on her lips.

"I like your boat. It looks pretty fast for the river," he said, peering at the colorful craft with its oversized outboard motor.

"You need to be able to outrun the gators and the redneck crazies sometimes," she said as he continued to examine the boat and its contents.

"You certainly have all sorts of equipment. These two poles made out of metal pipe look like they could land a dinosaur. And this chain and metal hook is not something we use much in Atlanta. At least, I can relate to the other two fishing poles," Jack said.

"The big poles are for sharks, if we get to the tidal part of the river. They will snap a regular deep sea pole in a second if they are in a bad mood. The chain and the hook are in case you want to play a little tug of war with the alligators. They are not in season, but it is fun to tease them out of their hidy holes," she said.

"I suppose the 30/30 rifle is in case they attack," Jack said as he glanced at the brown hunting rifle propped up against one of the seats.

"In season, we would shoot them with it once they grab the hook. Now, we would just use it to scare them into turning the hook loose. They all know about rifles. Also, it just makes sense to have it on board if you are way back in the swamps," she said.

"I'm sure there are nasty two legged gators out there also," Jack said.

"Oh, it's pretty peaceful. Mostly the folks I grew up with out there. But sometimes, there are suspicious people from Atlanta, who have had too much to drink," she said.

"I see. I will be on the lookout for those types. Are they in season?" Jack asked.

"They are always in season," she said, giving him a pinch on the back of his tight jeans. He reached to grab her back, but stopped when he saw the front door of the house open.

"You children better not be bringing back any alligators," was the high-pitched Southern warning which emanated from a small woman clad in a pink terrycloth bathrobe and orange flip-flops. Out of the pocket of her well worn robe she produced a pack of cigarettes and proceeded to light up and puff away enthusiastically. "Tacy won't let me smoke in the house, so I thought I would come out here and supervise you young people," she continued, as she took a long drag on her cigarette.

"Jack, this is my mom, Clarice Crandall. I was hoping she would be asleep when we left," Tacy said, with a gesture toward the robe clad figure.

"I'm pleased to meet you, ma'am. I will be sure and bring Tacy back safely," Jack said politely, walking forward to shake her hand.

"They all say that. Tacy, at least this one has some manners," the matron snorted as she snuffed out her cigarette and retreated to the house, the door slamming behind her.

"Now you have met my family. Do you still want to continue?" Tacy said.

"Of course, she was delightful in a Lester, Georgia sort of way," Jack said.

"People in town will be saying we are engaged," Tacy continued as she put Jack's cooler into the boat. "Let's get down to the boat ramp before it gets too hot," she said to Jack as he opened the passenger door to the truck.

It took less than five minutes for them to arrive at the public boat ramp on the river. There was one group of boaters ahead of them who were cautiously backing their boat down the concrete ramp. The group consisted of three large men all wearing various types of camouflage attire from hats to waders. The boat sank several inches into the water with its load of men and several coolers of beer on ice.

As Jack and Tacy exited the truck, Jack recognized the largest of the men as Captain Jamison, who was wearing a mismatched pair of camouflage pants and T-shirt, topped off by a worn baseball cap. He looked up and recognized them. "Boys, at least if we get into trouble, we know our crack medical team is out here on the water to save us," Captain Jamison commented as he released a large plug of chewed tobacco into the black water.

"And I am surprised the inmates haven't all escaped with this much security floating down the river," Tacy replied sassily.

"Well, Tacy, sometimes public safety just has to wait until we catch a mess of fish. Besides, those newbie officers need to learn how to run a chain gang without any grownups around," Captain Jamison replied with a broad smile. The man in the stern cranked the motor and they were off with a wave. Jack noticed that each of them was wearing a pistol and he saw the length of their own rifle beside the beer.

"Are all fishing parties down here so heavily armed?" Jack asked as they slowly motored out of sight.

"Oh, those boys are all right. I knew them all from town or High School. They all think of themselves as Daniel Boone. It helps them deal with having to ride herd on every thug from Atlanta," Tacy said.

"Tacy, you are just going to have to stop dissing my hometown. All thugs are not from Atlanta, just most of them. I have been at the prison long enough to know that there are several proud gangs from Augusta, Savannah and even Mexico," Jack said.

"Yes, and there is even one sad French-Canadian guy. He got picked up on the way to Florida with a load of drugs. He really hates the food and he keeps showing up for sick call in the summer claiming he is having heatstroke," she said as she unhitched the boat from the trailer let it slide backward on its pulley into the brackish water.

Once the boat was safely afloat Tacy unhitched the pulley while Jack held the boat steady. Tacy got back in the truck and expertly pulled the trailer out of the water and parked in a sandy area to the side of the ramp. After locking the truck, she hopped delicately into the boat as Jack pushed away with a paddle and she started the engine.

They slowly moved toward the center of the river and Tacy turned the boat and pointed it downstream. "What kind of fish do you want?" she asked as she increased the throttle slightly, causing the boat to cut smartly through the black ripples.

"Are we close enough to the ocean to get some sea trout?" Jack asked. "They are my favorite fish unless you are way out in the ocean and have a chance for some pompano."

"For sea trout we need to head further down the river, closer to the ocean, and near some oyster shoals. That is where they like to hang out. It won't take us too long," she said.

"I wonder what they eat that is around oysters? I know they can't be there for the oysters," Jack said.

"Probably the shrimp and other small fish feed on something on the outside of the shells," Tacy replied. She turned the throttle up slightly, creating a nice wind in Jack's face. Jack sat back in the padded chair and took in the rich smell of the river and the swamps. Jack watched two hawks circle slowly overhead, riding the now heated thermals over the river.

The banks on both sides of the river were crowded with old oaks whose gnarly roots and branches stretched out above the river for several feet. Jack pointed out to Tacy two huge hogs and three piglets who were rooting about in the underbrush. The biggest hog was tossing up dirt with its tusks like an earthmoving machine and the piglets were snorting around in the aftermath. The sun was now fully in the sky and the insect population was beginning to stir. Jack occasionally shooed away a mosquito, but mostly they were deterred by the wind of the boat's motion and Jack's generous application of bug repellent.

After about half an hour of cruising, Jack noticed that the woods on the banks of the river had thinned out to pines and scrub palmettos. The riverbanks were now a tan sandy color and the water in the river was now noticeably green instead of the previous black. Tacy pointed to a six foot alligator sunning himself on the sandy bank. She slowed the boat to a near stop and reached into the boat's cooler to produce a plastic zip bag.

"I'm going to toss him a little gator treat," she said as she put on a plastic glove, unzipped the bag and hurled the contents in the gator's direction. The putrid odor of the contents was so vile, even when being thrown at a distance, it made Jack sit up straight in his seat.

"What god-awful mess is in that treat?" Jack said as he watched the alligator slide off the bank headed for the floating meat.

"Just some nice sun ripened chicken heads and intestines. The nastier they are the better the gators like them," she said as she removed the plastic glove and increased the throttle. Jack watched the alligator retrieve his prize and return to the warmth of the shore.

They cruised for another fifteen minutes when Tacy pointed to an outcropping of oyster shells on the right bank of the river. She cut the speed of the motor and let the boat glide toward a sandbar near the oyster bank. "Maybe we can get some trout here," she said as she cut the engine and moved to the stern of the boat to retrieve the anchor. "We will anchor here and cast into the edge of the oyster bed," she said as she expertly dropped the anchor into the green water.

Jack looked around the boat for the two lightweight rods and checked the boat's bait well for bait. "I will get these rods rigged with live shrimp and we will see how we do," he said as he pulled a plastic bait bucket out of the well which was brimming with shrimp. He noticed that both rods were properly rigged with a float and sinker as he baited the two hooks and handed a rod to Tacy. He turned and propped his rod next to the cooler. When he turned back around, he blinked slightly as Tacy had now stripped down to her red bikini and presented herself to Jack and the world in general as a strikingly athletic and erotic woman with the slight exception of her somewhat nasty tennis shoes.

"All right, Ms. Swimsuit Beauty, I am going to strip down to my bathing suit and boat shoes. Hopefully, my radiant whiteness won't scare away the fish," Jack said as he removed his pants and shirt. Watching him, Tacy laughed with glee at his conservative bathing suit and general pallor. Despite her laugh she did notice that he was generally well built and in good shape for a practicing physician.

"I do like the blue shorts with the little whales. At least, it is not a tank suit. That's what we see with a lot of the Atlanta guys. I also think a good bit of suntan oil is in order," she said laughing.

Jack watched as she took the rod and expertly cast her bait ten yards off the edge of the oyster bed. It only took a few seconds before the float was underwater. Jack noticed that she did not jerk the line immediately, but waited a few seconds for the fish to swallow the bait, then jerked the line with a powerful pull, setting the hook. The trout exploded out of the water as she began to reel.

"They are out there!" she said excitedly as she brought the fish closer to the boat. Jack leaned over the side with a net and landed the wriggling creature.

"That's at least a five pounder," he said as he grasped the fish and held it up to Tacy.

"Get me baited up again!" she said, looking at the fish. Jack carefully removed the hook and placed the flapping fish in the boat's cooler. He then handed Tacy his already baited rod.

"Use this one while I reload," he said as they swapped rods. Tacy took the rod and once again cast the bait directly at the edge of the oyster bed near her previous cast. Jack watched while he baited his hook. However, it only took a few seconds for Tacy's float to again be pulled under the water.

"Damn, we are in the right spot!" Jack said as Tacy again set the hook and began reeling. Once again, he moved to the side of the boat with the net.

"This one is at least seven pounds!" Tacy said as Jack landed the fish with the net. "Let's get the lines out there again!"

Jack again handed her his baited line and then turned to the task of removing the hook from the flapping fish and securing it in the cooler. Once this task was accomplished he baited his hook and cast it toward the oyster bank. His cast landed a little closer to the sandbar that he would've liked, but still a proper distance from the oyster bank. He looked over at Tacy's float which was now floating quietly. "Now I'm going to catch up. It's hard to catch fish with your hook in the boat," he said as he took time to admire Tacy's now glistening body. His gaze was quickly averted by a strong tug on his pole. His float was now underwater but his line was running rapidly toward a clump of dead tree branches jutting out from the sandbar. He jerked the line helplessly. "Hell, that rascal has gone for a tangle in that bunch of tree branches," Jack said as he moved his pole back and forth feeling the tension on the line, but unable to reel the fish in.

"It's not very deep, I'm going to get it loose," he said as he secured the rod and prepared to jump into the water.

"Jack I wouldn't do that. The water is not deep, but the gators like to hang out at these oyster beds also. They like the trout just like we do," Tacy said with concern.

"So they're like the bad boys at the ATMs in Atlanta. I don't see any gators and it's not very far," Jack said as he jumped overboard and swam toward the tree branches.

"Jack, we can move the boat," she said as he swam away. At that moment, her float was again underwater. She yanked her rod and began to reel. Jack was now at the sandbar busily untangling his line from the branches. The fish on his line began to jump and flap in the water. It was a much larger fish than the two others and it was splashing wildly. She watched as Jack freed his line from the tangle and began swimming toward the boat with his prize trout held over his head. Tacy continued to reel her fish which was now jumping also. Jack was in the open water an equal distance from the shore and the boat. He was also about five yards from Tacy's fish in the water.

Suddenly, from behind the oyster bed Tacy saw a flash of movement. There was a huge splash and then her line went limp. She then heard another ponderous splash.

"Jack, there are two gators out there. Get rid of that fish," she screamed.

Jack looked over just as a huge alligator head surfaced about fifteen yards away with Tacy's trout embedded in its teeth. The gator's mouth opened wide and in one gulp the fish was gone. Jack threw his fish directly at the gator's head. It landed a few feet to the right. The fish struggled for a few seconds in the water and then disappeared in the jaws of a second alligator. Jack turned and calculated the probabilities between swimming to the boat or the shore. He selected the boat and began to swim.

Tacy had by now grabbed the rifle and was inserting a clip with trembling fingers. She undid the safety, aimed at the head of the largest gator and squeezed the trigger. She heard a metallic sound and felt the trigger freeze with a jam in the mechanism. "What do I do, Jack?" she cried, but Jack was too busy swimming toward the boat to hear. She looked desperately around the boat and her eyes fixed upon the flare gun.

In the water, the two alligators were not quite done with the fish and were moving slowly and carefully toward Jack's splashing white form in the water. Their reptile eyes, just above the water, followed Jack carefully. Jack could see the boat as he turned his head to breathe in his frantic freestyle toward the boat.

Tacy aimed the flare gun directly at the largest of the two gators. The flare shot out over the water in a stream of fire and then disappeared into the water near the alligators. Seconds later it floated to the surface still burning. Its hissing fire was all that was between Jack and the alligators. Tacy then reached into the boat's cooler and ripped open another gator treat and threw it into the water. It landed several yards from the alligators, but in a different direction from Jack. Between the first flare and the stench of the gator treat the gators stopped their movement toward Jack for a few seconds. Tacy reloaded the flare gun and again aimed directly at the nearest gator to Jack. Amazingly, the flare landed directly on the gator's snout and proceeded to burn and crackle with much greater effect than the previous flare. The large gator shook his head and sneezed from the smoke, dunking his head underwater. The gator then turned toward the shore and away from the boat, followed by the second alligator.

In a few seconds Jack lay panting on the floor of the boat. "Are you okay? Are you hurt?" Tacy said as he lay there, arms outstretched.

"God, I need a beer," Jack said meekly, still shaking from his close encounter with the reptiles. Tacy patted his head and went to retrieve a beer from the cooler. Even in his weakened state Jack could not help noticing as she moved about the boat in her red bikini. Exhaling, he sat up as she returned with his beer, also bringing one for herself. She sat down next to him, her long legs extended.

"Here is to escaping the jaws of death!" she said, clinking her bottle to his. Jack took a long pull on the beer. His shivering had now stopped and Tacy's closeness was beginning to have a major reviving effect on his physical condition.

"Tacy, I must say, I don't get many days like this in Atlanta. I am glad you learned to shoot a flare gun somewhere. Was that part of cheerleader training?" Jack asked, smiling as he put his arm around her.

She responded by running her fingers through his wet hair. "I was so afraid those gators were going to eat you. But I can see your strong will to live was able to pull you through," she said, looking directly at the bulge in his bathing suit. "And if they had eaten you, it would have taken months for me to find someone to replace you," she continued, as she moved her face closer to his.

Jack needed no further invitation. He pulled her close and kissed her eagerly, running his hands along her back. She responded passionately, her tongue pressing into his mouth. His fingers quickly undid the strings holding the top of her bikini. He ran his tongue across the tops of her now unencumbered breasts, noticing that they were completely tanned.

"Let's get these little whales off right now!" she said as she tugged at his bathing suit, pulling it down to his thighs. He wriggled free and reached out to embrace her.

Suddenly, both of their cell phones rang with the distinctive tone of the prison emergency system. "Dammit!" Jack yelled as he stood up to grasp his phone which was near the seat. He stood naked in the sun and pressed the button to answer. As he talked, a boat flew by loaded with the camouflaged security officers.

"Better get dressed for emergency call Doc!" he heard Captain Jamison yell as they hooted and waved. Jack held on to the side as their strong wake made the boat move sideways.

"Yes, I understand it is an emergency. I am on my way to the prison. I'm out on the river. I'm about a mile past Highway 189 Bridge. Yes, she is with me. We will meet you there," Jack said as he looked around the boat for his clothes. Tacy laughed as he hung up the cell and floundered about.

"At least, I wasn't the one exposing myself to the security staff," she said with a smile as she fastened her top and retrieved her clothes. "Something bad must be going on for them to pull everyone in. This only happened once last year," she said as she dressed and positioned herself behind the steering wheel. "Get the anchor and we will get moving."

Jack stumbled back toward the stern and reached to pull the anchor up, clumsily knocking it against the side of the boat which caused Tacy to grimace. He then carefully stowed it on the floor-boards near the stern and took his seat.

"When you say bad, what do you mean? What happened a year ago?" Jack asked.

"A year ago the inmates took over a building and set fire to a storage shed. There were six stabbings, four of them serious. Two of those were officers. Probably, the staff on-site could have handled it, but they wanted us there when they took back the building in case there were a lot of folks hurt," she responded.

"Sounds delightful," Jack said as she started the boat and pulled back the throttle.

"It wasn't too bad. I left the prison at about one in the morning," she said. The wind blew her hair back as she accelerated the boat. She kept the boat in the middle of the river, the deepest part, to avoid any sandbars on their run. Jack settled into his seat and continued to sip on his beer as he watched the scenery go by.

In about fifteen minutes they arrived at a sandy beach near a bridge over the river. Leading to the beach was a gravel road on which was parked a white prison van with its blue light slowly flashing. Tacy cut the throttle and eased the boat toward the beach. At the edge of the water was a telephone pole which had been sunk into the edge of the beach with a large steel ring on the side.

"I'm going to take it in slowly toward the pole. You jump out and we will tie the boat to the post and lock it with a padlock. Maybe the boat will still be here when we get back," Tacy instructed.

Jack gently jumped out into the shallow water and pulled the boat toward the post. The door of the van opened and a blue uni-formed officer waved at them. After Jack had pulled the boat onto the beach, Tacy jumped out and secured the boat with a chain and padlock to the post and ring.

"Let's take the rods and the gun with us or else they might disappear," Tacy said as she handed Jack the rods, taking the gun herself. In a few seconds they were seated in the van and were rapidly accelerating toward Georgia Maximum Security Prison.

TWENTY-EIGHT

AS THE VAN approached the prison, a black billowing cloud of smoke could be seen behind the Administration building. "Looks like the inmates are having a barbecue," the officer said as he pressed the vehicle up to the prison gate which opened quickly before them. A fire truck idled at the entrance of the prison with its red light slowly flashing. The officer pulled the van onto the sidewalk near the entrance to the Administration building. He parked the van and led the way to the security doors. With a wave to the officers inside, both the sally port doors popped wide open on both ends of the tunnel, allowing the group to rush inside the prison.

"At least the inmates aren't in the Administration building or they wouldn't be opening all the doors at once. They can only do that in an emergency," Tacy yelled as they ran down the tunnel.

"Great, a rule bending super emergency," Jack said, running along with the group. As they ran through the tunnel, Jack noticed that the red lights of the security cameras were all dark, and thought briefly that this seemed unusual. Once through the tunnel, the security officers inside the prison rushed them into the Medical Unit.

Jack and Tacy looked around in surprise once they arrived in the Medical Unit. It was quiet except for the whirring clicks from the white enamel overhead fans. They were the only medical staff in attendance. Softly, in the distance, could be heard sounds from the courtyard.

"Where are the injured folks?" Jack asked the officer had who had escorted them.

"Oh, there are plenty of those. The inmates have taken over the library and law library. They barricaded themselves in there. Apparently they knew as well as we do that the library is designed to be a safety area if there is a disturbance on the courtyard. They made a bonfire of library books. There have been some inmates stabbed. Luckily, the officers got out. We will get the injured inmates when we take the buildings back. Unfortunately, they had let one of those boogers from M building in the law library. He will be difficult to get back into the box. That damned Kirk has probably already fucked and killed some law library clerks," the officer replied.

Suddenly the noise from the courtyard increased. Shouting and screaming could now be distinctly heard. "Sounds like they are taking the building back right now," the officer continued.

"We better get ready. We need to get the ambulance bay open," Tacy said as she looked around. "Is it just me and the doctor for medical staff? What happened to Nurse Griggs?" Tacy continued.

"She was in a car accident. Contusions and bruises mostly. We were going to pull you in because of that, but then the riot kicked off and the Warden decided to bring you both in."

The sounds of the courtyard had now ceased but were replaced by the siren of an ambulance as it approached the ambulance bay. Tacy walked to the ambulance bay and opened the doors as the vehicle began to back up the ramp. She could see two other

ambulances with red lights flashing, coming through the gates toward the Medical Unit.

The officer's radio crackled and he responded quickly, "Ten—
four, we are ready. Bring them up," he said, pressing the black
button on his walkie-talkie.

"There are three injured on the way. One of them is that ass-
hole, Kirk. Hopefully somebody stabbed him good," the officer
said as he opened both doors to the Medical Unit. "I'm sure
they've got plenty of security on him."

Jack and Tacy moved about and opened the doors to three
examining rooms. Tacy unlocked the supply room and began pulling bandages and other equipment in preparation for the arrival of
the injured inmates.

It was only a few seconds before a crowd of officers arrived
with the three inmates on stretchers. Jack and Tacy stationed themselves in the hallway at the entrance to the Medical Unit as they
arrived. The first in the line of stretchers was inmate Thompkins,
minus his red panties, completely naked with blood streaming from
gashes in his face, chest and legs. He was contained in the stretcher
by a canvas strap which held him in place. It did not take much
examination by Jack and Tacy to determine that while his wounds
were no doubt painful they were for the most part, superficial and
not life-threatening.

"He beat me and raped me!" Thompkins screamed as he
pointed back to Kirk in his stretcher, fifteen feet behind in the
hallway. Kirk glowered back, surrounded by four officers.

"You tell them that and I will kill you, maybe some officers
too," Kirk snarled in a low voice as he was carried past Jack and
Tacy in the hallway. The officers, busy moving Kirk into the
Medical Unit, did not appear to hear his comment.

"Mr. Thompkins, we need to do a rape test on you and get
you bandaged up," Tacy said calmly as she gestured to the officers

to remove Kirk to an exam room. Kirk had several stab wounds, two of which appeared deep, and a very bloody nose.

Inmate Thompkins blinked and shuddered, realizing that he had made a serious mistake in reporting Kirk. "No rape kit, Miss Tacy. We got in a fight, that is all." Tacy looked over at Jack, hesitating as to what to do.

"Let's clean him up. We can't force him to take a rape test. But Kirk is a different matter," Jack responded.

The doors to the Medical Unit closed as the final inmate was admitted. Tacy and Jack took a quick look at the inmate law clerk, Jimmy Richards, who attempted a smile between grimaces of pain caused by a small gash on his stomach. "Kirk was burning the law books. I thought he would burn us all up, it took so long for the officers to take back the library. Thompkins did manage to nick Kirk a little, but it didn't do him much good," the clerk said as he was moved to the third exam room.

"We have three to clean up and send to the hospital. But since Mr. Kirk has been accused of a sex crime we need to take a sample of his blood," Jack said to the officer in charge who was standing in Kirk's room.

"You know Kirk won't agree to it and Thompkins is denying it happened. I don't know?" Tacy said hesitantly to Jack in a low voice.

"I'm the doctor and I will take full responsibility," Jack responded firmly.

Tacy turned and entered the examination room which contained inmate Jimmy Richards and closed the door. Jack moved into the room containing Kirk after retrieving a syringe and three blood sample ampoules from the emergency cart.

"Mr. Kirk, we're going to get you cleaned up and get a little sample of your blood. We will have you to the hospital in no time," Jack said calmly as all four officers held Kirk to the examination table. In his wounded condition they were easily able to restrain him.

"I ain't agreeing to no blood!" Kirk screamed as he attempted to wriggle free. The officers tightened their grip as Jack inserted the needle in his arm.

"Just relax and let's get this done the easy way," Jack continued as he filled the three ampoules with Kirk's dark red blood. Jack again noticed the red light on the security camera was dark above the scene as Kirk struggled helplessly. Jack then cleaned and bandaged the wounds and prepared Kirk for the ambulance ride with a large gauze patch over his nose.

The ambulance crew arrived and secured Kirk to another stretcher. They quickly removed him to the waiting ambulance with two officers riding inside the cargo area. "You shithead! I'm going to fuck you up and that whore, Tacy," Kirk screamed impotently as he was taken away.

"That will be quite enough, Mr. Kirk," Jack commented dryly as the attendants closed the door to the ambulance. By this time, Tacy had finished the preparation of inmates Richards and Thompkins and the ambulance attendants moved them quietly to the waiting ambulances. As inmate Thompkins was wheeled past he looked at Jack for a second with a small tear in his eye. "Thanks, Doc."

The entire response had taken about twenty-five minutes. Jack and Tacy watched the three ambulances make their way past the gates. As they watched, the security contingent departed, shutting the white metal entry doors to the Medical Section behind them. Tacy and Jack were now alone with only the quiet sound of the whirring metal fan overhead. "Well, you are now a combat veteran," Tacy said stepping closer to Jack. He could smell the lusty fragrance of her insect repellent as she came closer. He stepped toward her and put his arm around her back. His other hand ran lightly over the short blonde hairs of her forearm. "The way you smell like bug spray and the river is turning me on," he said, moving in to kiss her.

She pushed him away and walked toward the white metal doors to the clinic. With a click she locked them and turned toward him. Slowly she began to unbutton her white coat. "I do think we have earned ourselves a little treat," she said, tossing the coat on the floor. She then proceeded to unbutton her camouflage shirt revealing the top to her red bikini below. Slowly, she undid the strings on the red bikini top and tossed it on the floor. She kicked off her sandals and added them to the pile. "I am ready now for my own personal physical, doctor."

Jack stared at her, slightly amazed. He looked around the room and then listened for a second. The only sound was the overhead fan. "I guess I need to get into the spirit of correctional medicine," he said as he removed his white coat and began unbuttoning his shirt. He watched hungrily as Tacy slid down her jeans and then pulled on the red strings of her bikini bottom.

"Those damn whales again," she said, laughing as he stepped out of his khaki pants to reveal his blue bathing suit once again. He quickly removed it and tossed it on top of the pile of her clothes.

They stood there for a second or two under the bright clinical lights looking at each other. "No erectile dysfunction prescription for you today, young man," she said, stepping forward. As they came together their touch seemed to be amplified by the previous attempt in the boat, and by the starkness of the clinic environment. For perhaps an hour, they rolled on the floor, pressed up against the walls, climbed aboard the rolling stretcher and chased each other in and out of the examining rooms. They came to rest in the third examining room, together on the examination table with reams of examination paper shredded on the floor and running up the wall.

"Now that was a thorough physical," Jack said, sitting up slowly from the examination table, slightly out of breath. He looked around at the table on the other side of the room and noticed the ampoules of Kirk's blood. "We must not forget these. They were difficult to get," he said, jumping off the table and picking them up.

"Why did you force him to give a blood sample?" Tacy asked languidly as she watched Jack from the examination table.

"Science, my girl, science," Jack said as he stood naked before her displaying his prize samples in his outstretched hands. "The first one is my legal excuse. There was a claim of a sex crime, objectively verified by the observation of a naked victim with visible injuries. The samples were taken with only the minimum amount of force necessary to maintain positive control of the inmate under circumstances where we had probable cause to believe that he had recently committed a violent sexual assault," Jack continued.

"You have certainly learned the legal terms of the Court Order. But inmate Thompkins said he wasn't raped and refused the rape test," Tacy said.

"A mere technicality. We have a known homosexual, lying naked, with obvious trauma injuries, who claims to have been raped and then recants. Also corroborated by the threats of inmate Kirk. I think that is enough to get the sample," Jack said. "And of course, since force had to be used, we needed to get enough for three samples, in case there was any loss or destruction. Again, we are conservatively using force only once, rather than having to return for later samples. Besides, this is Kirk, who all the world hates, even the inmates. Now that we have these two extra samples they should be used somehow for the greater good. So I'm sending them to my friend Dr. Clayton at the CDC on Monday. They will check it out and see if there really is something special about Kirk. The first sample will, of course, be dutifully logged and sent with the requisite form to the Crime Lab."

Tacy watched as Jack strolled naked out of the examination room, placed the samples in the Medical Unit refrigerator and picked up an overnight package from the Nurse's station. She hopped off the examination table and went to retrieve her clothes. "I think you maybe should have been a lawyer. And that is good since you can be sure Kirk will complain to the Warden about the blood sample and probably also file a lawsuit. He filed a lawsuit claiming excessive force when he was restrained after killing Dr. Bridge," Tacy said as she went to the pile of clothes and dressed herself.

Jack padded about picking up his clothes which were more scattered. Within a few minutes he was also dressed, right down to his white jacket. He looked over at Tacy as she finished adjusting her outfit. "You are a wonderful lady and that was an incredible time we had together." He kissed her and felt her strong arms around him.

"There is plenty more available," Tacy said softly as she unlocked the doors to the Medical Unit and they stepped out into the hall, closing the doors behind them. In the Medical Unit, the red lights on the various security cameras continued unlit and dark, while the cameras continued to record the now empty area and the low sound of the overhead fan as they had since the entry of the first inmate.

In the Warden's outer office, a freshly printed fax lay unnoticed in the output tray of the fax machine on the credenza behind Darla Cooper's desk.

TWENTY-NINE

THE NEXT MONDAY was for all appearances a regular work day at the prison with no sign that any disturbance had occurred. Jack was at his desk promptly at eight, with Tacy and a lightly bandaged Nurse Griggs preceding him at their posts. On his desk were neatly written reports showing that the three inmates who had been transported to the hospital had been returned to the prison. The daily Sick Call Report was also there with a mundane list of colds, stomach aches and the occasional cut. Jack began his daily paperwork as he watched Tacy from his office with a satisfied smile. Once in a while they would glance at each other, each thinking about the previous weekend's activity. It was during one of these pleasant interludes when Jack's phone rang. On the line was the Warden's secretary, and her tone was not pleasant. "The Warden wants to see you right away in his office," she crisply commanded.

"We are just about to begin sick call," he began.

"He wants to see you now," she insisted. Jack hung up the phone and walked to the door, nodding to Tacy that he would be right back. Once he arrived at the Warden's office he found Mrs. Cooper standing behind her desk and cramming documents into the fax machine. "Go right on in. He is expecting you," she said without bothering to turn and face him. Jack turned the huge brass doorknob and entered the Warden's inner sanctum.

The Warden was seated at his large mahogany desk and was in the process of cleaning his .357 Magnum pistol which gleamed of chrome and oiled designer rosewood grips. He looked up at Jack, gave the pistol a last wipe with a chamois cloth and gestured for him to sit in one of the large leather arm chairs at the front of the desk.

"Dr. Randolph, I will start by saying that we are glad to have a doctor with your credentials and experience working with us. But as we both know, your being here stems from some of your own personal problems and the Judge's desire to make sure that the prison maintains proper medical coverage. I had hoped that this would be a win-win situation for all of us. It may still be," the Warden said slowly and clearly, looking directly at Jack. "I also know that except for the auto accident and Judge Valentino you would be a Buckhead doctor in Atlanta, not down here in Lester at the prison."

"Yes sir," Jack agreed.

"And I know a smart fella like yourself understands that down here you are on probation. You have to follow the rules or else you are looking at a serious situation," the Warden stated factually.

"Yes sir," Jack again agreed.

"And you know that this prison, myself, you, and all the employees of the prison operate under Court Orders from Judge Valentino. These orders were worked out and signed over a period of years and they control how we run this prison. You understand that?" the Warden asked.

"Yes sir," Jack said, thinking of the set of two large binders in his office which contained the Orders. "I am very familiar with the Orders concerning medical. I have studied them carefully. I have looked at the rest of the Orders and I am generally familiar with them."

"Then you will be quite familiar with the ones on the use of force on inmates to get blood samples," the Warden said aggressively, leaning forward slightly over his desk.

"Yes," Jack replied cautiously.

"I see from the Use of Force and Incident Reports of Saturday that you directed that force be used on inmate Kirk to take a blood sample. I say, directed, because security staff take the hit from the Judge if there is an inappropriate use of force. We had two officers indicted last year for excessive use of force," the Warden continued.

"I felt that it was required because Kirk had, once again, committed a sexual assault against another inmate," Jack responded confidently.

"And that inmate, the always reliable, Mr. Thompkins, recanted his allegations and refused a rape test. Am I correct?" the Warden continued. "And you had the officers use force and you took three blood samples from Kirk?"

"But Kirk threatened inmate Thompkins in my presence and then he changed his story and refused the rape test," Jack blurted back. This caused the Warden to look up and begin to clean his glasses with the gun cleaning cloth.

"Now that little detail was not in my reports and gives me something to work with," the Warden said, visibly relieved. "As I said, I got a Use of Force Report and an Incident Report from the officers today. Kirk wouldn't give the officers a statement but he wrote me a letter complaining with a copy to the inmates' lawyer, Arnold O'Berne, and the Judge. You are new at this little game. I don't have a problem using force on inmates and especially Kirk, if it is necessary. But it has got to be done by the rules and the Orders and we can't be retaliating against Kirk because he is a world class creep."

"I feel like we did it appropriately. I watched the video about using force and I have studied the Orders on use of force concerning medical," Jack replied mildly.

"Why did you take three samples?" the Warden asked.

"Just as a precaution, in case they were destroyed or lost. It would keep us from having to use force again. I believe Dr. Bridge did the same thing before," Jack replied.

The Warden cocked his head slightly to one side and appeared satisfied with Jack's explanation. "This sounds like an appropriate use of force. I had my doubts at the beginning. I will review the security videos from the Medical Unit and get back with you."

"The security videos?" Jack asked meekly.

"Of course. We have greatly increased the video monitoring system since Dr. Bridge was killed. Now, when we have a disturbance all the cameras go on for the entire time without the red lights. We cut off the red lights on the cameras so it would appear to the inmates that they are not recording. That way they don't destroy the cameras. It's all digital, so we can store a huge amount of information without any tapes. It's like an institution wide movie of everything that happened. I spent the morning with the videos of the take back of the library and law library. I could review it from three different cameras. It's like being a fly on the wall," the Warden said proudly as he pointed to a large black video screen on the wall, opposite the polished conference table in his office. "I'm sure these videos will save many an officer's ass from some of the allegations we get around here," he continued.

Jack blinked at the thought that his and Tacy's actual asses might soon be on display on the Warden's big-screen. Thinking quickly, he hoped to focus the Warden on the incident in question with the silent prayer that he would not take the time to review the entire day in the Medical Unit. "Yes sir, you take a look at that use of force from all angles. I felt the officers were pretty gentle with Kirk, and Kirk was very clear in his threat to Thompkins. It might be good to look at that part several times."

After the Warden indicated the interview was over, and Jack got up from the arm chair, turned and exited through the mahogany door. He watched Mrs. Cooper retrieve an incoming fax from the machine and peer at it intently. "Another damn Court Order from Central Office, ordering us to move a bunch of inmates to Court in Waycross on two days' notice," she said with irritation. "The Courts order us to produce inmates and staff at some Courthouse. That requires officers and a van. The Court sends the Transfer Order to Corrections Central Office in Atlanta. They let it sit around for a few days and then they fax the Order down here to us with a cover sheet telling us to produce the inmates and staff as directed by the Transfer Order. I get so tired of having to scramble on these. This is the second Transfer Order today. When I got here at seven thirty there was one from Judge Valentino sitting in the fax machine," she continued. Jack walked past her with other things on his mind.

Tacy noticed Jack's grim look when he returned to the Medical Unit. She followed him to his office and shut the door. "So what is going on with the Warden?" she asked. Jack sat on his desk and sighed, looking at her mournfully.

"How long do they keep videos of security?" he asked.

"I think it is thirty days. Why?" she said.

"In my little chat with the Warden he mentioned something neither of us knew. Mainly, that when there is a riot at the institution all the security cameras are turned on for the duration without their red usage lights being illuminated. The idea is to minimize the inmates destroying the cameras if they saw the illuminated lights. In other words, the cameras were on all the time, but we didn't know it. That may help with the use of force but if they fast-forward to the end of the afternoon, Lord help us," Jack explained.

Tacy sank into the metal chair across from Jack's desk. "I do remember that after Dr. Bridge was killed there was a memo and briefing about enhanced video security during emergencies. I guess I was thinking that was just for the compound. They did say something about the red lights not coming on. Oh my God! We are porn stars!" she said tearfully, putting her face into her hands.

"The Warden said he was reviewing the security videos for the use of force on Kirk. He may not go past that and then if he does there is the footage of getting the other inmates out the door to the ambulances and then us saying goodbye to all the security staff," Jack responded hopefully.

"But if he does ..." Tacy began.

"If he does, then the big-screen on the Warden's wall will shine with pagan images like never seen in a controlled prison environment," Jack said, finishing her thought.

"I wonder if there is some way we could erase part of the videos?" Tacy pondered.

"I gave some desperate thought to just that. Ignoring the fact that we would be destroying evidence which is certainly some kind of crime, we are looking at several video cameras and several digital recordings. Also, the video feed goes right into the Warden's office and I just don't think it is possible. I tried to focus his attention on the use of force. Our best hope is that he looks at that from every angle and gets bored with the cleanup and send off of these inmates in the ambulances," he said.

"I guess you're right," she said, sadly, as she got up from the chair and headed back into the Medical Unit.

Jack grabbed her arm as she went by, "Tacy, hey, it was worth it! To me, anyway."

"Me too," she said softly as she left the office, closing the door behind her.

Jack opened the drawer to his desk and retrieved the overnight package. He carefully printed the name and address of Dr.

Howard Clayton and the CDC from memory. Jack reached for his cell phone and dialed the familiar number. "Dr. Clayton, please." In a few moments he heard the friendly voice of Howard Clayton. "Yes, Howie, I am now a full-blown chain gang doctor. It beats being on the chain gang and it really is not so bad. The people here are pleasant and it is pretty exciting sometimes. I came across an interesting case and I'm sending you two blood samples. I am giving them the name John Doe 666. This guy tested positive for HIV twice before coming in here. Now he's tested negative on two occasions and it looks like he's completely clean. So here's the third round. If these samples are negative, he may be your Blood Cleaner. I think I got enough blood for you to play around with it and get some clues as to how he does it. But it is definitely worth a look," Jack explained to his friend. "Of course I took it legally. But let's just keep it as a John Doe until we know we have something. All right, Howie. Yes I am staying out of trouble. It is hard to misbehave when you are in Lester, Georgia," Jack said as he ended the call. Almost immediately, his cell phone rang.

"Yes, Mr. Davis," Jack said, recognizing the voice of his attorney. "Everything is going well. No major medical catastrophes so far. I was here for the riot but luckily the injuries were minimal," Jack said.

"Jack, I have some bad news. Cindy has taken a turn for the worse. They think she may not make it. Of course, you know that would jump your case up to involuntary manslaughter which would require the Judge to be looking at it again. We might be able to keep the same deal but you sure need to be a valuable commodity at Georgia Maximum Security Prison to do that. I would recommend you put in an extra effort as the doctor over there. I will keep you posted," the attorney stated.

"Should I go see her?" Jack asked.

"No, I think you need to stay put and do a great job of doctoring. Make sure the Warden wants to keep you. Also, you need to continue to be trying to remember where that thumb drive is hidden," the lawyer continued.

Jack hung up and looked at the overnight package he had prepared for the CDC. "To hell with it!" he muttered, picking up the package and heading out of his office toward the Medical Unit refrigerator. He took two of the samples and placed them in a plastic container with a frozen cold pack designed for such shipments. He sealed the plastic container inside the package and took it to the overnight pickup box at the nurses' station. Nurse Griggs, who was seated at the station, looked over at the package. "Sending something to the CDC?" she asked, looking at the address label.

"Yeah, I used to work there. Sometimes they help me out on a difficult diagnosis," Jack explained quickly, not wanting to draw any more attention to his package.

"I have heard Dr. Bridge used to do the same thing every once in a while. They have tests up there nobody else has," Nurse Griggs commented agreeably. Jack was relieved this was not an unknown activity at the prison.

"Dr. Randolph, we need to get moving with sick call. Also, we have the diabetes clinic today," Tacy said in an official tone. Jack looked around to see five inmates seated in chairs around the room. Three of the inmates were rather puffy and portly and obviously constituted the subjects of the diabetes clinic. Jack looked at his charts for the other inmates and noted they had only minor ailments.

"Let's get started," he said in a loud voice. He walked to the first examination room, taking a second to look at the security camera and shaking his head slightly.

THIRTY

THE CHURCH RECREATION Center for the Lester Antioch Baptist Church was a midsized corrugated metal building which also doubled as a basketball court. Jack had dropped off Tacy and her mother at the entrance, each dressed in similar floral print dresses while he parked the car. Tacy's outfit was a little more up-to-date with a red silk scarf and gold sandals. Her mother extinguished a cigarette as they entered the building.

Inside was a group of similarly dressed, mostly older ladies occupying a flock of varnished oak picnic tables, each equipped with several gray, folding metal chairs. At the front of the tables was a small wooden stage. On the stage was an ancient chrome microphone and a large table equipped with a metal bingo cage complete with a brass crank. On one side of the room was an oilcloth covered table, manned by Tacy's friends, Myrtrice and Alice, which was loaded with plates of small chicken salad sandwiches and frosty glass pitchers of sweet tea, lemonade and plates of cookies.

Myrtrice nudged Alice and gestured toward Jack. "That's Tacy's new doctor friend, Jack Randolph."

"Oh I like him. Let's hope Tacy gives him both barrels!" Alice replied as she admired Jack from afar.

"I am pretty sure that has already happened," Myrtrice said with a knowing smile.

At a small folding table to the side of the stage were stacks of bingo cards. An earnest looking, older gentleman with a bow tie was busily collecting five dollars for each card. Tacy and her mother waved and hugged their way to the bingo card table.

"I can't play more than two cards at one time now. I get dizzy," Tacy's mother explained as the group arrived at the table.

"Tacy and I will do three each. You can stick with two. That ought to give us good odds," Jack said as he purchased eight cards. They then maneuvered Tacy's mother to a front row table. Once she was situated, Jack and Tacy headed for the refreshments. Jack looked back to watch Tacy's mother examining each of the eight cards front and back, taking the time to read the comments about the quality of each card which previous owners had scribbled on the back.

"Myrtrice, Alice; have you met my friend, Jack Randolph?" Tacy said sweetly to the young women at the refreshment table who each looked up with a smile and a toss of their respective hairstyles.

"Not yet. But I am pleased to," Myrtrice said, holding out her hand, "I hear you two are getting along real well," she said with a slight cackle. Jack shook her hand politely realizing that his activities on the river had by now, forty-eight hours later, fully circulated throughout the county.

"We are just friends, you do know how that goes," Tacy explained carefully, giving Jack's hand a little squeeze. "Myrtrice and Alice have been my friends since grade school," she continued.

"Tacy is the sweetest girl I've been able to locate down here so far," Jack replied with a smile, squeezing her hand in return. With a nod to the ladies, Jack helped Tacy load two paper plates with sandwiches and juggle three lemonades as they headed back to the table. Tacy pretended not to notice as Jack skillfully produced a small flask from his coat pocket and deftly spiked their lemonades as he held each at knee level below the table for an instant.

It was only a few minutes after they were seated when a large man in a powder blue coat and a Western-style string tie appeared on the stage, turned on the massive chrome microphone and began calling the group to attention and prayer.

"All right, all you gambling church people, we're going now to thank Jesus for bringing us all together here tonight," he instructed. "Dear Lord, we thank you for this congregation of people who love You and each other. We thank you for allowing us this fellowship and ask you to bless us, even those that don't win tonight. We thank you for the blessings on this Church with the bounty brought by these games. We also ask that you especially bless Sam Tilden, husband of Laura Tilden, who is in the hospital tonight. Amen." Several vigorous amen's went off around the room and several of the older ladies prayed a little longer still. "My assistant will now spin the cage," he continued, as a slightly built, teenage girl in a green velvet dress spun the brass handle to the large metal cage which contained the bingo numbers. Once the cage stopped moving, he reached in and pulled out a black plastic ball. "Lester Eleven in the B column, number eleven," he announced as the sound of bingo cards shuffling filled the room. "Two plus two, I, twenty two," he continued. Jack closed the window on two of his three cards and pointed to the twenty two on Tacy's mother's card. This first game was a simple one, with any row, horizontal, vertical or crisscross, a winner. It did not take many pulls from the cage for a silver haired lady in the back row to announce bingo and claim her prize. Jack watched her smile as she retrieved the twenty dollar bill from the announcer and a ten dollar gift certificate from the Maximum Pig.

The drawings and games continued with each one a little more difficult. Jack, Tacy and her mother each came within one number of bingo, but the prize eluded them. The final game of the evening was to fill the entire card, with a grand prize of one hundred dollars and a twenty five dollar gift certificate from the Altamaha Central Hardware Store in Lester.

"I won once, a year ago. It was twenty-five dollars on a picture frame game. I haven't won since," Mrs. Crandall commented with a dry smoker's cough. Jack looked over at her cards and pushed over two numbers. The next two numbers were on his cards. He noticed her pushing them over on one of her cards also. Jack and Tacy were down to the last three numbers on their cards when Mrs. Crandall jumped to her feet.

"Bingo! Bingo! Bingo!" she shouted in a hoarse voice. She strode up to the stage waving her card. The announcer took her card and quickly checked it against the numbers called.

"I hope she hasn't made a mistake," Tacy said quietly to Jack.

"This card is correct. This concludes tonight's bingo. Come see us again," the announcer stated loudly, handing Mrs. Crandall her prizes. Jack and Tacy applauded as she made her way back triumphantly to the table.

"Good work, Mrs. Crandall, rarely have I seen such skillful gambling play," Jack said goodheartedly.

"I want a drink," the old lady announced to the laughter of Jack and Tacy as she waved her prizes proudly. "You young people can drop me off and then go on your way," she commanded. They followed the crowd which flowed out of the building with several people stopping to congratulate Tacy's mother.

In a few minutes they were on their way back home. "It is about time I won again. I do play every week," she chirped happily. "This certificate from the hardware store will come in handy too. I've been wanting to do some painting in the kitchen," she continued.

As she talked, Jack pulled onto the oyster shell driveway and stopped the car. He began to open his door to walk her to the front door, but a firm hand on his shoulder interrupted him. "I appreciate your being a gentleman, but I can get to the door from here," the old lady announced as she opened the back car door and blew Tacy a kiss. "Don't you be misbehaving," Mrs. Crandall instructed Tacy as she headed to the front door.

"Yes Momma," Tacy replied sweetly as her mother disappeared into the house. "I think she will be doing her own celebrating now," Tacy said with a smile as she watched the lights in the kitchen light up. "Where do you think we should go to celebrate?" she said lustily to Jack.

"I think the Medical Unit is out. I guess we might just head back to my place," Jack said.

"Will there be video?" Tacy asked teasingly.

"Lord, I hope not. But it is a State house. For all I know they may have it wired for surveillance also," Jack replied.

It only took a few minutes to arrive at the prison and for Jack to turn the car down the dirt road at the far side of the gate toward his State house. The red dirt road twisted through the pine trees, generally following the perimeter of the fence. As he slowly drove around the back of the compound toward the house, Jack's attention was mostly focused on running his hand down Tacy's thigh and her fingers running through his hair and across his shoulders. He did not notice the little puffs of dust on the road ahead and did not notice at all the patrol car parked back in the woods about two hundred yards from his front door.

"Are we there yet, Jack?" Tacy cooed as they approached the house. "This old dress is getting hot," she said, hiking up her skirt to reveal a pair of blue thong panties.

"I am getting hot also!" Jack said as he pulled the car up to the front door. Once the car was stopped Tacy's door was open and she was on her way to the front door. "Go on in, the door isn't locked," he said as he watched her approach the house. Once he had turned off the engine and the headlights, he watched her pull off the blue dress, tuck it under her arm and wave to him just inside the door wearing only her blue panties as she stepped into the house. Slick, the ever vigilant watch dog, woofed slightly at this sight and then followed Tacy into the house.

Jack shook his head and sighed, thinking of Oscar Wilde's remarks on temptation. He closed the car door and followed Tacy and the dog into the house. In a few seconds the lights in the house were extinguished. After about five minutes the patrol car in the woods started its engine and pulled out onto the dirt road very slowly, with its headlights off. In the moonlight the markings, "Sheriff Ossabaw County" could be dimly seen as the car traveled back toward the Highway.

THIRTY-ONE

MAJOR KNOWLES WAS just inside the border of
Ossabaw County when he heard the call on the radio. "Ten–
Thirty-One. Report of break in at storage shed at 301 Rodeo Road.
House owner reports suspect fled on foot headed for the highway.
Suspect is older white male in red plaid shirt. Owner thinks he may
be Henry Javits," the dispatcher announced to all patrol cars in the
County.

After a few minutes of driving, Major Knowles saw the rusted
sign to Rodeo Road just ahead. "Shit, I really don't want to fool
with old man Javits tonight," he said to himself aloud as he compared the description to one of the jail's most irritating frequent
flyers, Henry Javits. The Major was well acquainted with Javits as a
serial thief and world class alcoholic who always resisted arrest
violently and was often armed. Up a few hundred yards, lurching
along the side of the highway was the elderly perpetrator clutching
a large bag of stolen dog food. Major Knowles shook his head and
reached for the radio. As he was about to press the radio communication button his cell phone rang with the flashing secure line
indicator. "What can I do for you, Sheriff?" the Major asked.

"Knowles, Cindy is dead. And that jackass ex boyfriend of
hers, Tibbs, is headed from the hospital to her trailer. He is going

to tear it up looking for evidence. It sounds like he is drunk. I just got this little report from one of our friends at the hospital. Did you find the flash drive at the doctor's?" the Sheriff said.

"No, all I got was some pill company give away drive he had in his drawer. It is not the one on the video that Cindy had," Knowles replied.

"You get on over to Cindy's trailer and run Tibbs off. I know you have been through it carefully but I don't want him to have the chance to get lucky," the Sheriff ordered.

"I am not far away from her trailer. I have an idea about dealing with Mr. Tibbs," the Major replied as he continued to watch the stumbling figure on the side of the roadway.

"I will let you figure it out. We don't need Tibbs poking around in this mess anymore," the Sheriff stated with irritation as he ended the call.

The Major pulled up right beside the figure on the roadway and turned his blue light on. He took out his pistol and rolled down the window as he pulled off the highway and stopped. Manipulating the searchlight on the side of the police car directly into the subject's face, the Major rolled down the passenger window. The man froze in the bright light of the searchlight.

"Henry, what you got there? This is Major Knowles. Why don't you lie face down and I will give you a lift to the jail?" Knowles said in a loud and firm voice, all the time carefully watching Javits and keeping his pistol out of sight. The Major could see a large bulge in Javits' back pocket which was likely a gun.

Javits looked at the patrol car as though it had suddenly arrived from outer space. The glaze in his eyes and his sleepy response, "Will there be pork chops at the jail on Wednesday?" indicated to Knowles that Javits was wildly intoxicated to a point where he was not his usual combative self.

"Just lie down. We been expecting you. You know you are always welcome at the jail," the Major said soothingly. Javits lay down and the Major stepped out of the car, keeping his pistol out of sight behind his back. "That's good. Now put your hands behind your back so we can cuff up," the Major said smoothly as he approached the figure lying on the grass. The Major swiftly snapped a pair of metal handcuffs on the man's wrists and quickly pulled an ancient British officer's pistol from Javit's back pocket. "Who you going to shoot with this, Henry? I see it is all loaded up," the Major said as he placed the weapon in his own back pocket. A quick frisk of Javits' other pockets produced an interesting array of pills sufficient to thoroughly intoxicate several people. These Knowles also placed in his pocket.

"I keep it for protection. I have a right to keep and bear arms in America," Javits garbled drunkenly as the Major pulled him off the ground and placed him in the back seat of the cruiser. Javits immediately stretched out on the back seat and was soon unconscious. The Major took a quick look at the bag of dog food on the side of the road and then returned to the driver's seat and turned off the blue light. He pulled the patrol car back onto the highway and headed for Cindy's trailer.

It took about two minutes for the Major to arrive at the trailer. As expected, in the driveway was Officer Tibbs' black, mud covered truck. The door to the trailer was open and the Major could see the light of a flashlight moving slowly through the trailer. The yellow plastic tape with "DO NOT ENTER POLICE INVESTIGATION SCENE" continuously printed which had hung in front of the door had been ripped apart and hung limply at the sides of the door. The sign on the door which announced that the premises were an Investigative Site of the Sheriff of Ossabaw County now lay on the doormat, defaced slightly by a muddy boot print. The Major pulled his patrol car into the driveway and parked directly behind the truck. He exited the car and walked to the doorway. As he approached he heard the low growl of a dog. Knowles looked down and saw Rocco the greyhound on the ground, tied to a metal stake next to two large ceramic bowls which contained water and dry dog food. Ignoring the dog, Knowles entered the trailer. He could hear sounds and low talking from the side of the trailer toward the kitchen and bedroom. Looking around quickly, he could see that the trailer's contents had been pulled apart, with the sofa upside down and paintings lying on the floor. It was very different from his previous careful search where everything had been returned to its place.

"Tibbs, what the hell kind of trespassing are you doing at our investigation site?" the Major yelled in the direction of the noises. It only took a few seconds for a response, as a bleary eyed Tibbs stumbled from the kitchen toward the front door, still wearing his correctional officer uniform.

"You fuckers killed Cindy! I know it! So she wasn't in the drug trade with you? Just look at these," Tibbs drunkenly screamed as he lurched toward the Major. In his hands were two aluminum foil packets, one of which had been ripped open showing its contents of one hundred dollar bills. "When the power was turned off everything in the freezer thawed and spoiled. It smelled like shit. I guess that is why you missed these," Tibbs continued, his eyes wild with hatred, shaking the packages at Knowles. "There is lots more of these too! I am taking these to the GBI and Fitz Davis right now," Tibbs shouted as he drunkenly approached Knowles. That was a mistake.

With a swift chop to Tibbs' throat and a kick to his stomach, Knowles brought Tibbs to the floor in a second. Knowles put his foot on Tibbs' chest and easily restrained him as he picked up the aluminum foil packages and stuffed them in his jacket. Knowles reached in his back pocket and pulled out Javits' pistol, aiming it at the center of Tibbs' chest. Tibbs attempted to wriggle free but was helpless under Knowles' foot. Tibbs was able to slide his hand unnoticed into his pocket to switch on his digital recorder that he always kept with him at the prison. Tibbs looked up at Knowles, his reddened eyes full of pain and defiance. "Murdering shitass!" he shouted up at the Major, as the device recorded every word.

"Yeah, we killed Cindy. She was working a deal for herself with Fitz Davis. We set up a little dead deer and soap slide for that idiot, drunk, doctor of hers to drive through, right into the rocks. She would have been dead at the scene if that trooper hadn't arrived. As for you, you are going to be shot by Henry Javits who you surprised while he was robbing this trailer. Isn't this old pistol a classic?" Knowles said as squeezed off two shots into Tibbs' chest. Knowles then stepped over Tibbs' body and walked back to the freezer and retrieved the remaining aluminum foil packets filled with money. He looked carefully around the trailer, making sure his story would fit the scene.

Knowles stepped outside the trailer and once again the tethered greyhound let out a low growl. Knowles took a step toward the helpless dog. "Might as well put you out of your misery and add a little meanness to Mr. Javits' crimes," Knowles said as he shot the dog point blank with the revolver.

Knowles walked toward his patrol car, opened the back door and shook Javits awake while removing his handcuffs. Javits looked at him uncertainly with a face that was still printed with intoxication. "Henry, I am going to let you go, but first you have to do a few things for me. First, I want you to take some of your pills to liven you up," Knowles said as he reached into his pocket and selected four pills and held them out to Javits. Javits immediately snatched and swallowed all four. "Good. Now stand outside the car and give me your hand," Knowles ordered and Javits complied. Knowles stood behind him and directed, "Put your right hand out from your stomach, like this," he said positioning Javits' arm out at a ninety degree angle from his stomach and its plaid shirt. "You hold it just like that," Knowles said as he reached for the revolver. In one quick motion Knowles put his hand and the pistol over the back of Javits' hand and fired a shot toward the swamp. "Well it looks like you got gunpowder all over your shirt and hand," Knowles said as Javits looked at him sleepily. "Now you turn around again and face the car," Knowles ordered as Javits immediately complied. Knowles then took the barrel of the pistol and plunged it deeply into the soft dirt, nearly filling it. In his condition, and facing away from Knowles, Javits did not notice. Major Knowles wiped the gun with his sleeve to remove any of his own fingerprints and carefully returned the pistol to Javits' pocket.

Knowles then spun Javits around. He could see that the pills were having an effect as Javits' eyes were wider and meaner than before. "Now Henry, I am going to let you go. But there are other dangerous people looking for you. I would suggest that you run as fast as you can down that road and into the swamp," Knowles directed.

Javits looked at him with a wild look and then took off running down the road. Knowles could see him patting the pistol in his back pocket as he made his way. The Major then returned to his patrol car and picked up the microphone to the radio. "This is Commander Two, Ten-Forty Two. We have a homicide at Marsh View Court. Looks like officer Tibbs surprised a burglar at Cindy's trailer and was shot. Suspect may still be in the area. Notify the State Patrol since they may have a trooper nearby. I will secure the scene. I am sure Tibbs is dead but also send an ambulance. Ten-four."

It took less time than Knowles expected for the predictable result. In two minutes State Trooper, Doug King pulled up to the trailer with siren and blue lights at full tilt. He slammed the cruiser to a stop and exited with his gun drawn.

"Doug, I am sure Tibbs is dead. I will wait here for the ambulance. I heard some dogs barking that way over toward the swamp. There was an earlier break-in call near here that sounded like Henry Javits. Be careful, you know Javits usually is armed," the Major said pointing toward the swamp.

"That damned Javits!" Trooper King said as he took off, running toward the swamp, pistol in hand.

In a little over four minutes the ambulance arrived. As the EMT and Knowles were entering the trailer they heard two shots from the swamp. Knowles smiled slightly, sure that the sounds were not produced by an antique pistol. "Sounds like you may have another customer," the Major commented dryly to the EMT, as another State Patrol vehicle arrived at the scene carrying Fitz Davis and Jack Templar, the Regional Director of the Georgia State Patrol.

THIRTY-TWO

JACK AWOKE THE next morning and looked at his watch with a start. It was 9:05, over an hour past his starting time at the institution. He looked around for Tacy and saw only a note on the nightstand. "I needed to be in early and I didn't want to wake you. By the way, we need to do something about this State issue bed. Love, Tacy." He looked over at his cell phone and checked the alarm. He had mistakenly reset the alarm and it was now ready to go off at 9:30. He pulled on his clothes, stopping only to shave with his electric razor and finally reached his car, tying his tie as he went. None of this frantic movement in any way disturbed the dog, Slick, who continued to sleep and snore on a rumpled pillow on the floor.

It was nearly 9:20 when he finally arrived at the rotunda of the prison. The officer at the front desk looked at Jack over his reading glasses perched on the end of his nose. "Doc, Mrs. Cooper told me to send you to the Warden's office as soon as you got here. She didn't look too happy," the officer said in a kindly, sad way. Jack winced, knowing the probabilities of such a request and turned toward the Warden's door. "Miss Tacy got called in earlier when she arrived about seven. She left crying after talking to the Warden," the officer continued. Jack squared his shoulders and proceeded forward.

"Go right on in, Dr. Randolph," Mrs. Cooper said with an outrageously phony smile, her hand pointing toward the Warden's door. Jack slowly entered the Warden's office, careful to close the door behind him.

The Warden remained seated behind his desk, making no effort at the usual courtesies. "Doctor, I believe you know why you're here, but I will run through a few facts for you. First, I will give you a copy of a Contempt Action that Arnold O'Berne has now filed alleging excessive force and the illegal taking of a blood sample from his client, Henry Kirk. Of course, when I began our investigation I wanted to give you every benefit of the doubt, especially when we are dealing with Mr. Kirk. I was relieved with your explanation about how all this happened. So I took the time to personally review the security videos, just to be certain about what we would be required to be turning over to Mr. O'Berne for his presentation to Judge Valentino. Unfortunately, I couldn't find Kirk's threats of retaliation on the tapes. So I reviewed the actual restraint and blood sample videos several times from several angles. Then I got to thinking that perhaps the threats happened later so I started fast forwarding," the Warden said as he picked up his remote control and pointed it at the large television screen. He pressed the button and instantly a video image of Jack, completely naked and sporting a vigorous erection appeared on the screen. It was quickly followed by images of Jack chasing Tacy, who was also quite naked, around the Medical Unit and finally ending up on the examination table. "And this is what I saw," the Warden said dryly, again pressing the remote and freezing the screen with another nude frame of Jack. "I have already talked to Nurse Crandall and she has been discharged subject to any appeal rights she may wish to exercise," the Warden stated.

"But Sir!" Jack attempted to respond.

"Don't, interrupt, son," the Warden yelled, standing up at his desk. "How the hell am I going to defend this use of force in Judge Valentino's Court? That we are really running a damn medical whore house?" he continued. "Also, when I looked at the videos I saw you getting an overnight package after you took the samples. Now that is a little unusual, since the Crime Lab in Brunswick usually comes here for pickup. So I checked to see where that package went. You sent it to the fucking CDC for them to experiment on!" the Warden shouted, his face turning a bright red.

"Sir, I can explain," Jack responded shakily.

"You will have plenty of chances to do that in all kinds of Court hearings. These days they're kind of down on experimenting on prisoners. You are fired right now as far as I am concerned, but since you are here at the Judge's request I will give him the courtesy of calling him before you leave. As soon as I have talked to the Judge I want you out of here and that includes moving out of that State house we gave you," the Warden continued angrily.

"Sir, Kirk did threaten retaliation. I heard it myself and so did Tacy. It was in the hall as they were coming in. Maybe it is on that camera," Jack pleaded.

The Warden pounded his fist on the desk, breaking a pencil into pieces in the process. "Doctor, get the fuck out of my sight before I lose my temper."

Jack stood up and meekly took a slight glance at his nude figure on the screen and left the office. As he entered the outer office he saw Mrs. Cooper seated at her desk, equipped with her artificial smile, where she had obviously heard everything. "See you soon, Dr. Randolph," she said. Jack paused briefly to look over at the black officer in a Sheriff's Deputy's uniform who was seated in the waiting room. Jack looked at the man and felt that he recognized him, but in his confusion could not place him exactly as he walked back into the rotunda and began to exit the prison.

"I'm sorry Doc, we need to get your ID. You can leave the key to the house on the dining room table," the officer said in a kindly tone as Jack walked past his desk.

"Does everyone in Lester already know I am fired?" Jack asked, knowing the answer.

"Well sir, it is kind of a tight community. We all love Tacy, but you have made some friends here too. Nobody cares about you getting in Kirk's face. I just hope this turns out okay for you," the officer replied.

"Thanks Ben," Jack said, shaking the officer's hand and placing his badge on the desk.

A few minutes later, Jack opened the door to the State house and looked around with some sadness. It'd been a pleasant little place with its view of the river and his memory of Tacy. He looked at the table and now noticed that the lamps seemed to have been moved slightly. He had not noticed that last night. Jack went into the bedroom and looked around. Everything seemed to be in order. He opened the top drawer to the dresser and noticed something different. Inside, the contents were strewn about from the somewhat orderly way he had them arranged. Moving the contents around, he noticed that his flash drive was missing. He looked at the top of the dresser, checked his coat pockets, and finally rechecked the contents of the drawer. The dog was awake now and followed Jack around anxiously.

Jack was about to check the contents of his other coat pockets in the closet when his cell phone rang. It was Fitz Davis.

"Jack, Cindy is dead and they are upping your case to manslaughter. Plus, I hear you got yourself fired for putting on a naked show and abusing a prisoner. You are about the God damndest client I have ever had and that is saying a lot!" the lawyer said to him angrily.

"At this point I'm just glad to be outstanding in some area," Jack said in an attempt to defuse the call somewhat.

"It's going to be a real challenge for me to keep you from doing some serious, hard time, boy. You need to get back over here for us to talk. Also, have you had any luck with that flash drive? That is the only thing that will give you any kind of chance," the lawyer asked.

"No, but it looks like somebody went through my stuff and took an empty one I got from a pill company," Jack said.

"That does not surprise me. You meet me today at the Sheriff's office as fast as you can get here and we will turn you in on these new charges again. Call me on your cell phone when you are close to the jail," Davis instructed.

"I will be there," Jack said as he hung up the phone. He began to pack up his few belongings, piling the contents of the dresser onto the bed. He retrieved the large suitcase and duffle bag from the closet and began to randomly stuff them with the items on the bed. He stopped when he heard the screen door open. "Who is it?" he called with a little hesitation.

"Were you expecting the Warden?" Tacy responded as she entered the bedroom. "I see you have been given the boot also," she said, looking at his unfinished packing. "So what are we going to do? I hear you may be headed for the chain gang and it may be a little hard for me to find work here in Lester," she continued, her voice cracking. "Can I come with you? At least we can deal with this together," she said grabbing his arm.

"Tacy, I don't know. I have to be in Brunswick today to meet with my lawyer and turn myself in to the Sheriff, again, this time for manslaughter charges. I don't know how much good I would be for you. I seem to be a trouble magnet," Jack said, looking at her directly. "They are going to charge me with manslaughter since Cindy is dead."

Tacy's face darkened. "Then maybe you are done with me today. I hope you had fun!" she said angrily with tears in her eyes. "I thought we could fight this together!" she said turning loose of Jack's arm and running toward the door.

"Tacy, wait! Do you really want to be with me?" he replied, but she was gone. He watched from the porch as she entered her truck and turned on the ignition. Without looking at all, she backed up the truck and was down the dirt road in a cloud of red dust. Jack cursed and stomped. "Damn, can't I get anything right?"

Jack turned and walked back toward the house. He could see mail sticking out of the black metal mailbox by the front door. He stopped and pulled out the mail, looking over each envelope. At the bottom of the pile was an envelope with a certified receipt neatly stapled to it. He could see the letter had been addressed to him at the prison and signed for in the main mail room. It was a thick envelope from the Georgia Board of Medical Examiners and was obviously not good news. Jack opened it and sighed slightly as he read the not unexpected contents. It was a Complaint from the Medical Board with allegations that he had unlawfully treated a prisoner patient, Henry Kirk, and had unlawfully taken three blood samples, two of which had been sent to the CDC for unauthorized experimental purposes. It gave him thirty days to respond to the allegations. As Jack looked at the Complaint he noticed that he was not the only person named in the Complaint. He grimaced when he saw the name of Tacy Crandall as a co-conspirator, with a copy to the Nursing Board. "Shit, I even get my friends in trouble," he said to himself as he went back into the house.

Jack sat on the bed and ran his hands through his hair. He went over to the sink and put some water on his hands and ran a cool wet hand over his face as he tried to think his way out of his predicament. He remembered how his mother had cooled his forehead this way when he was a boy and had been sick with fevers. He tried to concentrate on the events of the night with Cindy and tried to remember the location of the flash drive. He could faintly remember her talking about it in the car. She must have put it somewhere. Obviously, whoever else was looking for it didn't have it or they wouldn't have searched his house. He looked over at the contents of the dresser on his bed. There were assorted socks, pocket knives, useless pens and other worthless items, including a pack of gum he had confiscated from Cindy at some point in the evening. "I hate it when girls chew gum," he said to himself looking at the open pack. Then it came to him. She had chewed the gum and wrapped it around the flash drive and stuck it away in the car. It might still be there! The thought immediately energized him and he quickly packed up his belongings. In a few minutes he was in his car with the tower of the prison in his rear view mirror.

THIRTY-THREE

JACK ARRIVED AT the Sheriff's office and sat on one of the vinyl black couches in the public area. It only took a few minutes for Fitz Davis to arrive and briefly enter the Sheriff's administrative office to announce their presence to the secretary and then position himself on the couch near Jack. Jack watched various relatives of prisoners come and go to retrieve their loved ones, each stopping at the Sheriff's Clerk's window to pay a fine or sign some bond papers.

Davis leaned over and in a very quiet voice explained, "The Grand Jury has now indicted you for Involuntary Manslaughter. The previous charges are still pending. This manslaughter charge is much more serious. You have now been fired by the Warden and there is now a fine mess of a Contempt Action that has been filed in Judge Valentino's Court by the lawyer for that inmate, Henry Kirk. I hear there is also a Medical Board Complaint. This all pretty much screws the deal I so carefully worked out for you. I am going to be doing real well to keep you out of jail until they try you which will be in about six months. I am sure we will be hearing all about this from the District Attorney and the Sheriff when we turn you in on the new charges in just a minute. Do you have any thoughts about your situation before we go in there?" Davis asked.

"Kirk threatened that inmate and that is why he changed what he said and refused the rape test. If the officers didn't hear him, it may be on the tape from the hall. So there was a real sexual assault and having Kirk tested was appropriate," Jack said quietly.

"Well then, what about sending the blood to the CDC and your being a world class porn star?" Davis responded.

"Doctors often get help from the CDC on difficult cases. I used to get samples from all over the world. It didn't require the patient's approval if a public health issue was involved. I have seen medical records that Dr. Bridge used to send the CDC samples herself," Jack continued.

"That is a possibility," Davis said, stroking his chin in a thoughtful way. "As to Tacy and me, we didn't know the security cameras were on. The red lights were not lit. Also, the incident was long over when we got started," Jack said.

"You did get some kind of briefing in orientation that the security cameras would work like that in an emergency. I know it is in the Court Orders somewhere," Davis said continuing to ponder the information he was being given for some slight reed of advantage to his client.

"I really didn't get a formal orientation since there was an emergency the minute I arrived. I got a tour of the prison and copies of the Court Orders. I mostly concentrated on the medical parts. Tacy told me that there was a memo about the security cameras being changed after Dr. Bridge's death. But she mostly forgot about it and she thought it was only the cameras in the compound," Jack continued.

"Also, have you figured out if you have any idea where Cindy's flash drive went? That could change the whole picture. They won't care about what you did if you have that," Davis said.

"I remember something about Cindy chewing gum. I want to have another look at my car," he said.

"We can probably get that. But I can assure you they have gone over what is left of your Mercedes very carefully," Davis replied.

"What exactly are we doing here today?" Jack asked, some-what confused about the various procedures of criminal law.

"You are turning yourself in on the new charge. Technically you will be arrested again. I think they will waive a new mug shot and fingerprints. Then we get to the issue of whether you go to jail until your trial or whether you get out on bond again. The Sheriff will want you in his jail. The District Attorney will go along with the Sheriff, but will not really care since he knows you will show up for trial. We will be doing an informal conference call with the Judge. It is not a hearing. He is attending a conference in New Orleans. He is going to be pissed at you for screwing up, but hope-fully not to the point of making you sit in jail for six months. If he seems headed that way I will ask for a bond hearing as soon as the Judge gets back while you look for that flash drive. That may give everyone a chance to calm down a little."

"So what if the Judge doesn't want to do that?" Jack asked.

"Then you go to jail today. But he will probably at least give you a hearing. Jude Valentino is very fair. He also knows you will be there at the trial. He just doesn't want to be picking up the paper when he has allowed you to be loose and see that you have screwed up again some way," Davis said. "By the way, I am going to do all the talking today. Let's go see the High Sheriff," Davis said pointing to the door of the Sheriff's administrative office. Jack followed Davis through the door into the office.

Once inside, Davis looked over at the secretary who was busy at her large teak desk. Behind her was a large oil portrait of the Sheriff in full uniform gazing majestically out into the room. "Ginny, could you tell the Sheriff we are here. I believe he is ex-pecting us," Davis announced as they took their seats on the red leather couch. The secretary stopped her work and disappeared into the inner office. In a few seconds she returned and motioned them in.

The Sheriff stood and shook hands with them from behind his huge antique mahogany desk and they sat down on another leather couch directly in front of the desk. On the floor was a large oriental rug similar to the one in Cindy's trailer. At the side of the desk Major Knowles sat in a large red leather arm chair. In his hands was a large file. He had not bothered to rise when they entered.

"Major Knowles has some paperwork for the doctor to sign and then we need to talk about whether Dr. Randolph will be our guest until his trial. Fitz, I understand you have set up a conference call with the Judge, the Warden and the District Attorney on continuing the present bond. Of course, we think he ought to be in our jail beginning today. So, are we ready to start the conference call?" the Sheriff said as he began to dial the number without waiting for a response. Davis nodded his acceptance and the group listened to the speakerphone as the conference call was assembled. In a few seconds the operator announced that all parties were present. The Judge then took control of the call.

"Gentlemen, I am sorry we are having to do this call. I was saddened to hear of Cindy's death," the Judge announced in somber tones.

"Judge, we appreciate your taking time out from the Judicial Conference in New Orleans to talk to us. I understand you will be down there for a few days," Davis responded.

"That is right. Maybe they can teach me something about all these computers we have in Court these days," the Judge continued. "All right, I understand we have a new indictment for involuntary manslaughter against Dr. Randolph and we have the question of whether he is to remain out on bond. This is an informal conference to get everyone's input and to see if we need to go to a formal hearing. Does everyone agree that is what we are doing?" he continued, setting the ground rules. "Mr. Lawson, as the District Attorney, you go first for the prosecution."

"Your honor, we think Dr. Randolph should be incarcerated until his trial. While he may not be a flight risk, he is someone who could be a danger to the community. If he were to cause another wreck or do something illegal, the public would be rightfully questioning why he was allowed his freedom. This is especially true since you gave him an opportunity at Georgia Maximum Security Prison and he seems to have squandered that, both by abusing an inmate and by outrageous sexual misconduct on the prison grounds in the medical area itself," the District Attorney asserted forcefully in a somewhat high pitched tone.

"I want you all to know that I previously received a call from the Warden about all of this. I will have him put that on the record if we have a hearing. Does anyone have a problem with me having discussed these matters with the Warden? It is our practice in the Class Action case involving the prison for him to give me a call when a problem arises," the Judge stated. "Of course, the Warden is also on this call if anyone needs his participation or he wants to jump in."

"Judge, we have no problem with you knowing exactly what is going on at Georgia Maximum Security Prison and talking to the Warden whenever either of you feels it is necessary," Davis responded. Quickly, the other parties indicated their assent.

"I am here if you need me," was the Warden's quiet response.

"Sheriff, what are your thoughts? It looks like you would be keeping him for about six months until the next available criminal trial date," the Judge continued.

"Judge, you worked with him and his lawyer to get him over to G-MAX. He has caused big problems over there. I don't want to be explaining to the press if he causes some more problems," the Sheriff stated as Major Knowles nodded his agreement.

Fitz Davis stroked his chin as he contemplated the Judge's tone and the arguments of the prosecutor and Sheriff. Clearly they had a point, but perhaps a little more time might improve things for the home team.

"Judge, I appreciate the District Attorney acknowledging he is not a flight risk and I understand that the Warden has fired Dr. Randolph without any sort of hearing. The prison is planning to provide any needed medical coverage out of Augusta Medical Correctional Institution until a substitute can be found. We could make Dr. Randolph available on the grounds at his State house at the prison, so he would at least be available if there were an emergency. So I would ask that you give him a full hearing on this bond when you get back from New Orleans in a few days," Davis said slowly with emphasis on medical coverage being handled out of Augusta which was about an hour and a half west of Lester. There was silence from the Warden on this point.

"The Warden didn't mention they were covering medical out of Augusta. That is a long way from Lester. Other than these consensual sexual high jinks allegations, I am not hearing any problems with his doctoring, am I?" the Judge asked.

"There are also allegations concerning a wrongful use of force in obtaining a blood test where there was no sexual assault," the District Attorney responded.

"Judge, that is exactly why we need a full hearing. There is no doubt that inmate, Henry Kirk, is a sexual predator. We think there is evidence that Kirk threatened and intimidated the victim. We need some time to gather that evidence," Davis forcefully argued

"All right. This is not something we can do on a telephone conference. I am setting it down for a full hearing the day I get back which is three days from today. I will keep the doctor out on bond until the hearing. Fitz, if there is an emergency at G-MAX, Dr. Randolph will be available to help until then? I also expect that he will stay pretty close to that State house on the grounds and not be roaming around the countryside," the Judge stated. Fitz Davis looked relieved. "Is that OK with you, Warden?" the Judge asked.

"We can handle Dr. Randolph for a few more days at least," the Warden assented.

Davis pressed his advantage. "Judge, there is also the matter of Dr. Randolph's auto from the crash. The Sheriff has had possession of it for some time now. We would like it returned so we can run some tests on it ourselves," Davis continued.

"Any objections to returning the car?" the Judge asked. The Sheriff looked over at Major Knowles.

"We are all finished with our tests, Judge. He can have it. I will have it on our wrecker tomorrow wherever he wants it," the Major responded.

"Good. I like to see everyone cooperating. Why don't you take it to the State house at G-MAX. That is where he is staying. Dr. Randolph can move it from there if necessary," the Judge said, concluding the matter.

"Thank you Judge," Davis responded. He was again quickly joined by the others in courteously thanking the Judge. Jack was free for another three days.

THIRTY-FOUR

JACK AND SLICK, the dog, were awakened the next morning at seven by the roar of the wrecker depositing the remains of his Mercedes next to his State house. The Deputy knocked loudly on the door and Jack jumped out of bed to meet him.

"Sign here," was the Deputy's laconic command as he thrust a clip board with an acknowledgement of receipt clipped to it toward Jack. Jack took the pen and signed his name. He walked over to the auto as the Deputy returned to the wrecker and was on his way. Jack watched the wrecker make its way up the dirt road to the hard road before opening the crumpled door to the auto. Jack looked around, carefully checking to make sure there were no observers. He ran his hand underneath the dashboard on the passenger side. At first he felt nothing but then as he moved his hand forward he felt a hardened lump firmly attached. He pulled it off using his fingernails. Embedded in the now blackened gum was Cindy's small, red, plastic flash drive. As he looked at it and dislodged it from the gum he finally had a clear memory of Cindy chewing the gum and putting it under the dash. Again, he looked around and walked back to the house.

Inside the house, Jack booted his laptop and inserted the drive. In a few seconds he had opened the drive and saw that it was full of spreadsheets and memos. There were also many saved emails. He clicked on one randomly and gazed at its contents. It was a deposit record from a bank in Panama. The account was in the name of a Panama bearer share corporation, Golden Ossabaw Corporation. It showed deposits in the past six months of two million dollars. He randomly clicked on an email. It was a confirmation of a user name and password for another Panama account for another corporation. He clicked on one of the memos. It showed payments, dates and amounts to a list of persons. He looked at the list and noticed the name of the St. Simons Coast Guard Commander, Stanford Dalton. His name showed a payment of one hundred thousand dollars. He clicked on one of the spreadsheets. It showed a cash flow analysis of recent purchases along with costs and payments. He clicked on another spreadsheet and it showed a list of accounts in the Bank of Lanier, along with the amounts deposited. The totals were in the millions. Jack closed his laptop and picked up his cell phone and dialed Tacy's cell phone number. He waited for an answer and when the voicemail came up he left her an excited message.

"Tacy, this is Jack. Give me a call. I have found something that will get us both out of trouble!" he said, his voice vibrating. He then called her mother's number. In a few seconds he heard Mrs. Crandall answer the call.

"Mrs. Crandall, this is Jack. Is Tacy around? I need to talk to her," he said rapidly.

"She doesn't want to talk to you! You have done her enough trouble already. Besides, she is not here. She was ordered to go to Judge Valentino's Court in Brunswick along with that damned inmate Kirk and one of his murdering friends. She left a while ago. She is riding in the prison van with the officer up front. There is supposed to be a Glynn County Sheriff's car following the van once they get to the Glynn County line," she said in a rasping tone.

"That can't be right. I know for sure that Judge Valentino is in New Orleans and won't be back until for two days," Jack said haltingly, digesting the information.

"How did she get notice of this?" Jack asked.

"The Warden's office gave her a copy of a fax from Central Office in Atlanta. There was an Order signed by the Judge ordering them all to be produced for a hearing at 9:00 this morning in Brunswick. They should be loading the van now if they are going to be on time," she replied as she hung up abruptly.

Jack looked at his watch and then shuffled through his Court papers to find the phone number of the Clerk's office. "My name is Dr. Jack Randolph and I have a case in Judge Valentino's court," he said slowly. "Is the Judge having a hearing today at nine with prisoners from G-MAX? I understand he is in New Orleans."

After an icy pause, the female voice at the Clerk's office responded. "I know who you are. You were the driver with Cindy. There is no Court today. I shouldn't be telling you this, but since you know, the Judge is in New Orleans. Why are you thinking there is a hearing today?"

"Because G-MAX got a fax of an Order from the Judge ordering them to bring inmate Kirk and another inmate, along with Nurse Tacy Crandall, to a hearing at nine today."

"They didn't get such an Order from us. I am the only one that does those and I didn't send one like that," the woman responded with irritation.

"Can you call G-MAX and stop that van?" Jack asked.

"You can have them call me to discuss it. I am not doing anything based on a call from someone who is charged with manslaughter in our Court," she said crisply.

Jack understood from her tone there was no use arguing. He hung up and dialed the Warden's office. He immediately recognized the voice that answered.

"Mrs. Cooper, this is Dr. Randolph. There is a van going to Court today. I just talked to the Clerk. There is no Court today because the Judge is in New Orleans. She also said that she never sent any Order for a hearing today. Can you please call her and confirm this? Tacy is supposed to be in that van. I think there is a problem here."

There was a long silence and then an obviously irritated response. "Dr. Randolph, I don't believe you have any business with our transports, even when you were a doctor in good standing here. That fax came from Central Office and not from the Court and I handled it myself. Maybe another Judge is handling it. Besides, the van is probably out the gate. I will give the Clerk a call and if you are right I will have the van radioed to turn around," the Warden's secretary icily replied without the slightest hint of urgency.

Jack hung up and looked around for something useful as a weapon. He saw a large knife on the kitchen counter and put it inside his coat. He then ran out to his car and quickly cranked it. In a few seconds he was on the dirt road and headed for the front gate of the prison.

THIRTY-FIVE

THE INMATE LAW library clerk, Albert Sams, stood near the chain link fence and watched the prison van pull up near the back gate. The officer exited the van and proceeded to the gate. The inmate watched the officer press the communication button to talk to the tower officer. The inmate watched carefully to make sure the tower officer was focused on allowing the officer to enter. With two quick flashes he threw the two tennis balls with their deadly cargo attached over the fence. The balls landed softly to the right side of the pickup area and were camouflaged by the tall grass into which they fell. Only a tiny bit of yellow from each tennis ball gave any sign of their presence, and only if one were carefully looking.

In a few minutes the van officer and another officer returned with Kirk and inmate, Jimmy Richards, the other law library clerk. Both inmates were handcuffed with metal cuffs with their hands in front. The two shuffled slowly in front of the officers toward the gate. The officers did not notice as the inmates caught sight of the yellow of the tennis balls peeking through the grass near the van. After a thorough pat down search of each inmate the officers moved the inmates through the gate and toward the parked van.

Tacy followed well behind the group as she went through the gate and entered the van on the passenger side. She watched as one officer ordered the inmates to sit on the grass while he opened the rear door to the van and carefully looked around inside for any weapons or contraband. The other officer stood by the driver's door to the van and called the tower on his radio.

"We are heading out to Court with two head of inmates and Nurse Tacy. I need to pick up my weapon for the trip," he said loudly into the device making sure the inmates were aware he would be armed. In a few seconds a basket was lowered from the tower which contained a service revolver in a worn, black leather holster. The officer strapped on the holster and climbed into the van. "I am expecting to pick up some extra security from the Brunswick Sheriff's office at the Glynn County line," he said into the radio as he looked over at Tacy. Tacy noticed the inmates moving their cuffed hands to the side and sliding around a bit on the grass, but she could not see them deftly hiding the tennis balls and their cargo under the shirts of their uniforms.

"Ten-four," was the response which crackled from the device. The officer started the engine as the other officer quickly ordered the two inmates into the rear of the van and slammed the door. The van pulled slowly up to the metal barrier by the tower and once it had been raised, the van and its passengers headed out around the prison perimeter and onto Highway 189 towards Brunswick. As the officer pulled onto the highway he checked the inmates in the rear view mirror and saw them quietly seated and facing each other. He noticed Kirk seemed to be wriggling a bit but this did not seem unusual. Satisfied, he looked forward over the shiny hood of the State van. There was nothing ahead but blacktop and pine trees for as far as he could see. He pressed the accelerator and felt the van slowly creep its speed up to the limit. "What kind of hearing are you and Kirk doing?" the officer asked Tacy, trying to make conversation while stealing a look at her tanned legs.

"I really don't know. I just got this Order to be present," she said, nervously clutching a copy of the fax and Order in her hand. "Nobody has talked to me about it. I guess I will just go and tell the truth. Maybe I should have gotten a lawyer," she said softly as she looked out the window.

The officer slowed the vehicle as they passed a decaying gas station and two small houses. Two black children were playing in one of the yards with a yellow dog as they passed. The officer glanced at the rear view mirror again and saw that the inmates were still quietly seated. "We should be getting an escort from the Sheriff down the road at the Glynn County line," he repeated, looking over at Tacy. She paid no attention and continued looking out the window at the endless pine trees.

They had traveled about three miles from the prison when, suddenly, from the back of the van, there was a scream. "Dammit Kirk! Don't kill me!" The officer slammed on the brakes and Tacy pitched forward into her seat belt. The officer maneuvered the van to the side of the road and turned his head to see Kirk holding a stiletto like, metal knife in his cuffed hands to the throat of the other inmate. The knife was attached with a nylon rope to a yellow tennis ball. A small wound on the inmate's neck, very near his jugular vein, was oozing dark red blood.

The officer parked the van and turned on the blue light. He reached for the van radio, as Kirk shouted at him. "Don't you be using that radio! You are going to be the one responsible for him getting killed. All I want is a running start for the woods and every-one will be OK."

The officer looked at Kirk with a slight smile as he pulled the service revolver out of its holster and pointed it at Kirk through the steel mesh which separated the driver and passenger from the in-mates. "Kirk, you ain't going anywhere and I could give a shit if you cut him up like a fish. Now I am going to open the back door and you and your friend are going to come out and lie face down and wait for me to have some back up," he said as he picked up the radio microphone and pressed the talk button. "This is Van 6. Code 10–31. Request backup. Kirk's got a knife on the other inmate. Location one mile south of Trudy's Gas station," he stated loudly so Kirk could clearly hear. "10–4, Backup on way," was the crackling response from the radio.

"You are going to let them out?" Tacy asked.

"I will shoot both of them if they do anything but get out and lie down in the dirt," he said, waving the revolver. "Kirk is not going to be killing anybody on my watch," the officer continued as he exited the van and walked around to the back. Tacy watched him and the inmates and then carefully pressed the automatic door locks. The officer looked into the back of the van to see Kirk still holding the knife at the throat of the other inmate. He did not notice the other inmate's grip around the yellow tennis ball to the side of his leg. The officer then gingerly unlocked the doors to the back of the van and pushed them open. Thinking ahead to possible results if the revolver were fired, Tacy had now positioned herself on the floor of the van with her head near the gas pedal. She did not want to find out if the metal mesh would stop a .38 caliber revolver bullet, even if it had been slowed slightly by traveling through an inmate.

With the doors open, the officer could now clearly see Kirk and the other inmate, still in the same position. "Both of you, come on out and if you make any fast moves I will shoot both of you!" he shouted at the two inmates as he pointed the pistol directly at Kirk. Kirk put the knife to his side and the two inmates began to slide forward on the metal bench seats toward the open doors of the van. "You better drop that knife before you come out of there," the officer ordered when he noticed Kirk still had the knife in his hand. The other inmate continued sliding closer to the doors and closer to the officer's face. Kirk defiantly still kept the knife in his hand as the officer watched. "Kirk, I will kill you if you don't drop that knife," the officer ordered, his focus now fully on Kirk and the knife as the other inmate slid closer to the officer on the metal bench, the yellow of the tennis ball showing slightly in his clenched hand. The officer fearfully tightened his grip on the pistol and sighted it on Kirk. He felt a sense of relief when Kirk dropped the knife to the metal seat beside him.

In one quick motion the other inmate squeezed the contents of the tennis ball directly into the officer's eyes. There was a tight scream from the officer amid the strong smell of ammonia and then the blast from the gun which tore through the roof of the van. The inmates quickly pressed their advantage, with Kirk grabbing the waving gun and the other inmate puncturing the officer's chest with the knife attached to the other end of his tennis ball. The inmates now stood above the officer as he writhed on the ground, clutching his eyes, his blue uniform awash with blood. Kirk aimed the pistol at him and then fired. The officer gurgled a cry and then was silent in a pool of blood. Kirk reached down into the dead officer's pockets and grabbed the keys to the van and the handcuffs. Immediately he began unlocking his own cuffs.

"OK Kirk, let's get going. It's a long way to Florida and we has got some good pussy to enjoy," the other inmate said, holding out his cuffed hands to Kirk to be unlocked and cocking his head over toward Tacy and the passenger side of the van.

"Sorry Jimmy. I won't be needing a law library clerk on my trip," Kirk said as he pointed the pistol at the inmate's chest and fired quickly. The blast tore through the inmate and knocked his now limp body back into the ditch by the road. Kirk watched him for a second to make sure he was dead, and then picked up one of the knives with a tennis ball attached which he stuffed into a back pocket. He then closed the van doors and slowly walked to the driver's side of the van.

Tacy had remained crouched on the floor of the van as she listened to the sounds of the fight. She reached for the microphone to the radio and clicked on it desperately, finally realizing that the radio would not function unless the motor was running. She heard the crunch of the gravel by the door and prepared herself to fight.

Fumbling slightly with the keys, Kirk unlocked the door to the van. Tacy made a quick lunge at him from her position on the floor which Kirk easily deflected with the butt of the pistol. He grabbed her by the hair and roughly tossed her into the passenger seat as he assumed his position in the driver's seat.

"You get yourself hooked in. We got a lot of traveling to do and I don't want you distracting me," he said to Tacy, shaking her violently with one hand. Tacy obediently fastened her seat belt and Kirk turned on the ignition and started the motor. He then grabbed Tacy again by the hair and put the knife on the dashboard in front of him. Picking up the microphone he calmly radioed the institution, "This is Unit 6. Situation under control. Cancel backup. We are proceeding to Court."

"10–4" was the immediate response which crackled back on the radio. Kirk then did a U-turn and headed the van back towards Lester. Tacy looked back and saw the two bodies lying in the grass and red dirt as they sped back towards town.

THIRTY-SIX

JACK PULLED IN to the front of the prison under the tower and mashed the communications button. "Has the van with Kirk and Tacy left yet?" he yelled into the machine.

"I shouldn't be telling you, Dr. Randolph, but they have been gone about twenty minutes," officer Beulah Burns in the tower replied.

Jack backed his car up and headed out toward the highway. At the highway he turned right toward Brunswick. There was only one vehicle ahead of him, a dusty green pickup which he quickly passed. His old car seemed to slowly float down the hot blacktop. He passed Trudy's gas station and saw the black children playing by the road. He drove for about a minute and then noticed a prison van approaching at a very high speed. He slowed his vehicle as the van approached and turned his head to look at the driver. The vehicles quickly crossed but in that instant Jack saw enough to give him a shudder. It was clearly Kirk driving the van with his hand on Tacy's head in the passenger seat. For a second his eyes met Kirk's and then the van was past in a flash of white metal.

Jack stood on his brakes and fishtailed the car around, skidding across the blacktop and onto the dirt, creating a huge cloud of red dust. It took him a second or two to regain control of his car and accelerate in pursuit of the van.

"Looks like I get to kill that doctor friend of yours," Kirk said with a snarl as he watched in the rear view mirror as Jack's car righted itself and headed toward the van. "Might as well have some fun with the blue lights," Kirk said as he turned on the blue lights and siren.

Jack was now about a thousand yards behind and the van was pulling away and heading for the gas station. The children heard the siren and saw the flashing lights and stopped their play to watch. The older child held his dog by the collar as the van approached. But when the van came within a hundred yards, the sound of the siren was too much for the dog and it broke away from the little boy and headed across the road. Without thinking, the child went right after the dog into the highway

"My God Kirk!" Tacy screamed as the child's body hit the front of the speeding van, and sprayed blood on her side of the windshield. The impact caused Kirk's hand to jerk the wheel and the van's right tire went off the road and clipped the mailbox which sat atop an ancient ceramic pipe. There was a crunching sound and then the van thudded along with a now punctured tire.

"Damn! I guess we will have to head down to the railroad track and catch us a train," Kirk said as he slowed the vehicle and turned down a dirt road to the right which cut through a swamp past the railroad. "But we will have us some fun first," he said, roughly putting his hand between Tacy's legs. "After I kill that doctor, of course," he said looking in the rear view mirror.

Jack looked over at the screaming children who had pulled the child's body from the road. An elderly black woman had emerged from the house and was crying with her hands to her face. He turned his car down the dirt road and managed to get within two hundred yards of the van.

Kirk somehow continued to drive the van down the dirt road. The blown tire thudded as the van cut through the dust of the road, causing the vehicle to slow. "These vans are supposed to run on three tires. I have heard the officers say that," Kirk shouted at Tacy over the thudding. "This one seems to be having a little trouble," he said as he slowed to cross the railroad tracks. Across the tracks was a field and then the tangled growth of a swamp. "I want to get in that swamp to deal with your doctor," he continued, pausing to see Jack's car gaining on the van.

About a hundred yards past the tracks Kirk pulled the van into the field and maneuvered it behind a large oak tree at the edge of the swamp. He slammed on the brakes and looked around the van. "There is a freight train headed for Savannah that will be coming through here in about thirty minutes. I have watched it from the prison many times before they put me in M building. There are always open box cars from deliveries in Brunswick and Jacksonville. You and I will be on board and having a fine time. But first, I do need to kill this damned doctor," he said, as he opened his door and pulled Tacy behind him. Tacy tried to fight back, but he knocked the wind out of her with one fast slap from the back of his hand. Kirk then positioned them both beside the van and began to take aim at Jack's car with the pistol resting on the hood of the van. Tacy could see Jack's car pulling into the field and heading toward the van. Kirk slowly squeezed the trigger and Tacy winced as Jack's windshield exploded on the driver's side. Kirk grimaced as the car continued toward them. "Damned lucky bastard," Kirk yelled as he watched the car approach with just the top of Jack's head visible above the dashboard below the shattered windshield. Kirk aimed carefully again and squeezed off another shot which clipped the side of the steering wheel about two inches from Jack's head. Tacy watched as Jack's car still chugged toward them. Kirk pulled out the handmade knife, cut a piece of the rope which attached the tennis ball and tied Tacy's hands, leaving about two feet as a leash. "We going to the swamp, Nursie! I still got one more bullet, and I am going to let him get real close this time," Kirk screamed to Tacy as he pulled her along behind him, waving the pistol and returning the knife to his back pocket.

Jack slowed his car as he came within fifty feet of the van and peered out over the dashboard. He could see Kirk waving the pistol and pulling Tacy into the swamp. He also noticed some movement in the lower, twisted branches of some trees and in the saw palmetto scrubs among the thick vegetation. He noticed further back in the swamp there was a patch where the ground was turned up like it had been plowed. He could see a huge oak which had fallen in a recent storm. It was directly in Kirk and Tacy's path and lay horizontal on the ground with its load of Spanish moss still hanging from the downed limbs.

Jack pulled his car right up to the van and, using it as a shield, opened his car door slowly and moved at a crouch on the ground beside the vehicles. He peered out to the swamp but now Kirk and Tacy were nowhere to be seen. Jack waited and watched quietly. There was no sound from the swamp but the screech of a few birds. Cautiously he crawled forward toward the felled tree. Jack continued his approach to the swamp, stopping from time to time to listen for signs of Kirk or Tacy. Listening carefully, he heard the crack of twigs and a rustling of underbrush, but when he looked into the swamp he saw no movement, only the slight swaying of the Spanish moss on the downed tree before him.

On the other side of the tree, Kirk was on the ground and finishing tying Tacy to a thick, moss covered branch. Her mouth was stuffed with part of a tennis ball which been cut and secured by a piece of the rope around her face as a gag. Completely immobile, her eyes were filled with tears of fear and rage. Kirk made a gesture of silence with his finger and ran his coarse tongue down her neck as his hands groped her elsewhere. His eyes laughed as she bit into the tennis ball in disgust. Peering out from a place under the tree where a rock pushed a section slightly above the ground, he could see Jack slowly approach. Kirk checked his pistol and tightened his grip on the knife. Kirk watched Jack step up on the trunk of the tree holding a knife and pause to look around from the higher vantage point. Kirk slid his knife into his pocket and coiled his muscles as Jack stood on the tree. In the far distance the sound of the train whistle miles away could faintly be heard.

Jack looked around and suddenly heard a muffled sound. He looked down, but it was too late. He saw a flashing glimpse of Tacy as Kirk grabbed Jack's belt and flung him over the tree onto the moist spongy ground. Jack's arms flailed out in an ineffective defense and his knife clattered on a stone on the ground near the tree. His next sight was Kirk standing over him, his shoe on his throat and the pistol pointed directly at his face which was turned slightly toward the swamp.

"I got one bullet and I wanted to save it for your face. Then I will have some fun with your girlie here on that train," Kirk said, his jaw quivering slightly in anticipation. With slightly dimmed vision Jack again saw movement in the scrub behind Kirk. Jack's hand eased into his pocket and grasped the striped pink plastic pig on the key ring from the Maximum Pig. He remembered the warning from the owner not to be using it in the woods. He pressed the little plastic pig several times with his thumb. The high pitched squeals penetrated the quiet of the swamp. Kirk looked puzzled and bent over and pressed the pistol closer to Jack's head. "What the fuck is that?" Kirk spat, as Jack managed one more, long, loud squeal from the little device, pulling it from his pocket. Jack looked up at Kirk and the oiled steel of the pistol. Kirk was smiling as he squinted at the striped plastic pig in Jack's hand. He did not notice the movement behind him.

There was the scream from Kirk and the sound of tearing and penetration as the tusks entered his chest from behind. There was the blast of the revolver which went a foot to the side of Jack's head. There was the deep, growling snarl of the giant hog as it lifted Kirk up with its tusks and dragged him back toward the swamp. There was the warm wet feel and smell of Kirk's blood on Jack's face and shirt. Then there was the high pitched squeal of several piglets scattering throughout the brush. One disoriented little fellow ran over Jack's leg, bounced off the tree, and headed back into the swamp. Jack turned his head and watched the huge hog continue to gore and stomp Kirk's now grotesque carcass. It was then joined in the kill by the equally large female.

Jack and Tacy watched for at least a minute as the animals had their way with Kirk before leading their brood back into the swamp. Jack and Tacy looked at each other quietly and thankfully for several minutes to avoid attracting the animals' attention before speaking. Slowly, Jack retrieved his knife from the ground and cut Tacy loose. Pulling her up, they walked over to Kirk's crumpled body and stared at this shredded face and broken limbs.

"I will never eat pork again!" Jack said, holding the porcine key chain in the air as Tacy hugged him tearfully.

THIRTY-SEVEN

MAJOR KNOWLES ARRIVED early at the River Compound. He was surprised to see the Sheriff's car parked at the entrance. As he unlocked the door he looked out at the dock and noticed that the Marine Interceptor was not berthed at the dock as usual. He entered the office and saw that the door to the Control Room was wide open. On the door was a folded note with "Major Knowles" written in the Sheriff's handwriting taped to the door. The Major unfolded the note and read the hastily scrawled contents. "They have the flash drive and a recording of you and Jason Tibbs at Cindy's," the unsigned note stated briefly.

"Son of a bitch!" Knowles yelled, crumpling the paper and throwing it on the floor. He calmed himself with the thought that there might still be time to escape. He remembered the precautions he had taken to create another identity in south Atlanta, complete with a small, safe room over a liquor store and a car, properly registered to this new identity. All that was needed now was his identification documents. His cash hoard for such an occasion was well hidden in Atlanta.

Knowles stepped inside the Control Room and looked at the screens which were all on and were focused on the River Compound. At first he was relieved to see there was no unusual activity, just the traffic on the highways and some small boats cruising slowly on the rivers. He looked around the room and saw drawers pulled out and papers everywhere. He went to the small safe which was open. He looked inside and found his disappearance passport and driver's license, along with Cindy's documents. The Sheriff's were missing. He ran his hands around the safe but could find nothing else. He looked at the passport and driver's license and began to think of his new life. When he looked back at the screens, things had changed.

He could now see at least five State Patrol vehicles converging on his location and three Coast Guard patrol boats approaching from the river. No doubt they were under the orders of someone other than Commander Dalton. Then suddenly the screens went blank.

Knowles rushed to the outer office and ran over to the metal door to the armory. He tugged on the door and found it unlocked and the light on. He looked at the shelves and could see that the Sheriff had helped himself to a load of weapons, mostly pistols but also at least one automatic rifle and several tear gas grenades. Knowles grabbed a bullet proof vest and a loaded, semi automatic shotgun. Hastily he crammed extra cartridges for the shotgun and his pistol into the pockets of the vest. He stopped when he heard the phone in the office ring. It was not the ring of the phone to the general office, but the distinctive ring of the security phone. He picked up the receiver to the white telephone. "Knowles, this is Fitz Davis. We have Cindy's flash drive. Those accounts are locked down. We also have a tape from Tibbs's pocket recorder when you killed him. So we know you caused the wreck that killed Cindy. That fits right in with your use of the Homeland Security system that night. The Sheriff is on the run, but when we catch him we might need your help. I don't think he has done you any favors. It would be a lot easier on you if you just came on out with your hands in the air so we can talk about this."

The Major paused for a second and then spoke clearly into the telephone. "I don't think so Fitz. That ain't my way," Knowles said as he hung up the receiver, cocked the shotgun, and took a step toward the door. Knowles looked out the small window and saw Trooper Doug King crouching behind the open door to his cruiser. "At least I can kill that damned sucker," the Major said aloud, strengthening himself for the attack and checking his weapons.

It was at that moment the lights went out. Seconds later the door to the compound was rammed down flat. The Major threw himself on the ground as a concussion grenade was fired into the office followed by two tear gas grenades. Staggering forward, his eyes blinded by the tear gas, he began firing at any movement. Squinting, he managed to get off one shot in Trooper King's direction. Knowles managed to fire one more round before the sharpshooters found their mark.

THIRTY-EIGHT

IT WAS A happy holiday scene at the wharf in Savannah. The shiny white cruise ship was bound for its regular two week cruise of the western Caribbean. The passengers' luggage was being loaded on the conveyor belt and the passengers were lined up for their security check and boarding. It was a long line but it was proceeding efficiently. Many of the passengers were in holiday attire and quite a few had obviously been celebrating their departure at the bars which lined the wharf. To keep the group entertained during the process several television sets were deployed on metal poles for the passengers to view. In addition, a Caribbean steel drum band pounded out island classics to the festive group.

A bald, older gentleman wearing a seersucker suit with a white polo shirt and aviator sunglasses watched with a slight smile as his ancient steamer trunk went past on the conveyor belt and into the cargo area of the ship. He could see it had caused no concern whatsoever to the uniformed operator as it passed through the electronic scanner and into the hold of the ship. He then turned his attention to the television screens before him. "What is going on while we are getting ready to have fun?" he asked an older woman who was accompanied by her even older friend. They were both wearing crisp white tennis shoes and flowery Mu-Mu type dresses. "Oh, you know. The usual bad stuff. Some sort of shootout between a Sheriff's deputy and Georgia State Troopers someplace in Georgia. Something to do with drugs. That's why I moved from Atlanta," the woman replied with a broad smile. Her friend nudged her to move on.

"Thank goodness I don't see much of that in my work," the man replied with an equally broad smile as he squinted at the monitor in the bright sunlight. There were images of a smoking building and a body being removed on a stretcher. The ladies giggled slightly as they approached the desk of the security officer and presented their documents. The man carefully watched the officer's procedure with the women and noted that the officer was not armed. In less than a minute the officer had shepherded both women through the metal detector and they were proceeding up the gangplank.

The man stepped forward and presented his ticket and passport. The officer noted that the man seemed to be in unusually good shape for his age. The officer looked over the passport and ticket and glanced for a second at a paper which contained pictures of two men in police uniforms. The picture of one of the men, a black man, had been crossed out.

"What sort of work do you do Mr. Simpson?" the officer asked in a monotone.

"I am a retired agricultural equipment salesman," the man responded.

"I am assuming you are traveling for pleasure, like everyone else?" the officer asked, knowing the answer.

"Right. Work is not involved. That is all behind me. My wife passed away and I wanted some time to myself," the man said softly with a friendly smile.

"Have a wonderful trip and be careful of the sun," the officer said, returning his passport. Behind him on the television, the screen was filled with the image of Sheriff Roger Odum and his grey pompadour hairstyle.

"I am always careful. Thanks," Mr. Simpson said as he proceeded through the metal detector and up the gangplank.

THIRTY-NINE

IN FRONT OF the Courthouse were three television trucks with their long silver antennae at full attention. A row of silver, metal police barriers had been hastily arrayed around the front of the building and five State Troopers provided extra security at the entrance.

Inside, the Courtroom was packed to capacity with news people and general gawkers. Jack sat with Fitz Davis at the counsel table on the right. At the other counsel table was Arnold O'Berne, the lawyer for the inmates, and Dewey Lawson, the District Attorney. Directly behind Jack, in the first row, Tacy and the Warden sat and waited for the arrival of the Judge. There were two Bailiffs stationed by the door behind the Judge's bench. A loud knock was heard and one of the Bailiffs proudly made the full ancient announcement.

"All rise. All rise. Hear ye, hear ye. The Superior Court of the State of Georgia is now in session. God bless this honorable Court, the State and People of Georgia and the United States of America," the elderly Bailiff intoned as everyone in the room stood while the Judge approached the bench, his black robe rustling slightly as he moved.

"Please be seated," the Judge said softly as he took his seat at the bench. He reached into a pocket and pulled out his narrow reading glasses and opened the large file in front of him. "I believe this was originally to be a bond hearing but now it appears that there are several matters to be taken up in the case of State vs. Dr. Jack Randolph and also some collateral matters in the G-MAX class action case. Is that correct?" he said to the assembled counsel as he peered over his spectacles.

Fitz Davis stood immediately in response. "That is correct, your Honor. The defense would move that the charges against Dr. Randolph be dismissed. I believe that recent events have fortunately shown him to be entirely blameless in this matter. I also understand that the District Attorney has no objection," he said, looking over to Dewey Lawson.

The District Attorney stood and faced the Judge. "That is correct, your Honor. We have no objection to the charges of involuntary manslaughter being dismissed. We now have credible information which shows that the accident in question was set up and planned by Major Knowles to eliminate a witness. Of course there is still the matter of the Defendant's driving under the influence ..." he said until the Judge cut him off.

"Are you trying to tell me that despite a local law enforcement official setting up an elaborate trap which resulted in a death along with serious injury to the Defendant you still want to prosecute him? Am I hearing you correctly?" the Judge said loudly as Fitz Davis also rose to his feet.

Dewey Lawson shuffled his file and looked back at the Court room where the media reporters were taking furious notes. "Hearing the Court's comments, we would dismiss that charge also. We just wanted to bring it up," he said looking down at his feet.

"So noted, Mr. Lawson. The charges against the Defendant, Dr. Jack Randolph, are dismissed. All the charges and with prejudice. He is free to go," the Judge stated making a notation in the file and handing a piece of paper to the Clerk.

"Judge, there is also the matter of excessive use of force against an inmate concerning this Defendant which is the subject of a Motion for Contempt under the Georgia Maximum Security Prison Class Action Orders. There are videos of that incident which have been provided by the Warden. These videos show the use of force to unlawfully obtain blood samples and they also show some collateral misbehavior on the part of Dr. Randolph and Nurse Tacy Crandall," Mr. O'Berne, the attorney for the inmates announced.

"I have reviewed those videos," the Judge said, looking down at Jack through his spectacles which were perched on the end of his nose. Jack started to stand but was restrained by a hand on his shoulder by Fitz Davis who was standing by his side.

"Your honor, this matter is essentially moot and also cannot now be legally proven. The complainant in this matter is dead, after showing himself once again to have been a vicious and violent man. A man who used the procedures of this Court to execute a violent escape," Davis clearly stated to the Judge.

"Dr. Randolph, why was it so important to send these blood samples to the CDC? I am not quite understanding that," the Judge asked. Jack looked at Davis who nodded his approval for Jack to explain.

"Judge, Mr. Kirk may be the Blood Cleaner for millions of people who are infected with the HIV virus which causes AIDS. Before I ordered these samples I had checked his file carefully. Kirk clearly was infected with HIV when he came into the prison system years ago. The law requires testing where sex crimes are involved, as I am sure you know. On two later occasions he tested negative. In other words, his body had somehow purged itself of the HIV virus. One of these negative tests involved the rape and murder of Dr. Bridge. The day I ordered these tests I was aware of those results and Kirk was again being accused of a sex crime by another inmate. I myself heard Kirk threaten the inmate victim who then refused a rape test. Often physicians send additional samples to the CDC of legally required tests, in essence for a second opinion. Dr. Bridge had previously sent them samples on other occasions. That was what I was doing," Jack said calmly.

"Did you ever get a response from the CDC?" the Judge asked, looking through the file.

"It is my understanding they would like as much of his blood and tissue that is available. He represents hope for a lot of sick people," Jack said looking out at the crowd and then back at the Judge.

"Warden, does Mr. Kirk have any relatives? Has anyone claimed his body?" the Judge asked.

"Your honor, I object. You can't just donate this man's body to science," Mr. O'Berne stated in lawyerly fashion.

"Would you like to take custody of his remains? Isn't such an unclaimed body the property of the State?" the Judge shot back.

"I don't think it would be appropriate for me to take custody," the lawyer stammered.

The Judge smiled slightly. "I didn't think so. I am dismissing the Motion for Contempt as moot and legally unproveable. I will do a written Order to that effect with a copy to the State Medical Board. As to any sexual misbehavior between Dr. Randolph and Nurse Crandall I find that completely irrelevant to the issues before this Court. I am also ordering these tapes to be sealed with access only to the Court and counsel. After a year they are to be destroyed. All copies are ordered destroyed at that time. Is that understood?" the Judge intoned. Both lawyers and the Warden nodded their assent.

"Is my client free to go?" Fitz Davis asked the Judge.

"I believe there is one more matter. Dr. Randolph has agreed to complete Dr. Bridge's contract to provide medical services at the prison. He has now completed two weeks of that agreement. Of course, the impetus for that agreement was these charges against him which are now gone and any evidence of any collateral employment misconduct is now under seal. Warden, have you found a replacement doctor yet? Do you have anyone interested?" the Judge asked.

"We don't have anyone yet, or any real prospects." the Warden admitted.

"Are you really trying to provide medical coverage out of Augusta as I was told the other day?" the Judge asked.

"That is right Judge. We have a doc that comes over twice a week," the Warden continued.

"Twice a week, for over fourteen hundred inmates? What do you do if there is an emergency?" the Judge asked, making a note in the file.

"They go straight to the local hospital." was the reply.

"Dr. Randolph, what are your thoughts on continuing your career in correctional medicine, at least until the institution can get you a replacement? It does seem from those videos you have made some friends at G-MAX in your brief stay," the Judge continued, looking over at Tacy as she sat with her long legs crossed in a crisp, black linen dress. This comment was greeted with muffled laughter in the Courtroom. Even Tacy laughed, as she blushed and put her hand to her mouth, her pretty eyes blinking wide.

"If the Warden can see to it to take Tacy and me back, I am available. I feel bad that she has had so many problems because of me. Lester, Georgia has been a lot more action packed than most people in Atlanta would believe," Jack said, looking back at Tacy. "But there is one more thing. It is important that Kirk's body be turned over to Dr. Howard Clayton at the CDC, especially since no one else claims it," Jack continued.

"Warden, do you have a problem with this? The doctor wants a package deal for himself and Nurse Crandall," the Judge asked in a tone where the answer was preordained. "No sir, not a bit." was the Warden's quick reply.

Mr. O'Berne stood and started to speak but was interrupted by the Judge.

"Dr. Randolph, of course you understand this Court cannot condone any wheeling and dealing with Mr. Kirk's earthly remains and your services. However, Mr. Kirk will have to be disposed of somehow and it appears that the CDC is an acceptable and appropriate recipient. Mr. O'Berne has stated to this Court that he cannot accept Mr. Kirk's remains and it appears there are no other takers. As such, the Warden is hereby ordered to transfer his body to the custody of the CDC for autopsy, examination and testing due to the nature of his crimes and for further respectful burial of any remains. Any further issues?" the Judge ruled to a quiet Courtroom. "Court is adjourned," he stated with a whack of his gavel. The Judge stood and turned to exit, and silently and without prompting, every person in the entire courtroom stood.

FORTY

THERE WAS A light wind blowing off the river, gently tossing the silver moss in the oaks beside Jack's State house. In an hour
it would be sunset and the view from the back porch would be
rivers of fire in the sky as the sun went down over the marsh. Tacy
pulled her truck next to Jack's car and looked over at the twisted
metal of the wreck which had started it all. The porch was freshly
swept and the door to the house was open.

"Jack, are you here?" she called as she stepped into the house.
She noticed the portrait of Robert E. Lee over the fireplace mantle
had been replaced by a large framed print of the ocean. "What have
you done with General Lee?" she asked as she entered and looked
around.

Jack appeared from the kitchen wearing a red apron along
with a trailing cloud of aromatic smells. In his hand was a bottle of
champagne. "General Lee now watches over my bed. I understand
he was quite a voyeur in his time," Jack said as he approached,
bottle in hand. He stepped toward her and pulled her close. "I got
you your job back. Are we still friends?" he said kissing her and
running his hand down her back. He pushed back slightly and admired her in the flowered sun dress which highlighted her tanned
body.

"Yes we are friends, you nut," she said kissing him back and running her hands down his back. "You saved me from that monster and you got my job back. I want to have your baby," she cooed. "But don't worry, I have taken my medicine so that won't happen right away."

"Actually, it wasn't me who saved you. It was the monster hog family. Never mess with a thousand pound adversary with tusks," Jack replied. "I have indentured myself to the prison to get your job back and make amends," he continued. "But I am getting to like it around here," he said kissing her and running his hands along the sides of her sheer dress.

She stepped back and with two quick tugs to the shoulder strings of the dress dropped it to the floor. Jack could not help but stare as she stood naked, once again, before him. "What do you like about it here?" she said coyly.

"Well, there is really good fishing and barbecue. They have gambling at the Church during the week. Housing is very inexpensive and the people are nice. There is very little crime outside of the prison as everyone packs a weapon. You can leave your doors open," he said as he took in her tanned, sexy presence. "From a clinical perspective, the place is a medical museum of pathology. You can see diseases here every day you can only read about in books in Atlanta," he said stepping toward her and running his hands gently down her soft, tight fanny. "Oh, and yes, some of the women are quite hot. Especially the athletic ones who like to fish."

"Would you like to try one on?" she said smiling as she ran her hands under his apron and began pulling him toward the bedroom.

"I had planned on champagne and dinner first, but I think you are changing my mind," he said kissing her passionately and following her to the bedroom after placing the bottle on a table.

"Are you sure it is your mind that is changing," she said pushing him back on the bed and removing his shoes and socks.

The dog, Slick, lay comfortably on his back on the floor, enjoying the scene, his breeding equipment fully exposed.

Jack looked up at General Lee as she removed Jack's pants. "I am sorry Sir, but I am going to surrender," he said in a heavy voice. Suddenly they both stopped as the siren at the prison went off with its familiar wail. "Damn," Jack said, as his cell phone went off with the special emergency ring.

Tacy sauntered over to the dresser and picked up Jack's cell phone. "Yes, Dr. Randolph and I will be right there."

In a few minutes, Beulah Burns turned her binoculars to the car pushing up a cloud of red dust around the perimeter of the prison. She then turned her view to the small cloud of smoke emanating from behind one of the buildings inside the fence. She put down the binoculars and picked up the black telephone receiver and pressed a worn speed dial button. "Warden, Doctor Jack is on his way. Nurse Tacy is right beside him. I think we got us a new doctor."

ABOUT THE AUTHOR

Davis Hewitt is a writer and attorney in Atlanta, Georgia. He is the author of the murder thriller, KILLING THE BLOOD CLEANER. Davis is a former Assistant Attorney General for the State of Georgia and has represented the Georgia Department of Corrections and the Georgia Bureau of Investigation and their wardens, agents and employees in hundreds of cases. He has also been lead counsel in numerous large, class action suits involving the Georgia prison system. To learn more about Davis, his books and events, please visit his blog at **https://www.davishewitt.com**